A THOUSAND TINY CUTS

CHRISTINA KAYE

MORE BOOKS BY CHRISTINA KAYE

CONTENTS

1

The bottoms of her feet were raw, and each time they hit the cold concrete sidewalk, pain jolted through her legs as if she'd been shocked with a cattle prod. The cold November air stung her lungs as she ran faster and faster, forcing herself not to look back. Her heart raced as her eyes scanned the dark, crowded street.

She found who she was looking for at the corner of Main and Broadway, sitting atop a chestnut horse. His uniform was dark blue, and he wore tall black boots which were hooked inside silver stirrups. He wore a black helmet with a chinstrap. His gaze was fixed on the onlookers pushing in closer to Triangle Park. All eyes in the crowd shifted to the giant thirty-foot Christmas tree the mayor was about to light in front of the water fountains. No one seemed to notice her as she ran up to the officer and grabbed his leg.

"Please, sir. You have to help me!"

Instinctively, the officer jerked his foot away and reached for his sidearm. But he must have seen the sheer terror on her face because he did not draw his weapon.

"Are you all right, Miss?"

"Please, help me. He's going to see me. He's going to take me back there. Please. Help!"

The man climbed off his equine mount, stood before the young girl, and took hold of her shoulders gently. "Who? Who's going to see you? Are you okay?"

"No!" Her eyes grew wide as two moons, and her bottom lip quivered. "He let me go, but what if he changes his mind? He might kill me! You have to save me. His name was Stan. That's all I ever knew. He never told me his last name, but please, sir. You have to get me away from here!"

The officer's right hand reached across to the walkie on his shoulder. "Dispatch, this is Officer Napolitano, badge number eight-niner-bravo."

"Go ahead, eight-niner-bravo."

"I'm at the corner of Main and Broadway. Possible 10-67 here. Requesting backup."

"Copy. I'll send a unit your way."

The officer looked at her with a hint of confusion in his eyes. Suddenly, the girl became conscious of the fact that she wore cutoff jean shorts and a thin, white tank top on a cold November night in Kentucky. Not to mention the fact that she was raving like a lunatic about some strange man and begging for help. It was no wonder the cop regarded her this way. But it didn't matter what he thought about her. What mattered was convincing him that she was in grave danger.

"What's your name?" He pulled a tiny spiral notebook and a pen from the front pocket of his uniform shirt and stood poised to write down her answer.

Her lips were so cold and stiff, she could barely formulate another word, but she managed to squeak out her answer anyway, as this was the most important detail of all.

"My name is Caroline. Caroline Hanson."

"Did you just say...Caroline...Hanson? As in *the* Caroline Hanson?"

She nodded. Finally. She'd said the words aloud.

The officer grabbed his CB radio again and spoke into it, his words coming out rapid fire.

"Scratch that 10-67, dispatch. Call Detective Mena Kastaros. Tell her I've got Caroline Hanson."

D etective Filomena Kastaros sipped coffee from a tiny Styrofoam cup, careful not to burn the roof of her mouth, as she'd done so many times before. The live footage on the screen was not zoomed in, but she could still see the young girl sitting at the interview room table with a grey wool blanket wrapped around her shoulders. The girl sat shivering and staring blankly at the wall. Mena took a step closer to the monitor. She tilted her head to the right to concentrate more intently on the girl.

She'd studied Caroline Hanson's picture for ten years, one month, and thirteen days. In fact, it was still tacked up on the bulletin board on the wall next to her desk. In the faded photograph, a five-year-old Caroline sat in a swing with her hands clutching the chains. The wind had blown strands of long brown hair across her pretty little face, but her features were clearly visible: tiny button nose, a toothy grin, and amber-colored eyes that had always reminded Mena of root beer.

Those root beer eyes had haunted Mena for over a decade. She would see them in her dreams and everywhere she went. On the rare occasion she'd run across a girl of about the right age who had similar eyes, she'd stop her and ask her name. So when this strange girl had shown up after all these years claiming to be Caroline Hanson, the first thing Mena had looked for in the picture the uniformed officer had sent her from his cell phone had been those eyes.

And there they were.

It wasn't fair. If this was really Caroline Hanson, it just wasn't fair.

Mena hated to think that way. She should have been thrilled, especially since the case had been cold for so long and Caroline had long been presumed dead. But the selfish part of her wondered why Caroline got to come home when Sadie never would. Sadie would never get married, have children, or grow old. She would forever be eight years old, and she would remain so in Mena's mind and heart for the rest of time.

"You think it's her?"

Mena startled then turned to see her partner, Detective Derrick Felton, standing next to her, staring intently at the monitor. He was in his civilian clothes—jeans, white sneakers, and a Vikings' jersey—and had apparently also received a call from their lieutenant demanding his presence. Mena guessed he'd just been to the barber shop, thanks to his closely cropped hair and neatly trimmed goatee. His gold detective's badge hung from a chain around his neck.

"It could be," Mena said. "Only DNA will tell us for sure."

"Cliff says he should have the fingerprints finished soon. Good thing her parents turned over that toothbrush when the case started."

"Yeah. I guess."

"You sound skeptical." He shoved his hands into his pockets and regarded Mena with a furrowed brow.

"It's just hard to believe. After all these years? Where did she come from? Where has she been? Who took her? Why did she show up tonight…downtown at the Christmas tree lighting, of all the times and places?"

"Why don't you just ask her yourself?" Felton jerked a thumb toward the monitor.

Mena sighed. "I'm going to. I just needed a minute to…"

"Watch her?"

Mena nodded.

"You going to call the parents?"

Mena shrugged. "Eventually. I need to know more first. Laura Hanson has called me every year on the anniversary of Caroline's disappearance to check in on the investigation. There's no way I'm going to call her without more information."

"Well, then. What are you waiting for?" Felton gestured toward the interview room.

No time like the present.

She set her coffee cup on the desk and walked up to the interview room door. When she looked back at Felton, he shooed her along with a smile, then gave her a thumbs-up. Mena rapped on the door and pushed it open.

Interview Room A was only about five foot by eight. Grey industrial-grade carpet lined the floor, bright white paint covered the walls, and the halogen lights in the ceiling cast a garish light on everyone and everything inside. At the metal table, which sat smack in the middle of the tiny room, sat the young girl Mena had been watching for thirty minutes.

Mena pulled out the chair opposite the young girl, sat, and scooted forward. She clicked the RECORD button on her hand-held recording device and set it on the table between them. With her hands clasped together, Mena leaned closer.

"Your name is Caroline Hanson. Is that right?"

The girl's eyes watered, and a single tear escaped, falling over her cheek. "Yes."

"Okay, that's good. I'm the detective who worked the…*your* case, back when you first disappeared. I know it's going to be difficult, but I need you to tell me where you've been the past ten years. I need to know who took you, where you were held, and how you wound up in downtown Lexington tonight."

Mena paused. The girl was clearly overwhelmed. She seemed to withdraw and curl in on herself with every word Mena spoke. And Mena knew better than to drill a victim this way. What had she been thinking? She was potentially too close to this case to be as objective as she should be.

Time to change tact.

"I see that Officer Napolitano gave you a blanket, but you're barely wearing anything and they keep these damn interview rooms so cold. Can I get you something warmer to wear? All I have handy is what we call 'marshmallow suits' but those are for suspects after we take their clothes for evidence. I could send someone to the store if—"

"I'm fine. Thank you, though."

"Okay. If you're sure. How about this. Let's start at the beginning. What is the last thing you remember from the day you were taken?"

The girl didn't respond at first, but Mena had the patience of a detective who'd interviewed hundreds of suspects and victims over the course of her fifteen-year career. So she waited. And waited. She watched the second hand tick around the clock. Finally, after at least thirty seconds had gone by, the girl's lips parted, and words began to tumble out.

"I remember the playground."

"That's good. Do you remember what the weather was like?"

"It was sunny, but a little cold. I had on my pink winter coat."

Mena's eyes widened, and she cocked her head slightly. "You remember your winter coat?"

"I'd just gotten it for my birthday. I remember because it was puffy and pink. Pink is my favorite color."

Mena recalled Laura Hanson telling her that Caroline loved

the color pink so much that she'd insisted her bedroom be painted the shade of Pepto-Bismol.

"Can you tell me anything else about that day? Anything at all?"

"I was playing on the big...I don't know...*thing*. The one with the slide at the top. My mom was there. I yelled her name, but she was busy talking to other moms. I wanted to show her how fast I could go across the monkey bars."

"Good. What happened next?"

"A man. There was a man. I didn't know him. But he said he lost his puppy. I felt sad for him, so I said I'd help. I just wanted to see the puppy."

The girl's voice was quiet, and her tone was almost child-like.

"It's okay." Mena reached out her hand and laid it on the table between them. Caroline's eyes darted to Mena's wrist where three tiny pink scars peeked out from under the sleeve of her black blouse. Mena jerked her arm back and pulled her sleeve down. "I know this part will be difficult, but can you tell me what happened after you left the playground?"

The young girl squirmed in her seat and looked away from Mena. "We walked for a few minutes. We looked in the bushes, then the trees. When we got near the street, a white van pulled up. He shoved me inside and slammed the door."

Tears streamed down her neck. She wiped them away quickly.

"He got in the van with you?"

The girl nodded.

Mena's curiosity was piqued. "Someone else was driving the van?"

She nodded again.

"Okay. You're doing great. Thank you." Mena stood and scooted her chair back toward the table. "I need to make a couple phone calls. I won't be long. Can I get you anything?"

"Where am I going?"

"What do you mean? You're safe here. You're not going anywhere," Mena reassured her.

"No, I mean...after this. Do I go home to my parents? Or some kind of shelter?"

"Let's not worry about that right now," Mena said. "For now, let's just concentrate on your story. We'll take it as slowly as you need to. It's going to get harder before it gets any easier, but you have my word, I'm right here. And I'm not going anywhere."

Mena exited the interview room, pulled the door closed behind her, and slipped the recording device into her pocket. She leaned against the wall to her right and thought over all the girl had said. Her mind drifted back to that day ten years ago when she'd kissed Sadie goodbye, not knowing it was the last time she'd ever have a moment like that. Hearing this girl – whoever she really was – describing her own abduction made Mena feel as if someone had stabbed a knife right into her gut and was twisting it one slow, sadistic turn at a time. Was this how it had been for Sadie? Had the same monster disguised himself as some poor schmuck looking for a lost puppy then snatched her up and shoved her into a waiting van? Thinking of the sheer terror Sadie might have experienced in that instant was almost too much for Mena to bear.

But if this *was* the same monster...if the same man who'd taken this poor girl from a playground, right out from under her mother's nose, was the same one who'd stolen Mena's happiness away from her, then she knew she had to find him. When she did, she was going to bring him to justice once and for all so no mother would ever suffer the same agonizing emptiness. If this girl, whether or not she really was Caroline Hanson, was the key to tracking him down and making him pay, then Mena had to get her shit together and focus on getting every bit of information she could from the girl.

This wasn't just a coincidence. Mena felt it deep down. It wasn't just her many years in law enforcement telling her that the cases were connected. It was something else. Something stronger than a cop's instinct for connecting the dots and following leads. No, it was a something much more magnetic and undeniably fierce.

It was a mother's intuition.

3

Stanley Pollard jerked his van into the driveway and pulled it into the garage. He pushed the button on the garage door opener and watched in the rearview mirror as the door slowly slid down, closing him inside. His hands still on the steering wheel, he gripped it tightly and watched as his knuckles turned white. Stan tried to steady his breathing, but it was no use. He was damn near hyperventilating. But he'd done what he had to do...for him and for Beverly.

Oh, God. How am I going to explain this to Beverly?

It wouldn't be easy. And she would certainly be pissed. But he'd had no choice in the matter. Not really. Plus, there was the fact that he had come to care for the girl. Not the way he loved his common-law wife, but he had developed strong feelings toward her, similar to what it must be like for most parents. Not that he had any experience on either side of that aisle. He'd never been blessed with children of his own, and *his* parents....well, he couldn't even think about his parents right now.

Fuck it.

He turned off the ignition, shoved the keys into his pocket, and climbed out of the van. He'd have to tell Beverly sooner rather than later, so he might as well rip off the Band-Aid. As he did every day, he kicked off his boots before entering the house. The smell of roasting meat and vegetables wafted through the air, and he heard Beverly humming in the kitchen. His stomach was clenched, and his nerves were frayed like a cut wire. This was one conversation he did not look forward to having.

"That you, Stan?" Beverly's sing-songy voice carried through the house.

"Yep, it's me," he said. "What's for dinner? Smells great."

"Roast with potatoes, peas, and carrots. Your favorite."

Stan rounded the corner and found his wife standing in front of the oven, stirring gravy in a large silver pot. Beverly was shorter than Stan, but not by much. She had gotten a bit thicker in the waist as she approached sixty, and she wore her brown and silver hair shorter and curlier than she'd ever done before, but Stan still found her attractive. She wasn't pretty, not in the traditional sense of the word, and Stan had never really had to fight another man for her affections, but she was loyal, and she was good to him, and that was why he loved her so much.

Well, it was one of the reasons, anyway. The other being that she had always supported his plans, even when they put them both at risk. But this...this thing he had to tell her...she likely wouldn't support him in this one decision.

"Where's the girl?" Beverly set down the ladle and planted her hands on her wide hips.

"About that," Stan said. "I...uh...I..."

"Do not tell me she got away! Stan! What on earth happened?"

"Just let me explain..."

He couldn't tell her the real reason. But it didn't matter. He could tell already there was nothing he could say to justify his decision to let the girl slip away. Instead, he hung his head and awaited her wrath.

"Explain? Do you realize what this means? We can't stay here.

They'll be coming for us. She'll tell them everything and we'll have to—"

She gesticulated wildly as Stan approached her and grabbed her shoulders tightly. "Beverly, listen to me. She didn't escape. Not really."

Beverly squinted her eyes and stared right through him. "What do you mean *not really*?"

"I sort of, well, I sort of let her go."

"Jesus, Mary, and Joseph." Beverly took a step backward. Afraid she was going to topple over, Stan gripped her shoulders tighter. "Ouch, Stan. You're hurting me."

Stan relaxed his grip somewhat. "Sorry, Bev. I was going into the gas station, and right before I got out of the van, I looked at her, and I don't know. I just...I can't explain it. I just let her go. That's all that matters."

This wasn't the real reason for his brash decision to release the girl, but Beverly wasn't going to understand any explanation he offered, so he'd decided to let it go at that.

"You've killed us both. You do realize that, don't you?"

"Bev, honey, you're being..."

"Being what? After all we've been through together? After I've stood by you all these years and helped you with your business. Both your businesses, actually. Now you go and do the most reckless thing you've ever done. No, I'm not being anything other than responsible and rational, which I can't say for you." She pointed a thick finger at Stan's chest. "Now that girl, she's going to tell the police everything. And do you think for one second they are going to let us get away? That they'll just forget about all of this," she waved her hand around the room, "and decide not to hunt us down?"

"She doesn't know where we live. She doesn't know anything about us."

"Foolish, stupid man." Tears sprang to Beverly's eyes. When Stan raised his hand to wipe them away, she slapped it down.

"Don't touch me. You need to fix this, Stan. Come up with a plan to get us out of this. I don't care what you have to do, where we have to go, but I'm not going to prison for this. It was all your idea, anyway."

"Now, hold on," Stan took two steps back and held his hands up between them. "It's not exactly like I had to twist your arm. You've benefited from this little business as much as I have. It's not like we could have made ends meet just on a mechanic's wages. Not with your online shopping habits, anyway."

"Wait just one minute, mister," Beverly snapped. "I don't—"

"You don't what? Spend hours on end watching those home shopping channels? Spend hundreds of dollars on kitchen gadgets, electronic gizmos, and those worthless little trinkets you collect?"

"My Hummels are not worthless trinkets! How dare you?"

Stan let his shoulders relax and sighed heavily. "All right, look, I'm sorry. I didn't mean to snap. I know it was stupid to let her go. But I'll figure something out. I'll take care of you." He took a step forward and wrapped his arms around her thick middle. "Don't I always take care of my Bevvy Bear?"

Beverly softened at his touch, smiled, and shrugged. "I guess. Yeah, you do."

She giggled when Stan nudged his nose underneath her chin and kissed her lightly on the neck. "Who's your man?" he asked.

"Oh, you are, you stupid sonofabitch," she said as she swatted him on the rear. She pulled back and looked at him. "You swear you'll get us out of this? Because I am not spending the rest of my life in prison. Besides, orange is not a good color on me."

"I swear," he said. "I'll do anything to protect you, Bev. I'd even kill for you."

4

Mena started at the screensaver on her desktop – a field of lavenders. She'd chosen this one because purple was her favorite color. It gave her something pleasant to look at after viewing grizzly evidence, disturbing crime scene photos, and cold, blue corpses. She drummed her fingers on the top of her desk as she contemplated her options. Calling the Hansons right now, before she had DNA results, or at least fingerprint matches, could give the parents false hope, only to have it snatched away if the girl was lying, or at least mistaken, about her identity. But not calling them immediately might be unfair and cruel. What if the girl really was Caroline Hanson and the parents found out Mena had not called them right away?

She couldn't help but put herself in their shoes. If this were Sadie, although that was entirely impossible since Sadie was never coming home, she would want to know immediately, even if it turned out to be a mistake. Better to have the chance to see for themselves. She determined she would call the Hansons, but be very clear about the precarious nature of the situation.

There was one more call she had to make first, though she hated to make it. Mena picked up the phone and dialed the number she had memorized for Child Protective Services. After a brief hold, she was transferred to the on-duty social worker, a woman Mena had worked with many times in the past named Danna Rodriguez. She explained the recent developments to Danna, who agreed to come to the station within the hour.

"If the girl turns out to be Caroline Hanson, that would make her seventeen, but she could possibly go home with her parents after we've interviewed the family, cleared the home, etc.," Danna told Mena. "If, however, the girl turns out to be anyone else, a minor child with no proven identity has no other choice but to be placed in a foster home until her parents can be located."

"Thanks, Danna. I'll see you when you get here."

Mena turned in her chair and began to rifle through the box that contained Caroline Hanson's entire investigation file, which a rookie had brought up from storage before Mena had made it to the station. Aside from the toothbrush, which they'd already lifted prints from earlier, the only other evidence was Caroline's hairbrush, which the Hansons had provided for possible future DNA testing on the hairs, if there were roots attached. But a forensic tech had already collected it and shipped it to Frankfort for expedited processing. Two large file folders stuffed full of dead-end leads and suspects who had been cleared filled the rest of the box. There had never been much to go on from day one. One minute, Caroline Hanson had been playing on the playground. The next minute, she had simply vanished. Not even one alleged sighting of the poor girl.

Someone cleared their throat loudly, and Mena turned to see Cliff Van Buren leaning with one arm resting against the top of her cubicle. Near retirement, the aging law enforcement officer, with a beer belly pushing against his white button-down shirt, had settled into a desk job as an analyst for the Lexington Police Department's Bureau of Investigations.

"Hey, there, pretty lady." Cliff ran his hand over his thinning white hair. "I got something for ya. But nothing comes free in life."

Mena wanted to roll her eyes. Cliff was not the most congenial man, but he was the best at comparing loops, whorls, and arches. Everyone simply tolerated his brash demeanor and crass comments.

"What do you want, Cliff? A slap on the back? An atta-boy?"

Cliff sucked his teeth and nodded slowly. "It's a nice start."

"All right, then. Good job, Cliff. Way to go. You're the best analyst in the whole wide world. Now, do they match?"

"Darn tootin. The prints are definitely a match. I found twelve matching points." Cliff seemed extremely proud of himself.

It was true. The girl really was Caroline Hanson. DNA would likely only confirm what Cliff had just told her. This didn't really surprise Mena. She'd known it deep in her gut the moment she'd seen those eyes. Nonetheless, the confirmation of her identity brought about a heaviness in Mena's chest and her limbs felt like they weighed a hundred pounds each. She recognized this sensation as one of sadness. Sadness once again that Sadie would never find her way back home and get to have the joyous reunion Caroline would likely have with her parents in the very near future. But her sorrow was quickly replaced with a deep-seated feeling of guilt for even thinking that way.

"Thanks, Cliff. You really are the best."

Cliff held his hand to his ear. "What's that you just said? Say it louder. I didn't quite hear you."

"Very funny." Mena grabbed the results from Cliff's meaty hand, walked over to Felton's desk, leaving Cliff to stand alone at her cubicle, and plopped the papers down in front of her partner. "It's her."

"Well, congratulations, Kastaros. You just solved a ten-year-old missing person case. You call the parents yet?"

"Not yet."

"You know, when I was in the military police, serving out of

Fort Drum, New York, we had this case where a young boy went missing from the base. Just...disappeared on his way home from school one day after getting off the bus. A military base, for God's sake. Anyway, we found the boy a couple hours later, apparently unharmed. But we didn't tell the parents. Not right away. My Sergeant Major wanted to interview him first."

"No offense, Felton, but—"

"Just hear me out. Anyway, when we finally contacted the parents about five hours later, they were beyond pissed. Dressed me down for fifteen straight minutes for not calling them right away. I felt awful, man."

"That wasn't your decision. That's not entirely fair."

"No, but it didn't matter to those poor parents who had made that call. I was the investigating officer, and he was found on my watch. Screw protocol. I should have called them the minute I found him hanging with his friends at the commissary."

"I get it." Mena suppressed an eyeroll.

"Then," Felton tilted his head and shrugged, "what are you waiting for?"

Good question.

"I don't know. It's just...can you imagine what it would be like to find out your missing daughter was still alive, even after ten long years?"

Felton's features softened, something that didn't happen often, and he sighed. "You're thinking about Sadie, aren't you?"

Mena refused to meet his gaze. She crossed her arms over her chest and looked out the window at the Lexington city scape, which tried like hell to be a metropolis, but fell miserably short. A flock of birds flew by in a V shape, and Mena tried to think about where they might be headed instead of where her mind was trying to take her. She'd already spent to much time there lately.

"Understandable. I can't imagine how you must be feeling right now. If you want me to call them, I will."

Her eyes snapped back toward Felton. "No, no. I'll do it."

This was her case. She'd earned it in a way no detective could ever earn a case in their entire career. Much as she loved her partner, she wasn't about to let him take that moment away from her, no matter how envious and shitty it was going to make her feel.

Felton shrugged and held up his hands as if surrendering after a hard-fought battle of wills. "Suit yourself." He turned back to his computer and wiggled his mouse so his Vikings logo screensaver disappeared, effectively shooing Mena away.

Knowing she could no longer postpone the inevitable, she walked back to her desk, picked up the phone, and paused before dialing the number for the Hansons. Though she'd spoken to Laura Hanson every January for over ten years, Mena never dreamed she'd be making this phone call. She wasn't even sure how to begin the conversation. Should she come right out and tell her Caroline was home? Should she hold back and simply ask her to come to the station? It wasn't like she had any precedence to lean on as she'd never faced a situation like this before. Mena tried to put herself in Laura's shoes, but then realized quickly she would never receive the phone call Mrs. Hanson was about to receive. This miracle was reserved for better parents. Parents who hadn't struggled with parenting while battling their own demons. Parents like Mark and Laura Hanson.

She picked up the phone, dialed the number she knew by heart, and listened as it rang once. Someone picked up before the second ring.

"This's Mark." His voice was muffled, and it was only when she heard the grogginess in it that Mena looked at the clock and realized it was well past eleven p.m.

Shit.

She tapped her cell phone against her forehead a few times as if by doing so she could knock out the stupidity. Mena had forgotten that most normal people would be in bed, not still working when it was damn near midnight.

She placed the phone back to her ear. "Mr. Hanson, this is Detective Mena Kastaros. I need to speak with you. It's about Caroline."

"Oh, God. You found her body, didn't you?"

Mena could hear Laura Hanson in the background begging Mark to hand her the phone.

"Just wait, woman," Mark snapped. "I'm tryin to talk to the detective lady. I'm sorry, Detective. Where'd you find her?"

"It's not exactly…actually…I just thought you should know that—"

"Just tell us what the hell is going on." Mark Hanson had never been the kindest of men, but Mena had always forgiven his brusqueness given what he'd been through. "It's been ten fucking years. We deserve some closure, so just tell me where you found her and where we need to go to identify—"

"Mark, I'm not sure how to tell you this," Mena began, treading lightly. "But Caroline is here. At the station."

A long, pregnant pause.

"What'd you say?"

"Mr. Hanson, Caroline is alive."

There was once again silence on the other end of the line. Then it sounded like the phone dropped. The muffled sounds of someone trying to recover the phone were loud, and Mena had to pull hers away from her ear.

"Detective Kastaros." Mena recognized the voice instantly, despite how broken and warbly it sounded, as if the speaker were trying in vain not to sob hysterically. "This is Laura Hanson. Did you say you found Caroline? Alive?"

"It appears so. We've done a fingerprint comparison, and this girl's fingerprints match the ones we lifted from her toothbrush back when—"

"We'll be right there."

"Perhaps you should wait until—"

The line went dead.

5

Less than twenty minutes later, after Mena had gently informed Caroline that her parents were on their way to the station, Mark and Laura Hanson practically ran toward Mena as the squad's young, bored, and very disinterested receptionist led them to her desk, held out her hand toward Mena, then turned on her cheap kitten heels and headed back to her desk. Probably to return to her Instagram scrolling. Standing before Mena, Laura Hanson wore grey sweatpants and a faded and torn University of Kentucky hoodie. Her blonde hair was pulled back into a high, messy bun, and her face was red and puffy, probably from crying the whole way to the police department. But her eyes were wide and full of hope. Mark wore dirty jeans and a red shirt with his concrete company's logo on the front. He stood with his hands on his hips, staring right at Mena. His expression told her he battled with a mixture of emotions, not the least of which was disbelief.

Mena stood, drew in a deep breath, and let it out.

"Mr. and Mrs. Hanson. I—"

"Where is she?" Laura Hanson looked at Mena, her hands

trembling as she bit her twisted bottom lip so hard, it was turning red.

"She's in one of our interview rooms, and we've told her you're here, but I think it's best if we meet with the social worker first before you—"

"Screw that," Mark said in a voice marred by years of chain-smoking and inhaling concrete dust. "We want to see our daughter. It's been ten years. We're not waiting another damn minute."

"Okay," Mena said with her hands held up in defeat. "I just want you to prepare yourselves. This girl, I mean...*Caroline* has been through a lot. We haven't even begun to scratch the surface and talk about her ordeal. I'm begging you...take it easy. Don't overwhelm her. Stand back and let me direct the conversation. At least, at first. Okay?"

Mark and Laura both nodded. Mena could tell by the way they both shook and jittered that they'd have agreed to just about anything at this point. She also knew they hadn't heard anything she'd said and that the only words they *could* hear were the ones likely playing over and over again in the loudspeaker of their minds: *our daughter is alive.*

"All right. Follow me."

Mena led the Hansons through the maze of workstations and down the hallway toward the first interview room on the left. She tapped on the door and opened it wide enough for Caroline's parents to see her for the first time.

Caroline's eyes widened and she sat up straight, as if she'd been caught doing something bad.

Laura gasped and her shaky hand flew to her mouth.

Mark's hands clenched into fists at his sides.

"My baby," Laura said.

Mena cleared her throat. "Caroline, your parents are here. But before we go any further, I think we should—"

"Mama?" Caroline stood. Her bottom lip quivered, and tears filled those beautiful eyes.

Before Mena could react, Caroline ran into her mother's arms. Laura enveloped her, and Mark wrapped his arms around both of them. The trio stood there embracing and crying as Mena stood watching, a mix of jealousy, sadness, and contentment swirling around inside her in a tornado of emotions. While she was glad for the Hansons and for Caroline, she was envious of this moment – a moment she would never experience, a moment some unknown monster had stolen from her a decade ago.

When the family finally pulled apart, Laura held Caroline at arm's length.

"It's really you. Are you okay? Did they...did they hurt you? Where you been all these years? We been worried sick. I can't believe—"

Mena took a step closer to Laura and laid her hand on her shoulder. "Let's give Caroline some time and space. One thing at a time." She knew Laura's intentions were above board, and she probably didn't realize how her questions might overwhelm her daughter.

Caroline stood staring at her mother with her head cocked to one side, as if studying her mother, trying to recall her face. Her lips began to tremble and once again, tears poured over her cheeks. She shook her head.

"I'm sorry, Mama. I'm so, so sorry. It's all my fault."

Laura cupped Caroline's frail face in her hands. "What? Your fault? Oh, baby...what on earth do you have to be sorry about?"

"I...I w-went with h-him. I...sh-shouldn't have done that. I'm s-so sorry."

Laura pulled her daughter in once again and swayed side to side. "Oh, sweetheart. It's not your fault at all. It's all my fault. I should have watched you better. It's not your fault."

Mark's eyes narrowed, and his lips twisted into a frown. Mena watched his shoulders raise and lower as his breath became faster and more labored. "What'd those bastards do to you?" His voice was low and even, and his skin was beginning to flush. "Who did this? I'll kill em. I swear to God, I'll kill em with my bare—"

"All right, Mr. Hanson." Mena stepped in front of him and laid her hand on his arm. "Let's step outside, shall we? You, too, Laura. I need to speak with both of you." She turned to face Caroline. "We'll be right back. I promise. We're almost done."

"I just want to go home," Caroline said. Her voice sounded tiny, like a child's.

"I know, honey. Very soon," Mena said.

She coaxed the Hansons out of the room and into the hallway, shutting the door to the interview room behind them.

"Listen, Mark. I know you're upset. Any father in your shoes would be. And trust me…I know from personal experience the anger that builds up inside you when something like this happens to your little girl."

"That's right," he said with a sigh. The tension in his shoulders eased and his gaze softened. "I forgot. Someone took your little girl, too. I'm sorry for your loss."

Laura slipped her arm around her husband and laid her head on his shoulder, not looking directly at Mena.

"I appreciate that. But we need to concentrate on Caroline right now." Mena shifted her weight from one foot to the other as she tried to remain focused. "I know you're ready to take her home, but I need to talk to her just a little more before I can let her go. I hope you can understand."

Mark and Laura looked at each other, then at Mena. They both nodded.

As if on cue, Felton stepped up to their group. "This is my partner, Detective Derrick Felton. Why don't you let him show you to the snack room? There are vending machines and coffee. Just try to rest and be patient while I finish with Caroline. Do you think you can do that for me?"

Again, they nodded.

"Great. I'll come get you when I'm done."

Back in the interview room, Caroline had returned to her chair on the opposite side of the table. Her face was ashen, her chin trembled, and her elbows were pressed in at her sides, making her appear even smaller than she already was.

"Caroline," Mena said after returning to her seat. "Before I can let you go home, we need to talk about the hard stuff. I promise, I won't make you talk about anything you aren't ready to discuss. There will be therapists down the road who can help with the really bad parts. But if I'm going to catch the bastard who took you from your family, I need all the help you can give me to find them and punish them for what they did. Is that okay?"

Without meeting Mena's gaze, Caroline chewed on her fingernail and shrugged her shoulders. "I guess."

"Okay, good. Let's start with what you can tell me. You told the officer downtown tonight that the man might come after you. And you said his name was Stan. First, tell me what Stan looks like, while it's fresh in your mind."

Caroline shrugged. "He was just kinda plain looking, I guess."

"About how old was he? My age?"

"Older. Maybe fifty? I dunno."

"That's good. Now think about distinguishing marks. Did he have any tattoos? Scars? Anything strange about him?"

"No tattoos." Caroline stared at the table, clearly uncomfortable. "And he was bald, mostly, but he had, like, red hair that went around the sides of his head." Caroline demonstrated by running her fingers along the back of her head from one ear to the other.

"This is all very good, Caroline. Keep going."

"He was short, and kinda skinny. And freckles. Lots of freckles all over the place. I don't want to talk about him anymore."

"That's okay. That's fine. Let's talk about how you wound up

25

downtown Lexington tonight."

Caroline hesitated. "I...he...we were riding around running errands. In the van."

"The same van they picked you up in all those years ago?"

"Yeah. It was all rusty on the sides. Always breaking down. But Stan knew how to fix it, so anytime it broke down, it would be running again in a couple days."

This got Mena's attention. "Stan knew how to fix it? Was he a mechanic? Think about it, Caroline."

She nodded. "I think so. He was always greasy and his hands...his fingernails were always black. But I don't think he worked at a shop. He never left."

Mena made a mental note: *Mechanic? Self-employed?*

"Okay, good. That's good. Now, back to tonight. What happened next?"

"When he stopped at the gas station, he left me alone in the car. He'd done that before...left me by myself. Normally, he threatened me. Told me he'd track me down and kill my family if I got out or cried for help. But he didn't do that this time. He gave me a...a look. Like, I knew exactly what he was saying with his eyes, ya know? But he didn't say that this time. Not out loud."

"What was different this time? Besides him not warning you as usual, I mean. Why did you run tonight? After all these years?" Mena hoped there was no hint of accusation in her voice.

"Because I knew it was almost time. He said I was almost ready. And I didn't want to..."

"Time for what? Ready for what?"

Caroline shook her head.

"It's okay, Caroline. You're safe now. Talk to me. What didn't you want to do?"

After a few drawn-out seconds, Caroline looked at Mena. "I didn't want to be sold."

"Sold? Sold to whom?"

"To the highest bidder."

6

Before Mena could figure out exactly how to respond to Caroline's statement, there was a knock on the interview room door. She held her finger up, stood, and cracked it open. Danna Rodriguez stood on the other side, holding a clipboard, and giving Mena a pleasant smile.

"I'll be right with you," Mena told the social worker. She closed the door and returned to her seat at the table. "Caroline, we absolutely need to finish this conversation, and soon. But there is someone here I want you to talk to first."

"Another cop?" Caroline's lips pinched together, and she tapped her fingers on the tabletop. Clearly, she was less than thrilled at the prospect of someone else trying to drag information out of her when all she wanted was to go home.

"No. But we do work together. Actually, she's a social worker."

Caroline's eyes went wide. "A social worker? Why do I have to talk to her? Are you putting me in foster care? I don't want that! My parents are right outside that door. Why can't I just—"

Mena held her hand up. "Just calm down. It's part of the process. We can't just let you leave here with nowhere to go. And I can't let you go home until Ms. Rodriguez has talked to you and your parents. It's merely a formality. But let's just take it one step at a time."

The tension in Caroline's shoulders eased and she leaned back in her chair. "Okay. I'll talk to her."

Mena nodded, stood, and opened the door again. Danna stood in the hallway, leaning one hip against the wall. She'd lost weight, Mena noticed for the first time. She hadn't worked with Danna in months, and the last time she'd seen her, the social worker's hips were much wider and her cheeks much fuller. Danna had also cut her hair in a chin-length bob, a style Mena had always wished she could pull off, but hadn't bothered trying since her thin, dishwater blonde hair seemed to do better if she kept it pulled back in a low ponytail most days. Subconsciously, Mena tugged at her hair, reminded herself she had no one to impress and no desire to anyhow, and pulled the door to the interview room closed.

"What've you got?" Danna asked, her clipboard held close to her chest.

"It's Caroline Hanson."

Danna's mouth fell open. "No. It can't be."

Mena tilted her head and raised an eyebrow.

"As in *the* Caroline Hanson? But how…I mean, I thought…"

What Danna didn't say, what Mena knew she *wouldn't* say, was that Danna, like everyone else, had assumed Caroline had met the same fate as Mena's daughter. She had told Mena as much. The year they both disappeared had been Danna Rodriguez's first year as a social worker. While it was her supervisor Lashonda Parker who had originally worked with the Hansons after Caroline disappeared, Danna had to know that she had been presumed dead, just like Sadie.

"I'm still trying to figure all that out," Mena said. "But her fingerprints match the ones we lifted from Caroline's toothbrush back when we first started. DNA is still pending, but that's a mere formality at this point. It's her, Danna."

The social worker's face softened. "I'm sorry, Mena. This must be hard for you. If there's anything I can do…" Danna shook her head and looked down at her feet.

"There is," Mena replied, more harshly than she intended. She sighed before continuing. "This poor girl and her parents have been apart for ten years. Understandably, she just wants to go home. I need to question her more if we're going to catch the bastard who took her and did God knows what with her for a decade, but it's almost midnight already and these parents deserve to have their baby home again. Can you help?"

Dann's shoulders rose and fell as she shook her head slowly. "Mena, it's not that simple. I have to interview the girl. I have to interview the parents. I have to make sure we're sending her to a suitable home environment. You know that. We can't just hand her over to them without—"

"I know, I know. I'm not asking you to break any rules. I'm simply asking if we could, I don't know, expedite the process a little. Grease the wheels, so to speak. Is there anything you can do for them?"

The social worker sighed. "For you, Mena, I'll see what I can do. If the parents seem okay, and the family home checks out, I'll let her go home tonight."

"I owe you one, Danna."

Danna Rodriguez held up her hand. "On the strict condition that I'm allowed to follow-up with the family in the home within forty-eight hours."

"Done. Thank you for that."

"Now," Danna said, tapping her pen on her clipboard. "I do have to talk to Caroline first. Standard procedure."

Mena gestured toward the interview room, turned the knob, and pushed open the door. Danna slipped into the room and closed the door behind her.

. . .

After checking on the Hansons, who were sitting in the waiting area shaking like June bugs, Mena headed back to her cubicle. When she passed Felton, he pushed away from his cluttered desk and leaned back in his chair.

"How's it going with the girl?" he asked.

She leaned against the wall of his cubicle. "Fine, I guess. Danna Rodriguez is meeting with her now. Parents are up next."

"Oh, yeah? That's good. That's good. She going home with the Hansons tonight?"

"That's the hope."

"Right on," Felton said, holding up his hand for what Mena could only assume was a high-five.

An uncomfortable moment of silence passed. Mena smiled, hoping her inner thoughts weren't displayed prominently across her face.

No such luck.

"All right, partner. Tell me what's going on in that head of yours," Felton asked.

Mena pursed her lips and shrugged, feigning nonchalance. "Nothing. Just happy for them, that's all."

"Mena."

"Derrick."

He tsked. "Come on, girl. You can talk to me. We been partners for what, four years now? I know what you're thinking. And it's okay to feel some kind of way about all this."

Mena stood up straight. "What are you talking about, Felton?"

He shook his head. " 'It's not fair.' That's what you're thinking. It's not fair that Caroline came home, and Sadie never will. It's all right, girl. Everyone understands. No one could blame you for having human emotions, Mena."

"I'm fine. I promise."

"All right. All right." Felton patted his hands on his thighs, like he was playing drums. "Play it your way. But I'm here if you want to talk."

"I said I'm fine."

"You know, I had this partner once who…"

Mena rolled her eyes, turned on the heel of her boot, and walked to her own cubicle, feeling guilty for treating Felton that way. True, his "back when I was in the Army" stories got old, but he was only trying to empathize and show his support. But Mena had spent the past ten years trying to prove to her colleagues at the department that she could put the past behind her and do her damn job. The last thing she wanted was for Felton, or anyone else in the department, to think she was coming unglued just because the Hansons were getting the happy reunion she never would. She was genuinely happy for them. And she wasn't going to let the past – a past which she could not change – get in the way of her work. Just because Caroline was home didn't mean the case would close. Far from it. The focus would simply switch from finding the missing girl to finding the monster who abducted her and held her captive for a decade.

He had to be stopped.

Determined more than ever to put an end to this man's reign of terror, Mena pulled out a yellow legal pad and a pen and wrote down every piece of information she'd gathered so far from her talks with Caroline. If it meant she stayed at the precinct all night going through the scant evidence and brainstorming ways to catch the sonofabitch, so be it.

But as she sat trying to focus on her notes, that old familiar itch surfaced for the first time in a long, long time. It reached up from the depths of Hell, clenched her willpower in its claws, and squeezed tightly. It wanted her to think about Sadie instead of Caroline. It wanted her to focus on her grief and guilt rather than on finding the man who had caused so much suffering for so many families. It screamed for her to stop what she was doing, give in to its mounting pressure, and do its bidding, consequences be damned.

7

Caroline wasn't sure how she felt about the social worker who walked into the room and sat down across from her. The woman seemed nice enough, but she didn't feel as comfortable with this strange person as she had felt with Detective Kastaros. The nice detective lady spoke to Caroline as if she'd known her for years. She'd even worried about her comfort and offered bring her clothes. Of course, it made sense. She said she'd been the one who had worked her case when Stan had taken her from the park all those years ago. She probably knew everything there was to know about Caroline, which was reassuring, in a weird sort of way. It brought her a sense of peace to know someone had been thinking about her and looking for her all this time.

"Detective Kastaros tells me you've asked what happens to you next. My name is Danna Rodriguez, and I'm a social worker. First, I want you to know, you can talk to me about anything."

"Why are you here?" Caroline asked in a tone which probably came across ruder than she'd intended. "I mean, are you here to send me to a foster home? Because I've already seen my parents and I want to—"

"No, no." The lady waved her hands in front of her chest. "We aren't quite there yet. And if we can avoid that, we certainly will. The hope is to have you home with your family as soon as possible."

"So they believe I am Caroline Hanson?"

Danna nodded. "Detective Kastaros just filled me in. Your fingerprints matched some we recovered from your parents' home when you first…"

"Was kidnapped?"

"Yes," Danna said. "What I'm trying to say is that, since you are not quite eighteen, we have to make sure everything is okay before we let you leave here."

"Like, make sure my parents aren't drugged-out losers? Or homeless? Or abusive?"

"Well, I wouldn't put it that way, but, yes."

"I don't know what my parents are like now, but they seem the same to me," Caroline said, her heart sinking at the mere thought of her family. "I remember them clearly. They were loving and kind. We never had much money, and my parents argued every now and then about bills and things like that, but they never abused me or neglected me, if that's what you want to know. They're good people. Or, at least, they used to be."

"And I'm sure that hasn't changed. I personally haven't spoken to them, but I will soon, and if everything is as good as you say, you can probably go home with them. Maybe even tonight. I know Detective Kastaros is rooting for that to happen."

"Yeah," Caroline said, looking down at the chipped polish on her fingernails then back at Danna.

The social worker tiled her head, folded her hands together on top of the table, and looked at Caroline with soft, kind eyes. "Caroline, is something worrying you? Do you not want to go home to your parents? Because if there's anything I should know, now's the time to speak up."

"No," Caroline said quickly. "It's not like that. Like I said, my parents were...*are* good people. I doubt that's changed. But..."

"Go on. You can tell me whatever's on your mind. This is a safe place, and I'm not going to judge anything you tell me."

"It's just that the whole time I was there, in that house, Stan and his wife told me my parents didn't love me. That they didn't want me." Caroline shifted in her seat. "They said if my parents really loved me, they wouldn't have let me go."

"Oh, Caroline," Danna said with a shake of her head. "That's not true at all. What happened wasn't their fault. Sadly, children are stolen from their parents every day. Even if your mother didn't have her eyes on you every waking second, that doesn't mean she didn't love you. It means she's human."

"I know that. Mostly. As I got older and read more and more books," she stopped staring at her fingers and looked right at the social worker, "Stan insisted I read books to learn as much as I could since I couldn't go to school." Then, her self-conscious and shy nature reemerged, and she dropped her gaze again. "I read about how much parents love their children, and I just couldn't imagine them letting me go on purpose. But still, I'm just..."

"It's okay, honey. You're just what?"

"I'm just worried they won't want me now. Not after I've been gone for so long. What if they think I...I did things with that man?" Caroline sat upright and her wide eyes stared directly at the lady. It was important she understand this part. "But I didn't! I swear. Nothing like that ever happened."

"I believe you," Danna said, holding up her hands as if Caroline might physically lunge at her. "You don't have to explain yourself to me. But, Caroline, your parents miss you more than you could ever imagine. Nothing you could have done, no amount of time away from them, could ever make them not love you. I'm certain this is true. That should be the least of your worries right now."

Caroline looked at Danna. Hot tears stung her eyes, but she blinked rapidly to keep them at bay. "Do you really think so?"

"I know so."

She nodded, sank back into her chair, and wrapped the wool blanket tighter around her shoulders.

"So," Danna said, clicking the end of her pen, "is there anything else you want to talk to me about before I talk to your parents? Now's your chance to talk about anything at all you want to discuss with me. If there's anything I need to know and you want me to hear your side first, now's the time."

Caroline shook her head.

"Okay, then I just have a few quick questions for you before Detective Kastaros comes back in."

"Okay."

"First, how well did you eat when you there? Did they feed you well?"

Caroline nodded. "Pretty much. They fed me three times a day. Regular food. Like, you know, spaghetti, fried fish, grilled chicken, sometimes pizza, if I was good. They said it was important to keep up my strength and not get too skinny. But they also weighed me once a week. Just to make sure I didn't get too fat, either."

Danna took a few notes in her portfolio then looked back at Caroline. "Good. Now what about exercise? Did you get any exercise at all while you were there? Did you ever get out in the sun?"

"No," Caroline answered. She was fully aware of how pale she was and the mere thought of feeling the warm rays of the sun on her skin again filled her with excitement. "I had to stay inside at all times. They even covered the windows so no one could see me. But there were lots of light from lamps. Why do you need to know these things?"

Dann clicked her pen one final time and set it down on the table. "Because I'm going to be working with you and your family for a little while until the dust settles. It's important for me to know what your environment was like so we can slowly get you acclimated to the real world again. Also, I need to know what to tell your doctors whenever you go for a checkup. It's just routine."

"Okay."

"One last question. And I know you've already answered this, but I have to be absolutely sure. Did Stan, or anyone, ever touch you in any way that made you feel uncomfortable? Did they hurt you in any way whatsoever?" Caroline didn't answer right away. "It's okay. Remember, you can tell me anything. I'm here to help."

Caroline glared at Danna. "I told you. Nothing like that happened. Can I just be done with this now? Where are my parents? I'm ready to see them now. I don't want to talk about this anymore."

Danna held her hand up. "Okay, okay. Fair enough. I think I have everything I need for now."

"What happens next?"

"Well, I need to talk to your parents now. And I have to go to the house and check things out – again, standard procedure. But I know it's late and that you're tired, so I'll try to get this done as quickly as possible."

Danna stood, collected her pen and portfolio, and started for the door.

"Um," Caroline said.

The social worker turned around and looked at her. "Is there something else you need to tell me?"

"No. It's just…I have a question…about Detective Kastaros."

Danna leaned against the wall and held her portfolio to her chest. "Okay. What's your question?"

Caroline wasn't sure why she was prying or why it was so important for her to know more about the detective who had worked her case for so long. It felt like an invasion of her privacy, but then again, if this woman was going to be digging into her life and her past, it only seemed fair that she know what kind of person Detective Kastaros really was.

"She seems, I dunno, sad. Is she…okay?"

Danna dropped her shoulders and sighed. "Why do you ask, Caroline? Did she say something that concerned you?"

"No. It's just," she didn't want to tell the social worker about the scars she'd seen. That wouldn't be fair. Besides, there could be any number of explanations for them. "Oh, I don't know. She just seems, like I said, sad. Something in her eyes when she talks to me. And it's not just that she's worried about me, which I totally believe is true. There's something else, isn't there?"

The social worker pulled her chair out again and returned to her seat. She set the portfolio and pen down and laid her hands on the table, one on top of the other. "I suppose it's only fair that you know. Though I really think you should ask her yourself. It's really not my story to tell."

"Please," Caroline insisted. "I don't want to bother her with this. And I want to know what's wrong so I don't accidentally say the wrong thing. She's been looking for me for years."

"Yes, she has," Danna said. "She never stopped."

"And maybe that's why I feel so comfortable with her when I don't even really know her. But I can tell something about me upsets her, and I just want to make sure I haven't done anything wrong."

"Oh, God, no," Danna said, sliding her hand across the table toward Caroline in a comforting gesture. "It's nothing like that. It's not you at all. It's just that…your case is very important to her for many reasons. Detectives learn all kinds of personal information about their victims during their investigations. It's common for them to feel a deep connection to them without ever actually meeting them. Does that make sense?"

Caroline nodded. "I think so."

Danna hesitated briefly before continuing. "It's just, there is one other reason this case means so much to her." She sighed again, and Caroline could tell she was conflicted about whatever she was about to reveal. "You see, a few weeks before you were kidnapped, her own daughter was abducted while walking to a friend's house."

"Oh, no," Caroline said. "That's awful. Did they ever find her?"

"That's the thing. Yes, they found her about a week later. But she was gone. Whoever had taken her had killed her and left her body on the ground next to the Kentucky River."

Caroline looked down at her hands. This was not at all what she had imagined. But it made sense now. The little pink scars on her writs…Caroline's heart sank at the thought of the detective, who seemed so strong and confident otherwise, feeling so depressed and lonely that she had tried to take her own life. Somehow, this knowledge endeared her to Detective Kastaros even more.

"I know," Danna said. "It's heartbreaking. But Mena, Detective Kastaros, is a very determined woman. Her tragedy drove her to eventually become a detective. One of the best I've ever worked with. But of course, seeing you here, returning home after all these years…I'm willing to bet that's why she seems so sad. Because it's not like her to show wear her emotions on her sleeve. I'm surprised you were even able to pick up on it."

"So seeing me come home upsets her because her little girl will never come home." Danna nodded once. "I totally get it. It makes sense."

"But don't you worry," Danna said with a smile as she stood again and reached for the door. "You're in good hands. There's no one I would want in my corner more than Detective Kastaros."

"What's her name?" Caroline asked as Danna turned the knob.

She turned and looked at Caroline. "Her name is Mena, but I think you should—"

"No, I mean, her daughter. What's her daughter's name."

Danna's features softened. "Sadie. Her name was Sadie." She

smiled at Caroline again and waved as she stepped out into the hallway and closed the door behind her.

Caroline slumped in her chair. The story about the detective's daughter made her heart ache. But it made the detective seem more human, more vulnerable to her. And somehow, it made Caroline feel safer knowing they had a deeper connection than she'd even imagined. Detective Kastaros's own daughter had been kidnapped. And only a few weeks before Stan had taken her from the playground. What were the odds of that happening? Like, a million in one, probably.

Then, like a lightning bolt striking the ground on an otherwise clear day, it hit her. Suddenly everything came rushing back, and she realized it wasn't a coincidence, after all. She remembered something. Something Stan had said to her one day shortly after he'd taken her from that park. And just like that, she connected the dots. She knew why this case meant so much to Detective Kastaros.

She was looking for the man who'd killed her daughter. She was looking for the man who'd abducted Caroline. And Caroline now realized what Detective Kastaros had probably known for years.

Stan had killed her daughter.

8

It was almost 3 AM when Mena turned the key to her brownstone door and slinked inside. She kicked her boots off in the entryway and shed her coat, hanging it on a hook on the wall near the stairs. Catsby wasted no time in running up to Mena and rubbing his jaw against her ankle. She reached down and picked up the white, hairless Sphynx which she'd named The Great Catsby as an homage to her favorite book. Truth be told, the idea had come to her when she'd stumbled across a list of "funny cat names" on her Facebook feed one night. His first name had been Bob. Though some would think of him as just a pet, to Mena, Catsby was a constant reminder to look past life's distractions and find what was true. Like Jay Gatsby watching the glow of the light from Daisy's house across the lake, Mena's cat was the one light that beamed in the darkness. It was not lost on her, however, how sad it was that this was true and that the soul she was closest to on this earth was an ugly, creepy-looking cat, who truly only cared about being fed, having a clean litterbox, and occasionally being scratched behind the ear.

The feline purred incessantly when she bent down and scooped him up into the crook of her arm. Petting his bald skin, which was a blessing due to her extreme allergy to all things furry, Mena ambled down the hallway and toward the kitchen.

"Busy day today?" she asked him.

Meow.

"Tell me about it." Mena set Catsby on the floor, opened a can of Friskies tuna-flavored cat food, plopped it into his bowl, and patted his head for good measure. "Eat up, boy."

Her phone pinged. She slid it out of her back pocket and looked at the screen. It was a text from Danna that read: *Caroline is safe and sound at home. Patrol car parked out front. Will check in Monday morning. Get some sleep.*

Mena's shoulders relaxed, and she let out a long-held breath, knowing that Caroline Hanson was now safely home in the arms of her loving parents gave her comfort. Parents who had waited over ten years for this day. Parents who had, in all likelihood, long ago assumed their daughter had met the same fate Sadie had met. Thinking of her daughter again made Mena feel like someone was squeezing her tightly around the chest, cutting off her oxygen supply, and making her dizzy. From the moment Mena had heard Caroline's name come out of the dispatcher's mouth hours earlier, images she didn't want to relive had flooded her mind. Mena always tried to remember Sadie the way a mother wants to remember her child: bright, happy, and full of life. But those are not the adjectives that one would use to describe what Mena had seen play in her mind all day, like some sort of demented home movie played on an old-timey projector.

First, there was the image of Sadie laid out on a cold, steel slab in the morgue the night Chief Medical Examiner Len Watts had called Mena down to identify her body. A white sheet covered Sadie's tiny frame until Watts had pulled it back, revealing her pale but angelic face. Her blonde hair was disheveled and in rats' nests, but the thing that had been burned permanently into Mena's mind, as if someone had used a soldering iron to permanently etch it into her memory, were the black, blue, and green bruises around her tiny neck.

Worse than this were the photographs Mena had forced her lieutenant to show her of Sadie's body as it lay on the river bank along I-75 near Clays Ferry Bridge. Picture after picture showed Mena's little girl laying face-up on the muddy grass, staring up at the midnight sky as if watching the clouds dance across the moon. Her legs were twisted in almost unnatural angles, and her arms were splayed out at her sides as if she'd been making a snow angel. Sadie was still wearing her white, puffy winter coat, buttoned up to the top, just the way Mena had fastened it before naively allowing her to walk to her friend's house earlier that day. The memory of the guttural cries that had escaped Mena's throat when she'd seen these photos and noticed that her little gloves and scarf were missing still made her stomach churn.

"She's cold! She needs her gloves!" Mena had screamed as Lieutenant Iverson had struggled to hold her tightly. *"My baby is so cold. Please, please find her gloves."*

Mena's phone rang. Assuming it was Danna again, she glanced down at the screen, prepared to click the side button and reply after a few hours' sleep.

No such luck.

Instead of Danna, the caller ID displayed the number of Shady Oaks Nursing Home, where Mena's mother Helena had been a resident for six months.

Shit.

"This is Detective Kastaros," Mena answered.

"Detective, this is Nancy Vancleave here at Shady Oaks. I'm sorry to bother you at such an early hour…"

"It's okay. I just got home. Is everything all right with Mom?"

"Well, actually, that's why I'm calling. Your mother has taken a bit of a fall. We're sending her to—"

"Excuse me," Mena interrupted. "But how exactly does a

seventy-five-year-old woman who is confined to a hospital bed have a 'bit of' a fall?"

"I…I'm not…sure, exactly. All I know is that the CNA went in to check on her and—"

"*The* CNA? As in, just one? How on God's green earth is it that one CNA was…you know what? Never mind. Just…tell me where you're sending her."

"We've sent her to St. Joseph Hospital on Broadway and—"

"I'll be right there."

Mena clicked END without saying another word and dropped her phone to the granite countertop so hard, the corner of the screen cracked.

"Fuck!"

Suddenly, and without warning, that old familiar itch surfaced again, and there was only one thing in the forefront of her mind. Mena knew these thoughts were not only wrong but dangerous. And years of therapy combined with anti-anxiety meds and antidepressants usually kept these obsessive thoughts at bay. But considering the pounding her psyche had taken in the last twelve hours - from Caroline Hanson reappearing, to the deluge of thoughts about Sadie, to now learning her mother had somehow fallen at the nursing home – Mena was not in a stable enough place to push back these troubling tendencies.

Catsby meowed at her as she stormed down the hallway toward the bathroom. Mena opened the cabinet over the toilet and shuffled around the orange pill bottles, Q-Tips, and tampons until she found what she was looking for. She seized the small wooden box she kept hidden behind the bag of cotton balls.

Gingerly, she smoothed her fingertips along the lid to the box, pried it open, and peeked inside. Her hands trembled as she reached in and grabbed the razor blade, held it up, and examined it. Part of her knew she should flush the damn thing down the toilet. But the biggest part of her knew this tiny metal item had more control over her than it should. This wasn't the first time. It wasn't the second, or even the third. And as much as Mena hated to admit this to herself, it would not be the last.

Mena pulled her shirtsleeve up and pressed the razor blade to one of the few remaining clean spaces between her scars. She breathed in, breathed out, then dug the razor's tip just deep enough to cut through the first layer of skin and dragged it about an inch across her inner wrist. As the blood slowly appeared and trickled down her arm, Mena felt a wave of adrenaline crash over her, followed by another wave of excitement that left her breathless and quickened her pulse, and finally, a wave of relief that brought a faint smile to her lips and made her knees wobbly.

She drew in a deep breath, counted to ten, then grabbed her go-to bandages, slapped one over her freshest cut, and headed back to the kitchen. There, Mena grabbed her gun and badge, slipped her phone into her back pocket, and headed for the door.

9

The detective lived in a much nicer place than Stan had expected. He wondered how she afforded her three-story brownstone on a cop's salary. It hadn't been that hard to find her. The online article about the girl's return home had mentioned Detective Mena Kastaros by name. After that, all it took was a phone call to his old friend Hirano, who'd helped him build The Rainbow Room and hide it on the dark web. In less than thirty minutes, Hirano had texted him the detective's home address, a picture of her in her dress blues in front of an American flag, as well as some interesting personal facts about her.

As he stood across the street, hidden behind a tall, thick, oak tree, he watched through the window on the third floor as her silhouette flitted about the tiny room, which he assumed was her bathroom. He couldn't see her features since she'd been smart enough to draw the blinds, but she sure spent a lot of time standing in her bathroom. He wondered what in the hell she was doing at this late hour. It was nearly four in the morning, for God's sake.

The floodlights on the tiny front lawn illuminated her brownstone enough that Stan could tell it was a brick construction unit with black window shutters and a matching door. There were no decorations on the grass, the porch, or anywhere else on the exterior. No wreaths, flags, or statues. Not even political signs in the yard left over from the recent election, like some of her neighbors' yards boasted. Nothing at all to personalize her home. Perhaps she liked to keep things as simple as possible. Neat and orderly. The inside of her house would tell the real story, but he couldn't get in while she was still there. Or at least, while she was awake.

When the light went off in the upstairs bathroom, his pulse raced, and his hands grew itchy. Of course, he'd have to wait a bit and give her time to fall asleep before he could even consider entering the house. He hadn't thought much past that point, or what he'd do once he got in, but he just knew he had to stop her before she found him and Beverly and they both spent the rest of their lives in prison. He'd promised to protect his wife, and that was exactly what he was going to do, no matter what it took. The first time he'd killed, it has been an accident. Anger and fear had gotten the best of him, and things had gotten out of control. But he'd learned from his mistakes. Stan didn't relish the idea of killing anyone again, least of all a detective. He knew he'd been lucky to get away with it the first time. This time, if he wasn't as lucky, he'd not only face life in prison, but quite possibly, a needle in his arm.

A light came on downstairs.

Go to bed already, will ya?

Seconds later, the light went out again. The front door opened, and Stan slunk further into the shadows, suddenly worried the oak tree wasn't quite doing the best job hiding him. He risked a glance in her direction and saw a woman hurrying out of the house, shoving a gun into its holster, then zipping her coat all the way up and flipping her hood down over her head. It had to be Detective Kastaros. It was pitch dark out, and from this distance, there was no making out the features he'd seen in the policewoman's profile picture. But he felt certain it was her.

Where are you going this late at night?

Probably got a call about one of your cases.

Was it about him? Had they found something out already? Beverly had been right, the more he'd thought about it. True, they'd gone to great lengths to cover their tracks and keep any of the girls from learning any details about themselves, their location, or anything else that might one day lead to their undoing. Caroline Hanson was one smart cookie, though. Not like all the rest. She'd had a natural intelligence about her and a desire to learn, which Stan had foolishly encouraged by bringing her books to read. He had thought he was doing her a kindness because, after all, no one wanted to purchase a stupid girl who couldn't hold a simple conversation. Men liked girls with at least something inside their skulls. But what if she was even smarter than he had thought? What if she'd figured out where they lived? What if he or Beverly had accidentally let something slip in front of her one day that could lead the police right to their doorstep?

Stan watched as the detective sped away from her parking spot in front of her house. Watched her taillights as her car traveled to the end of the street, took a right, then disappeared around the corner. This was his chance. He'd wanted to catch her alone when she least expected it and threaten her into letting the case drop. Into leaving him and Beverly alone. And if it had come to violence, then so be it. What mattered most was buying them some time to at least formulate a plan. But now that she was gone, he was forced to do something else. For now, anyway.

Stan looked all around for signs of life, then, finding none, he darted across the street and ducked behind a bush in the detective's front yard. He was careful to avoid the glow of the floodlights, though. Scanning the yard and the sidewalk, he noticed that if he hurried and stayed slightly to the right, he could make it to the front door without being caught in the beams of light. His heart pounding and sweat beading on his forehead, he drew in a deep breath, let it out, and made a mad dash for the front door.

When he made it to his destination, he jerked his headfirst right, then left, on high-alert for anyone who might still be up at this insanely late hour. Seeing no one around, he reached into his back pocket and pulled out his wallet. Remembering the instructional YouTube video he'd just watched, he selected the flimsiest card in his wallet – his Kroger grocery discount card – and slid it between the door and the strike plate. He glanced over his shoulder and once again ensured no one was walking or driving by, then angled the card and bent it to a nearly ninety-degree angle. Applying what he hoped was just the right amount of pressure, he wiggled the card back and forth until he heard the faintest click, telling him the trick had worked. Thankfully, the detective had not engaged her deadbolt, which was a miracle in and of itself, considering her line of work. But he'd noticed she'd left her brownstone in a hurry, so he could only assume she'd forgotten to do so in her haste to get wherever the hell she was going. Stan took a third and final look around him and hoped that, even if someone did see him entering, he'd been so quick about his duties, anyone would simply assume he might be a friend, family member, or anyone else who belonged there and that he'd used his own key copy to enter.

He pushed the door open gently, praying there was no alarm system activated – the last possible security trap that could trip him up. After a few seconds went by without a loud, screeching sound piercing the night, he breathed a sigh of relief and stepped over the threshold.

On any other night, Stan was certain he couldn't have gotten away with breaking into a house, let alone a detective's house. If anyone would be likely to have high-level home security, it would be someone who worked in law enforcement. But the planets had all aligned for Stan tonight. No floodlights. No nosy neighbors. No deadbolt. No alarm system. Had the Detective Kastaros not fled her brownstone in the middle of the night in such a rush, Stan would likely have never gotten this far. Perhaps the universe was looking out for him and he'd be able to accomplish his mission and find a way to save him and Beverly from lifelong prison sentences.

Stan crept slowly down the hallway, using the flashlight app on his cell phone to light the way. To his right, stairs led up to the second level – most likely where he'd find the detective's bedroom. He thought for a moment, wondering if he should look for her computer, which would probably be in an office that could be anywhere in the house. His other option was to make a beeline for her bedroom, where he could maybe find something he could use to persuade her to leave him and Beverly alone. Who knew what kind of secrets people kept in their underwear drawer? Even hard-boiled detectives like Mena Kastaros had to have something incriminating for which they would do anything to keep from seeing the light of day.

The bedroom it is.

He turned and made his way up the stairs, slowly and steadily, so as not to make any noises. True, the detective was not home, but what if she had kids? Or a boyfriend?

Shit, I didn't think about that.

The last thing Stan wanted was to get into a life and death struggle with some beefed-up police officer she might be sleeping with. The information Hirano had provided him made no mention of a husband or a live-in partner, but that didn't account for friends-with-benefits or brand-new boyfriends...or even girlfriends. Stan decided he'd just take a quick peek into her bedroom. If he saw a man sleeping in the bed, he'd hightail it out of there before anyone was the wiser. Then, he'd have to come up with another plan to get this dogged detective off his tail.

Looking down the hallway once he made it to the second-floor landing, he noticed three doors – two on the right and one on the left. The one on the left had to be the bathroom since he'd already seen the detective's shadow in that window earlier. That meant there were two bedrooms, one of which had to be hers. He crept down the hallway until he came to the first door on his right, which stood wide open.

Stan shined his phone light into the room and saw a small bed, a dresser, and a nightstand. The room was sparsely decorated, from what he could tell in the darkness, and the comforter was tightly tucked into the mattress. Several throw pillows were stacked neatly at the head of the bed, and he saw no signs of it having been slept in recently. This was not where Mena Kastaros slept. This was clearly a spare bedroom.

Stan looked at the time on his phone. He'd already been inside for five minutes. He had to pick up the pace. What if she had just realized she needed milk and was already on her way back? She'd shoot him where he stood without blinking, and she'd be justified since Stan had technically broken into her home. He decided to pick up his pace. Beverly would be lost without him, so he couldn't let himself be killed.

He turned on the thick heel of his work boot and made his way to the last remaining room on the second floor. This time, the door was shut. Stan reached out, grabbed the doorknob, and turned it slowly. With a gentle push, the door parted wide, and the light from outside shone into the room, illuminating it enough for him to see a larger bed, an armoire, and a walk-in closet to the left. The bed was unkempt, and the sheets hung halfway off the bed. Pillows were scattered across the room. She clearly was not a "make your bed every morning" kind of girl. Stan shined his light around the room, looking for anything he could use to his advantage.

His eyes landed on the nightstand to the right of the bed, and he took two steps toward it. Something shot out from under the bed, causing Stan to stumble backward and nearly fall to the ground. He caught himself just in time by grabbing hold of the footboard of the bed. His pulse raced, and a drop of sweat dripped down his forehead and off his nose onto the carpet as he tried to steady his breathing. Stan shined the light over to where the thing had run, and there, in front of a large swivel mirror, sat a creature that somewhat resembled a cat, but it had not one single hair on its entire body.

What the fuck is that?

He took a step forward to examine the strange-looking creature, but when he was only inches away, it hissed at him. He realized then it was, indeed, a cat, though it was the creepiest fucking cat he'd ever seen. Stan kicked at the freakish animal just enough to scare it away, and it thankfully did as he'd hoped. The animal from Hell slinked out of the bedroom and into the darkness of the hallway.

Stan turned his attention back to the nightstand. On top was a lamp, a box of tissues, a cell phone charging cord, and a framed picture. But he was more interested in what the detective might be hiding inside the nightstand. Slowly, he slid the drawer open and shined the light from his phone downward. Using his gloved index finger, he scooted the items around. He found two bottles of pills: a sleep aid and an antidepressant.

Well, well, well. Someone has serious issues.

But the fact that Detective Kastaros was depressed and had trouble sleeping at night meant nothing. Half of the population was on one form of antidepressant or another. Besides, it likely stemmed from her job. He continued looking around and found a bunch of hair ties, two batteries, and a pair of silver hoop earrings. Stan dug further back and finally found something of more interest to him – a black leather-bound journal.

A wide grin spread across his face, and his heart rate accelerated as he untied the leather bindings and flipped through the pages. He was in luck. The journal was nearly full. It started in January of last year, and every page contained entries all the way up until two days ago. As intrigued as he was by this discovery, and as much as he desperately wanted to read her innermost secrets and thoughts in the hopes of finding something he could use to his benefit, he knew he didn't have time. Instead, he tucked the journal behind him in the waistband of his jeans and pulled his sweatshirt and coat back down to cover it.

Jackpot.

But just as he was about to tiptoe out of the detective's bedroom, curiosity got the best of him, and he felt the sudden urge to look at the picture on top of the nightstand. Who knew? Maybe it would give him some glimpse into her private life. Some tiny detail that might be helpful to Stan. He shined his phone light on the photograph, and his heart stopped. A sudden coldness hit him to his core and his mouth fell open. He shuffled back a couple of steps and nearly lost his balance but regained it just in time to pick up the frame and stare at the picture more closely...just to be sure his eyes weren't playing tricks on him.

The frame held a photograph of a young girl Stan knew all too well. It had been ten years, but this was a face that was seared into his memory; one he would never forget for as long as he lived. Staring back at him with wide, hopeful eyes full of life and promise was the girl who haunted his dreams and plagued his mind almost every waking minute of the day. The only girl Stan had ever had to kill.

But wait. Why would the detective have a framed photograph of that girl on her bedside table? Even if she had worked the case after her body had been found, it made no sense for a police officer to keep a picture of a victim on her nightstand. Unless...

A sudden urge to vomit overwhelmed Stan as realization smacked him across the face. The girl he'd killed was Detective Kastaros's daughter. How on earth had he managed to not find this out before now? Of course, he'd avoided any mention of the girl in the news during that time as the guilt over what he'd done had overwhelmed him. Still, he'd killed the daughter of a police officer, and now that same officer was working on the case of

Caroline Hanson and, presumably, trying to identify and locate Stan and Beverly.

If she knew…if she had figured out all those years ago that the person who killed her daughter and the person who had taken Caroline Hanson were one and the same, she surely would never rest until he was in prison, or better yet, six feet underground. If that *was* the case, there was nothing Stan could do to scare or intimidate her enough to stop tracking him down. No, she'd want revenge. She'd want to be the one who personally watched the life fade from his eyes. Suddenly, Stan's entire scheme went flying out the window. He was screwed. Big time. Worse yet, there was no way he could protect his beloved Beverly from the consequences of his actions.

Stan had to come up with a new plan. Had to find a way to protect them both. But first and foremost, he had to get the hell out of this detective's house as fast as possible before she returned home. With what he now knew about her, she wouldn't hesitate to shoot him between the eyes and not even think twice.

He set the picture down, twisted it so it was at its original angle, shut the drawer, and quietly made his way out of her bedroom. Stan tiptoed down the stairs, out the front door, and out into the darkness of the night.

It wasn't until he was halfway home that he realized he had only one course of action. It wasn't ideal, and it would be painful as hell, but knowing there was a dogged detective out there, hell-bent on avenging her daughter's death, Stan knew he was out of options.

It was time to go home.

10

Stepping into her home for the first time in ten years felt to Caroline like stepping into a parallel universe. Her mother and father had already walked through the doorway and were standing in the living room, looking at her with wide eyes and big grins and motioning her forward. Caroline tried to ignore the cameras, bright lights, and reporters who had encircled their front porch and were clamoring for a picture, a statement, or anything at all they could get from the poor young girl who'd just reappeared after a decade. Apparently, word had gotten out about her return before she'd even left the police headquarters.

With butterflies in her stomach and a racing heart, Caroline stepped over the threshold and into the safety of her childhood home. She started to shut the door behind her, but her mother stepped forward and leaned out into the chilly night air.

"Y'all come back later. Let my poor baby get some rest. We'll make a statement after she's slept some. Thank y'all for coming out." She smiled for the cameras and waved goodbye before shutting the glass door, then the heavy wooden one. "Whew," she said.

"What a circus. I figured there'd be some folks hanging about. It's just like when you—"

A thick, heavy, and uncomfortable silence fell all around them.

"When I was kidnapped," Caroline finished.

Her mother's features softened, and she reached her arm out, laying her hand gently on Caroline's shoulder. "Yes, baby. And I'm so sorry. It's all my fault. I've lived with this guilt for so many years. I thought my baby girl was gone forever, and I only had myself to blame."

"But you didn't…"

"Your mother has blamed herself this whole time for what happened." Her dad stood between Caroline and her mom, looking down at the ground as he spoke, his hands shoved into the pockets of his jeans. "She believes it's her fault since she was the one who took you to the park."

"It's not your fault, Mom." Even though Laura Hanson was her mom, the title still felt odd coming out of Caroline's mouth. Maybe because she'd been gone so long. Or maybe because she'd convinced herself she'd never see her parents again. "I don't blame you, not for a second."

"I know, and I love you for it," her mom said. "But I was the one who took you there. I was supposed to watch you. And I *was* watching you. But then Kelly and Ginny showed up, and I hadn't seen 'em in such a long time. I just started talking to 'em and I lost…" Tears began to flow freely over her mother's cheeks and down her neck. She didn't bother to wipe them away. "I lost you. I thought I'd lost you forever."

"It's over now," Caroline said, surprising herself with her own strength. "I'm not saying things will be easy. I don't really feel all that comfortable here yet. But you're my parents. I remember you, and I love you. I certainly don't blame you." Now it was Caroline's turn to cry.

The three of them stood in a tiny circle, each of them sniffling and wiping their eyes for several seconds before her father cleared his throat and clapped his hands together, causing Caroline to flinch.

"Now, it's real late, and it's been a long and exciting night. I say we all try to get a few hours of shut-eye. Detective Kastaros said she'd stop by tomorrow morning, so we'd best let Miss Caroline get to bed." He looked at her and smiled, his eyes warm and kind, just the way Caroline remembered. "Do you remember where your old room is, sweetheart?"

Caroline nodded.

"Good," her mom said. "I'll go with you. I'd like to say good-night and tuck you in, just like we used to. That is, if you are comfortable with that."

She wasn't sure if she was completely comfortable with the idea of being tucked in like a child by her mother whom she hadn't seen in ten years, but it seemed to mean a lot to her. Plus, it sounded kind of sweet, and what harm could come from being tucked in by your own mother, even if it had been ages since it last happened?

"Sure," Caroline said with a shrug. "Why not."

Her mom smiled so big, her entire face seemed to light up, and Caroline knew she'd made the right decision.

"Right this way," her mom said, gesturing toward the hallway.

Caroline took one last glance around the house. Everything looked exactly as she'd remembered. Not the most expensive, classy decorations one could ask for, but it was homey and cozy. A place where she remembered feeling safe as a child. A place where she felt safe now, oddly.

She followed her mother down the short hallway until they reached her room on the right, just as she'd pictured it in her dreams while she was…gone. It was like she'd stepped through some sort of portal where she was zoomed back to her child-hood. The walls were still that odd shade of pink Caroline had begged her mother to paint them when she was about six years old. Her bed was still set up caddy corner, just the way she'd liked it. All her favorite trinkets and girlie things were neatly organized on top of the white dresser, and the posters of Edward and Bella were still tacked up on opposite sides of the room.

Her mother must have seen her staring at them. "You remember how we argued over those posters?"

Caroline nodded, keeping her eyes on Edward's chiseled face. "You said I was too young to see the movie, but I'd already read the book. I'd checked it out from the school library and hid it from you for the week it took me to read it. When you found out, you were really mad."

Her mom nodded. "At first. But you wore me down eventually and convinced me you were an 'old soul' and that you understood more than most girls your age did. You were right. You were more mature than the other girls in your class. Maybe that's why I thought I could let you play at the park without watching you every second."

Tears filled her mother's eyes once again, and she stared down at her feet as she tried to maintain her composure, probably for Caroline's sake.

"It's okay," Caroline said, laying her hand gently on her mother's arm. "It's really okay. I'm here now. No reason to be sad."

"Oh, honey." Her mother looked up at her, reached out, and pulled her into a tight embrace. "I can't believe you're really home." She cried on Caroline's shoulder for a good minute or two before pulling back and looking her square in the eye. "We have so much lost time to make up for. I want to take you to the mall. We'll go shopping. We can go to Joseph Beth and buy you a book to read. I remember how much you loved to read. And we can go to Ramsey's, your favorite restaurant. You can order the fried chicken and—"

"Slow down, Mom," Caroline said as kindly as she could. "We have plenty of time for all that. Let's just enjoy some time together and get to know each other again for a while before we venture out into the world. Besides, I'm not sure I'm ready to go out in the public just yet. I hope you understand."

"Sure, sure," her mother said, nodding and wiping her nose with her sleeve. "Let's get you into bed. You must be exhausted, and I'm probably making it worse."

Her mother bent over, pulled back the white and pink checkered comforter, and patted the mattress. Caroline hesitated for a beat, then climbed into the bed, thankful her parents had brought her a change of comfy clothes when they'd picked her up at the precinct. Her mom tucked the comforter up under Caroline's arms, then patted it down on both sides of her body, the way she had when Caroline was little.

"There," she said. "All snug as a bug in a rug."

The old saying brought a tidal wave of emotion crashing down over Caroline. She'd longed to hear those words for as long as she could remember. And now, here was her mother, tucking her in tightly and saying those exact words she'd dreamed of. Caroline broke down into unexpected sobs, and her mother wrapped her arms around her and held her tightly until they subsided.

When they finally did, Caroline laid her head back on the pillow and apologized to her mother.

"You don't ever have to apologize for anything, sweetheart. You cry all you want. I'm here for you. You've been through a lot, and I don't know exactly how we'll manage these first few days, but we will. We're a family. And we're together again. That's what matters most."

"You're right," Caroline said, smiling back at her mother. For the first time since she'd come home, she really saw her. She looked exactly the way Caroline had remembered, only a bit older. Her hair had blonder highlights and tiny crow's feet and laugh lines were etched into her face. But she was still beautiful to Caroline. Oh, how she had missed her mamma.

"I'll let you get some sleep," her mom said, patting her daughter's leg and standing to leave the room.

But before she could step out, Caroline stopped her. "Mom?"

She turned around and smiled at Caroline with raised eyebrows. "Yes, sweetheart?"

"Do you think he'll come back?"

"Who'll come back?"

Caroline hesitated. She didn't even like thinking about Stan, let alone talking about him. But this cocoon of safety wasn't foolproof, and she still didn't understand why or how Stan had let her go that night.

"Stan...the man who..."

Her mother's shoulders slumped, and she exhaled, took two steps forward, and sat down on the bed again. "Oh, Caroline. That's just not possible. You're safe here. There's a policeman parked right in front of the house. Detective Kastaros insisted after that social worker came and met with us here and agreed you could come home. And your father keeps a gun next to our bed. He'll keep us safe. But you don't even have to worry about that." She bent forward and kissed Caroline on the forehead. "Besides, that only happens in the movies. He's not coming back for you. Ever. Trust me on this. You're safe here. Now get some sleep."

Her mom blew Caroline a kiss, turned off the bedside lamp, and walked out of the room, leaving the door slightly ajar. Caroline rolled over onto her side so that she was facing the window. Her mother's words were comforting, for sure. But wouldn't every mother say the same thing? What if Stan changed his mind? What if he realized how stupid it was to let her go and he came to silence her and keep her from talking to the police? Not only was she afraid that Stan may come for her, she was afraid her parents might get caught in the crossfire. She'd just gotten them back. No way could she lose them again.

Sure, it was a little surreal returning to this house after all these years. But it was her home. She knew in her heart this was true. And these were her parents. They loved her. Any doubts she'd had about their ability to welcome her home, or about their love for her, was slowly fading away. It was clear by the way they reacted tonight that they loved her as much now as they had ten years ago, if not more. Caroline decided at that moment that she was going to do whatever it took to get back to "normal" and make her parents proud. They deserved a happy ending, after all. And so did she.

She closed her eyes, and though it took a while for her nerves to settle, eventually, she fell asleep, safe in her bed, where she belonged.

11

St. Joseph Hospital was one of the oldest hospitals in Lexington, but it was still one of the best and the one most of the town's senior citizens turned to for health-care in their golden years. Mena rushed through the automatic double doors to the nurses' station and asked the first nurse she saw where she could find Helena Kastaros. As she waited for the hospital worker to slowly make her way around the desk and over toward the entrance, Mena looked around the waiting room and saw several people waiting for news of their loved ones. The walls were painted a muted yellow, and several reprints of Monet paintings hung on the walls. The décor created a homey, comfortable atmosphere likely meant to subconsciously calm the frayed nerves of visitors and family members.

A woman with large bags under her eyes finally made her way over to Mena and directed her through another set of double doors, but this time, a nurse had to swipe her key card for access. When Mena found her mother, she was behind a curtain, laying on a gurney, propped in an upright position. She rushed to her mother's side.

"Oh, my God, Mom. Are you okay?"

She shooed Mena's words away like an annoying gnat. "Eh. Everyone is overreacting. I took a little tumble, that's all. A few bumps and bruises. No worse for the wear."

Mena looked at her mother, with wires connected to her and an oxygen tube in her nostrils, and her heart sank. "Mom. They're not overreacting. You fell. At your age, that's nothing to—"

"My age? Give me a break, Filomena. I may be seventy-five, but age is just a number. I still don't see why I must stay in that God-awful nursing home. I was perfectly fine at home by myself. If anything, you're the one who overreacted the first time I fell, and you abandoned me at the old folks' home. Do you remember that?"

"Yes, I remember, Mom. But I didn't abandon…never mind. Tell me what happened tonight. How did you fall?"

"Pfft. It was nothing. I just had to use the little girls' room, that's all. I got a little wobbly on my feet, and I fell. Simple as that."

"You're not supposed to go to the bathroom by yourself. Why didn't you use the call button?"

"I did! I pushed it three times, to be exact." She crossed her hands over one another and squared her shoulders. "No one came. And I wasn't about to piss on myself. I'm not *that* old, you know."

"So, no one came when you pushed the call button three times?"

"They rarely do."

Her body tensed, and heat flushed through her chest, but knowing her mother's penchant for exaggeration, she tamped it down and pushed forward. "Okay, so you got up to pee, you got…wobbly, then you fell. Then what happened?"

Mena's phone pinged. This time it was Felton, saying: *Just checking on you, partner…let me know you're okay.*

Mena typed out a quick: *I'm fine. Thanks. See you Monday.*

Laying the phone face down on her leg, she looked back at her mother, who had fixed her with a look Mena knew all too well. It said, *"You're always working. You never have time for your mother."*

"Mom, what happened next?"

Helena looked away from Mena and shook her head. "You're a busy detective. You shouldn't have to be here right now. I'm fine. Just go home. Come see me this weekend. We'll play Scrabble, like we always do. And I'll beat you, like I always do."

"Stop avoiding the question. What happened next?"

She let out a dramatic sigh. "Well, I guess I fell asleep."

"You what? You fell asleep?" Mena's heart rate picked up, and she grinded her teeth together. But after a beat, she took two deep breaths and relaxed her jaw. "Mom…what time was it when you got up to use the bathroom?"

Helena shrugged her shoulders. "I don't know."

"Mom."

"Okay, okay. It was around ten."

If there had been anything breakable around, Mena would have picked it up and thrown it against the wall. "Are you sure it was ten o'clock?"

"Yes, I'm sure. I know because I looked at the clock. It read 10:03 PM. I may be old, but I'm not blind, Filomena."

"I know. I know." Mena leaned forward and squeezed her mother's frail hand. "Do you mean to tell me you fell, then you just laid there for almost five hours? Mom, I want you to be certain about this because they didn't call me until after three in the morning."

Helena raised her chin. "I know what I'm saying, darling. Yes. That's what happened."

"For the love of…" Mena lifted her phone again and pushed the contact for Shady Oaks's Administrator, Nancy Vancleave's cell phone. It rang twice.

"Hell, Detective. How's Helena doing?"

Mena stood and paced back and forth at the foot of Helena's

bed. "Do you mind telling me how in holy fuck my mother fell five hours ago, and you only just found her after three?"

"Detective, I'm not sure what you're—"

"Oh, just save it." Mena stopped dead in her tracks and fought to keep her voice low. "I've had my doubts about your little establishment for the last few weeks. I pushed them aside because you promised to take care of my mother. But this?" She spoke through clenched teeth. "This is just going too damn far. Effective immediately, Helena Kastaros is no longer a resident at Shady Oaks."

"Now, wait a minute, Detective. I'm sure we can—"

"I'll be by in a day or so to collect her things. And you can be sure you'll be hearing from my attorney soon," she said, shouting the last words louder than she meant to.

Mena pushed END and dropped the phone onto her mother's bed.

"That's my girl," Helena said.

"Yeah, well, I learned from the best. The only question now is, where in the hell do you go when they release you from here?"

"I'm sure there are plenty of other nice establishments in the area." Helena looked up at the ceiling and shrugged. "You'll think of something, I'm sure."

Mena knew her mother well enough to know exactly what she was not saying but implying. She rolled her eyes and her mother did not miss this insulting gesture.

"Filomena Agnes Kastaros," her mother snapped, "you can be so ungrateful sometimes, you know that? My parents came here from Greece when I was only two years old. After they died in that horrific car crash, I lived alone from the age of seventeen until I had you."

Here it comes.

"I know, Mom." Mena took a deep breath and counted down from ten.

"I raised you all by myself. And that wasn't easy, considering I was forty when you were born." There was not a trace of embarrassment on Helena's pale face. "Sure, I should've had things settled by then, but instead, I had you. And I barely made ends meet, working as a housekeeper by day and waitress at night." Her voice rose with every passing phrase. "I had to pay the rent on that tiny one-bedroom apartment with no help from anyone. It was always just you and me and I..." Helena looked down at her frail hands, fidgeting with the hem of the thin hospital blanket.

Mena looked over at her mother and sighed. "Don't worry, Mom. You're coming home with me."

Helena looked back over at Mena and a small smile appeared on her thin lips. "Well, if you insist."

12

The next morning, after tucking Helena safely into her armchair with Perry Mason reruns playing on the TV in front of her, Mena looked down at her mother and said, "Mom, are you sure you're going to be okay until I can get a nurse in here to help out?"

Helena swiped her hand through the air. "Yes, fine, fine. You know, I can get up on my own, if I need to. I'm not crippled."

"I know that, Mom, but even at Shady Oaks, you were supposed to have aides helping you get up and around. Look what happened last time you got up on your own."

"Pish, posh," Helena said, turning her head and looking away from Mena. "I've got that fancy cane you bought me for Christmas if I have to get up for anything. And I'll take it nice and slow. Does that make you feel any better?"

"Not much, but just promise me you'll take it easy. I'll have a nurse out here by tomorrow at the latest."

"Go on, dear. You don't want to be late," her mother said with a smile Mena could not decipher.

"All right. Just please, be careful. Call me if you need anything at all. I set your phone right there on the end table."

Helena tapped the smart phone Mena had bought her two years ago with a crooked finger. "Yep. It's right here. Now, go."

Mena kissed her mother on her forehead, gathered her gun, badge, and wallet, and headed for the door. She turned and took another worried glance at her mom, then slid on her fur-lined winter coat and stepped out onto the front porch. The cold winter wind stung her cheeks, waking her up more than any five-dollar coffee ever could. She jogged down the front steps and made a mental note that she'd have to have a ramp installed for Helena, sooner rather than later.

The Hansons lived in Woodhill Subdivision, one of the lower-middle-class neighborhoods in Lexington. Not like the projects, but nothing like Henry Clay District, either. Mena parked her beige Towncar on the street in front of 214 Cedar Wood Drive. As she climbed out of the driver's seat, she eyed her surroundings and kept one hand on the gun at her hip. Even though she'd not been a beat cop for many years, those old instincts had never died. After nodding at the officer in the cruiser parked in front of the house, she walked up the sidewalk that ran straight through the middle of the yard covered in patchy, dry, yellow grass, and right to the front door of the Hansons' house.

Mena knocked on the glass front door and, immediately, the heavy, incessant barking of what sounded like a rather large dog thundered from behind the door. She could hear a man's voice shouting at the dog to "shut up" and assumed it was Mark Hanson doing the yelling. A few seconds later, the big wooden door opened, and Mark stood there with one hand on the door and another latched onto the black, spiky, leather collar of a Rottweiler who was lunging and snarling and throwing thick, white saliva everywhere.

"Laura! Come get this damn dog! Detective Kastaros is here!" Mark looked at her with a sheepish grin. "Sorry. We got Zeus here for protection a few years back. In this neighborhood, you can never be too sure. But he's a damn handful. Laura!"

"All right, all right, I'm coming! Jeez."

Laura Hanson appeared from the kitchen, wiping her hands on a hand towel. She grabbed the dog's collar and shooed him into his cage. "Hey, Detective. I was just making breakfast. Got some biscuits and sausage gravy and some bacon. Wanna join us?"

"No, thank you." Mena smiled as politely as she could.

"You sure? How 'bout coffee, at least?"

"Coffee I can do."

"Well, come on in. It's cold out."

Mena thanked the Hansons and stepped over the threshold. Out of instinct, she glanced around the living room. Though it wasn't necessarily a pigsty, the place was full of worn-down furniture and chintzy decorations. Above the maroon couch, which had several dog claw marks and rips in the worn leather, hung a replica of a Michael Kincaid painting, which prominently displayed a log cabin with a stream running past it. Duct tape covered a hole in the brown, threadbare recliner. A large red candle made the living room smell like apples and cinnamon. It looked – and smelled – like many of the homes Mena had visited in the area throughout her career – an eclectic collection of furnishings, likely bought at thrift stores or yard sales, yet clean and somewhat tidy.

"Please, have a seat," Laura said as she snatched up a basket full of clothes from the couch and set it on the floor, making room for Mena.

"Actually, I came to talk to Caroline. Is she here?"

Laura's expression changed from one of sweet, southern hospitality to one of curiosity and concern. "Yeah. She's in her room. But why d'ya need to talk to her? She's done been through a lot these last ten years. And you talked to her Friday night. I don't want my baby to go through no more…"

Mena held her hand up. "Laura, please. I understand your hesitance. Keep in mind, yes, we're thrilled that Caroline is home safe and sound with her parents. But this man who took her all those years ago is still out there somewhere. Talking to Caroline may be the only way we will be able to find him and whoever he is working with and make them pay for what they did."

Laura's features softened a little and the tension in her shoulders relaxed slightly. "All right." She turned and faced the hallway. "Caroline! Come in here, honey!" Turning back to Mena, she said, "I'll get you that coffee now. Mark, come eat."

Mark followed Laura into the kitchen, and Mena sat on the edge of the sofa. On the glass top coffee table sat a copy of Sunday's *Lexington Herald-Leader*. Prominently displayed on the front cover was a picture of Caroline which a reporter had taken as she walked with her parents from the front porch of their house to their red, beat-up Chevy pickup. In it, Caroline looked like a deer caught in headlights while, strangely, Mark and Laura were smiling at the camera and waving.

People react to trauma differently, Mena reminded herself.

"Hey, Detective."

Mena looked up to see Caroline standing before her, wringing her hands together nervously and biting her bottom lip.

"Hey, kiddo," Mena said. "Sit down here and talk to me for a sec."

Mark sat in the recliner and Laura set the coffee down on the table and started for the couch. "Actually, if you guys don't mind, I'd like to speak with Caroline alone."

Laura's eyes widened. "That Mexican social worker lady already talked to her alone. We have a right to be here, don't we?"

This part always frustrated Mena. Yes, the parents did have the right to be present while their minor child was interviewed, but from Mena's experience, children were rarely willing to open up and be honest in front of other adults, especially Mom and Dad. "True, but I just need a few minutes. Please. It would really help."

"C'mon, honey," Mark said, gently grabbing Laura by the upper arm. "Let's go have a smoke."

"But breakfast—"

"It can wait. Give her a few minutes, for God's sake."

"Fine. One cigarette."

As Mark gently guided Laura out the front door, he turned to Mena and held up two fingers, hinting he'd get Laura to stay out for at least two cigarettes.

Mena nodded. When the door closed behind them, she turned to Caroline, who had sat on the far end of the couch.

"How are you doing, Caroline? Everything going okay here?"

She nodded. "Mom and Dad are even nicer than I remember. They hover a little, but I understand. They just missed me, that's all."

"That's good. Now, we don't have much time, so let's get right to it. When we left off the other day, you were telling me that this man, this…Stan…was about to sell you to the highest bidder. What exactly does that mean?"

Caroline's eyes welled with tears and she blinked them away. Sniffling, she said, "When we turn eighteen, he sells us to whoever pays the most money on the internet. We have a little birthday party, then the girl leaves with Stan. I don't know what happens after that. No one ever comes back. But I can guess."

"What do you think happens?"

"Well, while I was there, he took really good care of me. He made sure I ate well, but not enough to get fat. He made me exercise every day, even if it was just walking circles around the room. He took my measurements once a year. And the woman with him – Beverly - she washed and brushed my hair every day and clipped and painted my nails every now and then." Caroline looked down at her fidgeting fingers. "They talked to us a lot about how to behave and speak properly. They taught us manners. They even taught us how to dance with men and how to make them feel special. I think he was grooming us to, you know…"

Mena choked back the bile that rose in her throat and forced herself not to show the sickening feeling that washed over her. "You think they were going to sell you as a sex slave?"

Caroline nodded, but wouldn't meet Mena's gaze. Mena wanted nothing more at that moment than to swoop Caroline up into her arms, hold her tight, and rock her back and forth. Instead, Mena reached out her hand and laid it gently on top of Caroline's. "I promise you, honey. We're going to find Stan and Beverly and whoever else is responsible for what happened to you. You have my word."

Caroline looked down at Mena's hand, then finally looked her in the eyes. "Your wrist. It's all bandaged up. What happened. Did you…"

Mena jerked her arm back more sharply than she intended and slid her shirtsleeve down to cover the bandage. But it was too late. Not only had Caroline once again seen the evidence of her darkest secret, but she appeared to understand exactly what had happened. There was no denying it now. No putting unringing the bell. Mena had a choice to make. She could either ignore Caroline and maintain the detective/victim boundaries, or she could let her guard down for once in her life and be human, if only for a minute, and hopefully establish some sort of connection with the girl.

"It's a long story," Mena finally said.

"But I didn't think adults did that. I thought only girls my age cut themselves."

Mena nodded. "Me, too. I thought I was the only one. Turns out, it's this whole thing…adult self-harm, they call it."

"Why would you…"

"I'm sure you heard about my daughter, Sadie."

Caroline's beautiful eyes went wide as moons. "Yeah, that

social worker lady told me. I'm so sorry. I feel sort of guilty, actually."

"Why on earth would you feel guilty?"

"I, well, I sort heard Stan talking about a little girl who…"

Mena's heart began racing a mile a minute. Her hands trembled. "What? What did Stan say about Sadie?"

Tears streamed down her thin cheeks, but she didn't wipe them away. "I'm not sure it was her. I just feel so awful that I got away and she…she…"

"What do you know, Caroline?" Mena knew Sadie was gone from this earth, but that was all she knew. She'd never even had confirmation that Caroline's abductor and Sadie's killer were one in the same. Until now.

"He…he said…he said there was a girl, right before me. He never said her name, but he said she, um, she couldn't be a good girl, like me."

Mena bit her lip and her stomach roiled as she listened to Caroline. It was all she could do not to bolt out the door, get into her cruiser, and just drive. But she had to hear this. "Go on."

"Stan said, if she had been a good girl like me, he wouldn't have snapped her neck."

13

The world spun around Mena, and her empty stomach lurched at the mere thought of that monster's hands wrapped around Sadie's little throat. Just as she was about to excuse herself to the bathroom, the Hansons came back inside, a smile spread across Laura's face.

"Channel 18 is here," she said, looking directly at Caroline.

"The news?" Caroline asked in a tone Mena could not decipher.

Great. Just what I need right now.

"Yes, baby. They want to interview you about…well, you know."

"Laura," Mena said cautiously, "I don't think that's such a good idea right now."

"Why not? After all she's been through, my baby deserves to get to tell her story. Besides, we already got a call from *Dateline* and *Nancy Grace*. She'll be doing a lot of interviews soon. Might as well start local, don't you think?"

"No," Mena said, "I don't think." Laura crossed her arms over her chest and pouted at Mena. "Listen, Laura," Mena stood, "Caroline has been through God only knows what for the past ten years. We're only just beginning to scratch the surface of what she endured at the hands of that...*animal*. And he's still out there somewhere. The last thing Caroline needs right now is exposure of any kind. It's bad enough she's on the front of the Herald-Leader." Mena pointed down at the newspaper on the coffee table.

Mark took another step inside and pulled the front door closed. "Baby, maybe Detective Kastaros is right. Let's give our little girl some breathing room for a bit first."

Clearly unhappy her husband had sided with anyone but her, Laura shot Mark a piercing glance. She seemed to ponder her options briefly as she rubbed her mouth with one hand and placed the other on her hip. After a few seconds of silence, Laura turned to face Caroline again. "All right, honey. Looks like we'll have to wait a little while before you go in front of the camera." She turned her attention to Mena. "But me and Mark...we can do interviews, right?"

"If you really feel—"

"Great! We'll go talk to the reporter now while you finish talking to Caroline. You're almost done, right?"

Mena nodded.

"Okay, then. Oh, I'd better put on some makeup real quick. Or maybe..." She looked at Mark. "Or do you think I'd would look more sympathetic without the makeup. Just, ya know, how I look normal."

Mena shook her head minutely and crossed her arms as Laura fussed over the prospect of being in front of the cameras. If the news stations ever came to interview her about what had happened to Sadie, she'd tell them where to go, how to get there, and exactly what to shove up their asses when they arrived. Yet, here was Laura Hanson, relishing the idea. But again, Mena reminded herself that people react to trauma differently and she did her best to reserve judgment.

After Laura and Mark stepped back outside, Mena glanced

out the window and watched as they stood arm in arm on the front porch. A crew member pointed a camera directly at them, a boom mic operator hovered his equipment over them, and a reporter Mena vaguely recognized stood poised with a microphone at an angle that would ensure she was off-camera.

"She's doing the best she can," Caroline said.

"What do you mean?" Mena sat back on the couch.

"I mean, my mom…well…I don't really remember a lot about the time before. But I do remember some. She's always been good to me. She's a good person. Mom just…she just…wants to help, I think. She told me she wants to help catch him and save all the other girls."

"Let's talk about that for a second," Mena said. "You've mentioned the other girls a few times. How many girls were at the house with Stan and Beverly while you were there?"

"Three," Caroline said without missing a beat.

"Three? Why three?"

"He said three was a good number. Two weren't enough. Four were too many to handle. So he kept three in the house at all times. One at each stage of the process."

"Stage of what process?"

Caroline broke eye contact. "The grooming. He always had one new girl, usually around eight or nine. One he'd just taken from wherever he could grab them. One was in the middle of training. That girl would be about twelve or thirteen. Then, he'd have the one who was ready to leave. As soon as the girls turned eighteen, that's when they'd leave, and I'd never see them again. I watched two leave. I was next."

"And that's why you ran when you got the chance. Very brave, Caroline."

"Thank you." She looked down at her fidgeting fingers.

Mena glanced out the window at Mark and Laura, who stood on the front porch, enveloped in one another's arms as the reporter stood a couple feet away, speaking into her microphone. She shifted her attention back to Caroline.

"Now, the two girls you saw leave...do you remember their names?"

Caroline shook her head, staring now at her bare feet. Mena noticed she'd removed all the chipped nail polish. "Not their real names. He gave us new ones as soon as we got to the house. He told us to forget our old names. Our families didn't want us anymore, so our names didn't matter." There was a long pause. As Mena waited for Caroline to continue, she looked around the room and noticed there were no framed photographs of the family or even Caroline as a child. "My name was Violet."

Mena looked at Caroline. "Violet?"

Caroline nodded. "The two girls before me were Silver and Scarlett. And there were two younger girls at the house when I...I left. Their names were Ebony and Hazel. I...I shouldn't have left them...I...oh, my God...those poor girls..."

Caroline bent forward and sobbed into her hands. Her shoulders heaved up and down, and her head shook side to side. Mena scooted closer to her and wrapped her arms around the girl for the first time since she'd shown up at the station Friday.

She held Caroline while she cried. Mena's vision blurred as she tried to fight back the tears that threatened to spill over her cheeks. She dug into her pocket, pulled out a clean tissue, and handed it to Caroline, who wiped her face, though she continued to sob in Mena's arms.

"Caroline," Mena said. "You are not to blame for anything. You did the right thing. You saved your own life. It was a very brave thing to do. And with your help, we're going to find Stan and Beverly and we'll save Ebony and Hazel."

Caroline sat up, her face red and blotchy, snot and tears streaming down her face. "You think so?"

"I know so. But I need your help to find them. So as hard as this is, I need you to think hard. Is there anything you can remember, anything at all, about where this house might be?"

"No," Caroline answered, shaking her head. "Nothing. Any time he took me anywhere, he would put me in the back of the van. There were no windows in the back. And he didn't let me look forward. I had to face the back the whole time. He'd park in the garage, close the garage door, then he forced me straight in through the door to the inside. I never saw the outside of the house or anything."

"That's okay. That's good, actually."

Garage. Attached. Door to the interior.

"What else. Any little details about the house can help us track him down. Think."

"The basement." Caroline hugged herself tightly as if the memory Mena had conjured had frozen her to the bone.

"The basement?"

"Yeah. The basement. He kept us down there all the time. The door to it was right there as soon as we entered from the garage. I never even saw the kitchen or any other part of the upstairs."

"Good. How about when you had to use the restroom?"

She shook her head again. "There was a bathroom downstairs. It had a shower, but no tub. Yellow tile covered the floor and walls. A white plastic shower curtain. A toilet and a small sink. No mirror. The only time I got to see myself was when Beverly would brush my hair. She'd hold up a small hand mirror and I'd get a quick look."

"What about food? Where did you eat?"

"Down in the basement. Beverly would cook upstairs in the kitchen then bring our meals downstairs. We always had to eat in our room. We all shared one room."

"That's all very helpful, Caroline. You're doing great. One more question for today. Then you get some rest." Caroline nodded. "Think really hard. Close your eyes." The girl did as

Mena asked. "Now. Did you ever hear neighbors? Don't answer right away. I want you to concentrate. Think hard."

At first, Caroline shook her head. "No. I don't think so…"

"Anything. No matter how small. Did you ever hear lawn mowers outside?"

Her eyes brightened. "Yeah. I did. But sometimes it seemed bigger…louder than at other times. Like there was more than one mower." She seemed zoned out, concentrating on some place or thing far, far away. "And laughter. Sometimes I heard little kids laughing and playing. I remember because when I ten or eleven, the first few years I was there, I used to get so jealous. I wanted to go out and play, too. But we couldn't leave the basement." Her head snapped up, her eyes widened, and she smiled ever so slightly. "And a dog! There was a little, yappy dog there recently. It wasn't there for years. But the last couple of years, I heard a little dog barking over and over again." She turned and looked at Mena. "Does that help?"

Mena smiled and placed a hand over Caroline's. "More than you know."

14

Stan didn't bother to take his boots off when he entered his house this time. Instead, he hurried inside, down the hall-way, and into the bedroom where he found Beverly standing in the master bathroom in front of the mirror, curling her hair. When she saw his reflection, her eyes widened, and she set the curling iron down on the counter.

"Stanley Dale Pollard," she said, her hands on her wide hips. "Where on earth have you been all night? You had me worried sick! Don't tell me you already found another girl, because this is not the time to be—"

Stan rushed up to Beverly and stood inches away from her. "I'm sorry I worried you. I couldn't sleep last night for worrying about how to protect us both, so I snuck out of bed and went for a drive."

Beverly raised an overly plucked eyebrow. "A drive? You went for a drive in the middle of the night?"

"I know. But listen, I called my friend. You know, the one who helped us set up the website?"

"Japanese fella, if I recall," Beverly said with a puzzled look.

"That's him. Anyway, I had an idea, and he helped me track down the detective who's been assigned to investigate us. I found her name in an online article." He shook his head as if to clear the cobwebs. "He gave me her home address. I went there and I watched her house for a while and I—"

"You did *what*? What were you thinking? What if she'd seen you? And what exactly were you planning on doing?"

"I didn't really have much of a plan. I just thought maybe if I could scare her or find some way to convince her to leave us alone, I could—"

"And if she didn't listen?"

Stan shook his head and looked down at his boots. "I didn't think that far ahead."

"You really are some piece of work. What if she'd caught you? You'd have been hauled right off to jail!"

"It's worse than that," Stan admitted. "Much worse."

Beverly's shoulders drooped, and she tilted her head. "How, Stan? How could it get much worse than you being handcuffed, in the investigating detective's house, nonetheless, and sent to prison for the rest of your life?"

"She could have killed me. Would have killed me. I'm certain of that now."

"Well, I guess that's a possibility."

"No, you don't understand, Bev. I found something when I was in her bedroom. A couple somethings, actually."

"You went into her bedroom?" Beverly took a step back and held up her hand. "I don't think I want to hear any more of this."

"One thing I found might be able to help us. The other…"

Beverly leaned against the doorjamb and fanned her face with her palms spread wide. "Now I really don't want to hear this."

"I found a journal. Her journal. I haven't had a chance to read it yet, but it's full. All the way up until two days ago. This woman is an obsessive writer. If she writes that much, surely there's something in there that we can use to—"

"What's the other thing?"

Stan didn't answer at first. He simply stared at Beverly, clenching his fists at his sides and chewing on his bottom lip. Then he opened his mouth, shut it, then opened it again, like a fish struggling to breath on the hook. "You remember that girl? You know the one. About ten years ago. Right before we got Violet?"

Beverly's eyes narrowed, and she pressed her lips together into a thin line. "Stan, we…we said we'd never talk about that again. Why on earth would you bring that awful business up now?"

Stan sighed heavily and looked up at his wife. "That detective? Kastaros? That girl was her daughter. There was a picture of her, framed, on the nightstand."

It took a minute for Stan's words to sink in, but when they did, Beverly faltered as she took three steps, reached down to find the bed, and slumped onto the edge of it. "Oh, my God. I can't believe this." She didn't look at Stan. Her gaze wandered up toward the ceiling for a few seconds, then she closed her eyes tightly. "How is that even possible? What are the odds?"

"I'd say a million in one. Worse than that. We should play the lottery today."

Beverly's eyes snapped open and she looked Stan square in the eye, wagging a finger in his face. "Don't you joke at a time like this, Stanley Pollard."

"Sorry." He took a seat next to Beverly, but a couple inches away. "I know. It's awful. Seeing her face again after all these years. You know, I didn't really mean for that to…"

"Enough," Beverly snapped. "Do you know what this means? Do you?"

Stan nodded.

"Well, I don't think you do. But I'll tell you what it means. It means that if she has made the same connection you have, she's out for blood. She won't stop until she finds you. Finds us. And

God forbid she catch you in some dark alley with no other cops around. That woman will kill you."

"Don't be so dramatic, Bev."

"Dramatic? I'm being realistic, Stan. And one of us needs to be. You said it yourself. If that detective has her way, she'll see you buried before she sees you in cuffs." Beverly folded her hands in her lap. "Now, I may not have ever been blessed with children of my own. God saw fit for me to marry a man who was shooting blanks."

"Hey, now," Stan said. Her words had hit their intended mark.

"Sorry, love, but it's true. That doesn't mean I love you any less. Hell, that's half the reason I agreed to help you with this little venture. I get to take care of these girls and help give them a better life. But if I'd had children of my own, I can promise you right now...if someone took that child away from me, regardless of their reasons for doing so, I'd stop at nothing until I found that person and made them pay. You can bet your bottom dollar that's exactly how this detective feels now if she knows what we know."

"I know. Trust me, I know." Stan looked down at his fidgeting fingers.

"Then what are we going to do now?"

He looked at his wife. "I still have her journal. There might be something in there we can use. Something we can blackmail her with or scare her with."

"You can look," Beverly said, "but I think we're way past that now. So what's your big plan if that doesn't work?" Stan stared at her blankly. "Oh, Lord, no. I know that look. Go on. Tell me."

"I've had an idea. You're not going to like it, but I think it's our only option at this point. Just hear me out."

Beverly crossed her arms over her ample chest. "Oh, yeah? And just what might that be?"

"I think we have no choice but to call Walter."

Stan waited for Beverly to shake her head, to jump up from

the bed, to shout in his face – any one of her typical reactions any time he suggested involving Walter. But instead of reacting in her usual way to his suggestion, she drew in a deep breath, let it out, and patted his hand.

"Make the call."

15

Mena charged into the station, down the hallway, through the door, and into the detectives' section of the building. Her muscles were tight to the point she felt they might snap. Her senses were on high alert, and her jaw was set. She was determined to make progress in the investigation with the information she'd just learned from Caroline.

Felton stepped into her path with a cup of coffee in hand. Mena nearly bowled him over but stopped short just in time to avoid a collision.

"Sup, partner? Or are you just flyin solo these days?" He arched an eyebrow and one side of his mouth tilted upward.

Mena fixed her gaze on her partner. "What?"

"Lieu said you went to the Hansons' this morning alone," he said, sarcasm oozing from each word. "I checked my cellphone for any missed calls, but would you believe there wasn't one missed—"

"Shove it, Felton."

"All right, all right. I see how it is. And here, I was going to offer you this cup of coffee. I saw you park out front and being the friendly, *cooperative partner* that I am, you know, I just thought I'd *share* with you. You know, my *partner*."

"Point made, Felton," Mena said with a sigh. "Loud and clear. You can come next time. It was just on my way in, that's all. Wasn't trying to leave you out of the investigation."

"You swear?"

"Are you going to ask me to lock pinkies or something? Because you can forget that right now."

"Nope. Just thought maybe we could go over the tips that have been pouring in since Friday. We've got over three hundred fifty tips already. Can you believe that shit?"

She deadpanned him. "Yes, Felton. I can believe that shit. Caroline's case is making national headlines. The Hansons told me this morning they've already gotten calls from *Dateline* and *Nancy Grace*. Of course every Tom, Dick, and Harry with a police scanner who thinks themselves an armchair detective is going to have some 'tip' for us. Bet at least ten of those tips are from psychics. Am I right?"

Felton looked down at his feet, his hands shoved into his pockets. "Thirteen."

Mena realized she'd let her determination influence her attitude toward her partner. He'd done nothing to deserve her brusque reaction. She softened her tone. "That's what I thought." Mena patted Felton on the shoulder. "Let the rookies go through the tips for now. I have an idea." Mena snatched the coffee cup from his hand. "Thanks, by the way."

"What the—"

"Follow me."

Felton tsked as Mena turned and headed for her cubicle.

"Hold up," he said. "Slow your roll, Kastaros."

"Keep up, Felton." Mena ensured her tone was playful this time.

"Shiiiiit."

"Now," Mena said as she arrived at her desk. "When I talked to

Caroline this morning, she gave me a lot of useful info on the house where Stan and Beverly held her and the others."

"She knows where they kept her?" Felton leaned back against his own desk, his arms folded over his chest.

"Not exactly. But she gave me details about the inside of the house and even the neighborhood. Check this out." Mena dropped her things on her desk and turned to face her partner. "She remembers a lawn mower, children playing, and a yapping dog."

Felton raised an eyebrow. "That's...great...Mena...I...mean..."

"Think about it, Felton. What do all of those things point to?"

For a military veteran with years of experience as an MP and as a civilian detective, Felton could be slow on the uptake sometimes. He shrugged his shoulders and Mena resisted the urge to slam her palm into her forehead.

"Suburbs. They're keeping them in the suburbs." Felton just looked at Mena. The upstairs light still hadn't come on yet. Mena sighed and shifted her weight from one foot to the other. "Think about it. Dogs barking, children playing, lawnmowers running," Mena realized she was gesticulating wildly and lowered her hands, "those are all sounds you'd hear in a typical suburban, middle-class neighborhood. Sonofabitch has been hiding in plain sight."

Felton shook his pointer finger at Mena. "Yeah, yeah. I bet you're right. I mean, on one hand, it seems pretty high-risk to hold young girls captive right under all those neighbors' noses. But on the other hand, what better way to avoid suspicion than to blend in with Mr. and Mrs. Jones? I like the way you think, partner."

Mena nodded, staring at the middle distance, in deep thought. "I want to pull vehicle registrations on every early model, white, windowless van in the metropolitan area. We can narrow the results down from there based on vehicles registered to residential addresses."

"We can also probably assume that if he owns a white utility van like Caroline described, he's probably using it for some business venture. Not many regular folks drive around in vans like that."

"True," Mena said. "I bet you dollars to donuts he's still registered his company vehicle to a residential address, though. Some business you can run from your home." Mena began pacing in short bursts back and forth in front of her cubicle. "I highly doubt this asshole has time to work a nine-to-five job where he has to punch into a time clock every day. This guy would want to be home with the girls and Beverly as much as possible." She stopped right in front of Felton. "I'd say if we narrow the list down even further to white company vans registered to residential addresses within the city limits, we may just have a list we can work with."

"Well, I mean, we know his name is Stan. Surely there can't be *that* many men named Stan on that list," Felton added.

"True, but we can't know if he gave the girls his real name. Probably didn't. Too risky. But, yeah. Anyone named Stan on that list…we're banging on his door by the end of the day."

Felton pushed away from his desk and stood before Mena with his palm held high. "Hell, yeah. That's what I'm talkin about."

She hesitated. Then, despite herself, Mena raised her hand and slapped Felton's hand.

"See what a little teamwork can accomplish, Kastaros?"

Mena narrowed her eyes at her partner. "Just quit while you're ahead."

16

A s Beverly finished primping and sprucing herself up for God only knew what reason, Stan sat on the edge of the bed, flipping through the small, leather-bound journal he'd stolen from Detective Kastaros's bedroom. He'd already made the crucial call to Walter, but Beverly never went anywhere without curling her hair and "putting on her face," so before they took the most drastic measure to secure their safety, Stan wanted to at least try to see if the journal held any information he could use to save their sorry asses. Preferably, he'd find entries about how Detective Kastaros was sleeping with her boss, how she'd mishandled a case and a killer wound up walking scot-free, or better yet, that she had a penchant for stealing evidence or taking bribes. Deep down, Stan knew this was a longshot, at best, but hey, stranger things had happened. And he'd watched enough crime shows to know it happened, and usually with officers who would be the last one anyone would suspect of such deeds. He had to at least give it the old college effort.

The journal started with January of this year, so she likely kept one for each calendar year, as many people did. Not that Stan had ever felt the urge to write in a diary. Journaling was for girls or for sissies, neither of which described him. Besides, he never understood people's obsession with writing down their daily routines and every thought that passed through their minds. It was a symptom of society's increased sensitivity and decreased ability to use common sense. He was thankful, however, that this detective was one of the sheep blending in with the flock because if he could find even the tiniest hint that she was a dirty cop, he could find a way to blackmail her with it, and she'd have to choose between arresting Stan and potentially losing her badge, or better yet, her own freedom.

He returned his focus to the journal and began skimming through the entries. Thankfully, her handwriting was neat – beautiful, even. She wrote with blue ink in a clean, swirly cursive he could easily read. Stan ran his calloused finger down the page, stopping every so often when a word or phrase caught his attention.

...not sure I did the right thing. Felton said I should have waited to make the arrest, but I know in my bones that Bullock is guilty as sin. At least Lieu backed me up and the County Attorney agreed to prosecute, so...

Boring. He flipped the page and skimmed through more.

...and that's exactly why I don't date. What a douche. I know it's the twenty-first century and all, but men these days don't even know what the word "chivalry" means. Dutch? Who goes Dutch on a first date anyway? Loser. I'm never going on another...

She was lonely. If she weren't hunting Stan down, he might feel somewhat sorry for her. But she was. So he didn't. He kept reading.

...think Felton has some sort of weird crush on me. I swear, sometimes I catch him looking at me a little longer than he normally does. Felton's cute, if you like that whole baggy pants, sports jersey, white tennis shoes, and goatee thing he's

got going on. But, I mean, it's Felton, for God's sake. He's like a brother to me. I could never...

Nothing helpful at all. This was exactly the kind of thing Stan couldn't understand. She sounded like a teenage girl more than a hardnosed detective out for vengeance. He flipped several more pages, then read some more.

...missing Sadie today, more than usual. It would have been her eighteenth birthday today. I can't believe my baby would be an adult. She'd be going to college this fall. Then maybe getting married. Maybe kids. Hell, I could have been a grandmother. Now, I never will be. I swear to God in Heaven...if I ever find that rat fuck who took my baby's future from her, I will...

Shit. This wasn't exactly what Stan needed to be reminded of right now. He kept flipping, almost afraid to keep reading.

...know I shouldn't. It's not going to bring her back. It's not going to erase the pain completely. But for those few seconds after I do it, I feel...nothing. Not pain, no sadness, no emptiness, just...peace. No one knows. No one even suspects...

Now this was the kind of thing Stan had been looking for. What was Mena Kastaros up to that she was hiding from everyone in her life?

...but if that's the ugliest skeleton in my closet, I think I'm doing pretty good. I'm a great detective. I'm honest. I'm attentive. I'm determined. I've never committed a crime. Hell, I've never done drugs...unless you count weed those last two years of high school, which is pretty much a blur. So, if my biggest, baddest secret is that I cut myself every blue moon to ease the pain, I guess I'm doing pretty good. Well, maybe not good, but at least I'm surviving, which is more than I can say for my baby...

Fuck. Fuck. Fuck. Fuck.

He slammed the journal shut. So much for that idea. Basically, all he'd learned about Mena Kastaros was that she was a lonely, sad woman who cut herself to ease the pain behind closed doors but did everything else out in the bright light of day and by the books. His hopes of finding something incriminating to save him and Beverly had flown out the window. Nothing in this journal would help him. And now, she'd eventually realize her journal was missing. If she was any kind of decent detective, she'd figure out someone had broken into her house and stolen it, which only made his situation even more urgent.

There was nothing left to do. Nowhere else to turn. He was out of options, and there was no denying that Walter held the key to his freedom. No matter how hard this next step was going to be, he'd have to take it, even if it took him way past the point of no return.

17

W hile she waited for Felton to work his magic with the vehicle registration database, Mena sat at her own computer, watching Laura and Mark Hanson's interview on Channel 18's website. Her official reason for seeking out the interview was to scroll through the comments, just in case any of them seemed suspicious. Mena knew from the hundreds of suspect interviews she'd conducted, that perpetrators often followed news coverage of their crimes and their victims. So the idea that Stan might actually be watching, and possibly even commenting, was not beyond the realm of possibility. But if Mena were being honest with herself, she'd have to admit that a small part of her was uncomfortable with Caroline's parents' interview.

Mena watched as Mark spoke first. He talked about how happy they were to have their daughter safely back home. He told a couple of anecdotal tales about Caroline: how she loved cookie dough ice cream, how she loved their dog Zeus, and how, despite everything she'd been through she was "just a normal, everyday kid." Mena didn't miss, though, how Mark found a way to not-so-subtly drop the name of his concrete company when answering one of the reporter's questions. As Mark spoke, Laura hung her head and stared at the ground. Occasionally, she wiped away a stray tear.

The reporter, Ashley Babcock, asked probing but sensitive questions about how Caroline was coping with being back home and if she was going to seek professional help to deal with her trauma. Intermittently, throughout the interview, the image on the screen switched from the Hansons standing on their front porch to pictures of Caroline taken around the time she was abducted, contrasted with blurry images captured by amateur reporters as she entered and exited the police station on the night she returned home.

The reporter turned her attention to Laura.

"Mrs. Hanson, I know this is tough, but if you could say anything to the man who took your daughter away from you ten years ago, what would you say to him?"

Laura's gaze lifted, and she looked right at the camera. Her brow furrowed, and her lips drew into a tight, thin line. "I'd tell him he will rot in prison for the rest of his pathetic life. After that, I'd say things a Christian woman like me has no business sayin. He's a scumbag, and the police will catch him, sooner or later. Until then, he'd best be makin' things right with his maker. That's all."

The Hansons disappeared, and a picture of a Facebook page appeared on the screen.

"A GoFundMe account has been established for Caroline Hanson to help pay for counseling and any other expenses the family may have during this emotional time. Back to you, Susanne."

The video ended. Curious, Mena opened a new browser and went to her Facebook account. In the search bar, she entered Laura Hanson's name. Seconds later, she was looking at Laura Hanson's page. Sure enough, right at the very top of her timeline was a post with the GoFundMe account link prominently displayed. Laura had written:

Thanks to all our family and friends who have been there for us the past ten years and for your prayers and support. As you all know by now, our little angel Caroline came home to us recently. We got the best blessing God could give us when we found out Caroline was alive. We never gave up hope. But now she's going to need counseling and lots of things we're not able to provide because me and Mark don't make much money. His company, Hanson Concrete, doesn't get much work during the winter and as you all know, I haven't been able to work because of my back. Any little bit will help. Thank you for your love and support.

Below this message was a picture of Caroline, taken recently. It was a close-up shot, and in it, Caroline smiled, though it didn't quite reach her eyes. Her long brown hair was pulled back in a ponytail, and she wore a white headband and tiny silver hoop earrings. No makeup. Mena could almost hear her saying, "Please don't take a picture of me."

The message underneath her picture read:

CLICK HERE TO SUPPORT *CAROLINE SMILES*.

Mena clicked.

She was taken directly to the GoFundMe page for *Caroline Smiles*. The picture Mena had just been studying popped up even larger. To the right, it said, "$5,000 of $50,000 goal." There was a large DONATE NOW button below that. Mena was tempted to click and donate every penny she had, but she knew it wouldn't be proper. At the bottom of the page, below Caroline's picture, was a long typed-up paragraph where someone had gone into greater detail about Caroline's ordeal and exactly why this anonymous benefactor had started the account. According to the narrative, Caroline would need money for food, clothes, transportation, therapy copays, and other expenses. The author encouraged readers to donate, no matter how little, to *Caroline Smiles* to help this family in their time of need.

Mena cringed and shook her head. Perhaps it was some small, petty part of her that was jealous and unable to look past her own tragedy in the wake of Caroline's serendipitous return. Or perhaps it had more to do with the fact that, when she considered Laura's excitement over the news interviews, combined with this GoFundMe account, it seemed to add up to the Hansons possibly taking advantage of their few moments of fame and using it to their advantage.

But since their daughter's disappearance a decade prior, Mark and Laura had been the epitome of grieving parents. Maybe they did see something fortuitous in the prospect of earning some extra, much-needed cash in the midst of Caroline's return. But who could really blame them? They had been through hell, and as Laura had mentioned in her Facebook post, they'd fallen on even harder times since Caroline disappeared.

Mena chastised herself for hearing hoofbeats and thinking zebras. It was a common pitfall for detectives – seeing something innocuous and mentally turning it into some puzzle piece that held greater meaning than it actually did. The Hansons weren't greedy or opportunistic. They were just down-on-their-luck parents who needed as much exposure and help from family and friends as they could get.

Mena's phone vibrated on her desk. She looked down to see her mother's cell phone number staring back at her. She held the phone to her hear as she closed the web browsers.

"Mom? Is everything all right?"

"Mena, I think I might have had a little accident," Helena said in a steady, even tone.

Mena shot up out of her chair, her stomach twisted into tiny knots. "Mom, what's wrong? Are you okay?"

"Oh, yes, yes. At least, I think so. But I think you might want to come home as soon as you can."

"Why, Mom? What is going on over there?"

Helena cleared her throat. "I might have started a little fire. That's all."

18

Mena steadied her breathing as she drove past the elementary school with its yard full of children bundled in parkas and scarves, past the frosted grass of the park, and rounded the corner. The stoop of her brownstone appeared as she came around the bend of her quiet street. She slowed down as she looked for a parking space. The house seemed quiet, there was no smoke billowing from the windows, and there hadn't been any emergency vehicles blaring in the vicinity.

She parked her cruiser a couple doors down from her brownstone. Her fingers were tighter around the steering wheel than she realized, and her knuckles ached as she fumbled with the seat belt release, getting in her own way as she tried to hurry. She bolted from the vehicle, slammed the door behind her, and ran to her house.

Mena took two steps at a time up the stoop. With her hands shaking, she jammed her key against the door's keyhole twice before she managed to thrust it into its slot. She burst through the door. She smelled something burning, and a thin layer of smoke lingered in the air.

"Mom! Mom! Where are you?"

As she made her way down the hallway and into the kitchen, she found her mother sitting at the small breakfast nook, waving one hand through the air, and using the other to work on a sudoku puzzle.

"Mom?"

Helena looked up and smiled. "Oh, hello, darling. Sorry about all the smoke. I had a little accident making lunch."

"Apparently. What happened?" Mena surveyed the kitchen until her eyes landed on the sink. In it lay a baking sheet and several slices of blackened toast.

"I was trying to make some toast and jam. But I guess I lost track of the time."

"Did you set a timer?"

"I couldn't find one anywhere in your cupboards. You know, you really should get a decent egg timer."

Mena sighed, walked over to the sink, and opened the window. "Mom, no one uses those anymore. They use the timer on the oven. Or the ones on their phones. You have one, too. Remember? I showed you how to use it."

Helena swiped her hand through the air. "Pfft. You know I can't figure out all this new-fangled technology. Who needs a phone that can do all that stuff anyway? All I really need is to be able to place a call."

"Mom..." Mena decided it was pointless to continue down this path. Instead, she walked over to the back door and slid it open, making sure to leave the screen closed so Catsby didn't get out.

Then it hit her. Catsby hadn't run up to her as he usually did whenever she walked through the door. In fact, she didn't see him anywhere.

"Mom, where's my cat?"

Helena shrugged. Worried Helena may have accidentally-on-purpose let Catsby out, as she'd made no bones about hating cats in the past, Mena panicked and headed for her bedroom. She opened the door, half expecting to see her hairless friend curled up on her bed, but there was no sign of him anywhere. Mena went from room to room, her pulse quickening each time she opened a door and saw no sign of her cat.

When she ran out of places to look, Mena stood in the threshold of the spare bedroom. Tears burned at the rims of her eyes. She sucked in her lips and held her breath for a moment. Then, she heard a soft meow.

Mena froze. Where had the sound come from? She listed more carefully, wondering if she'd missed a hiding place or a closed closet in the other rooms. The sound came from the garage. She hurried to the garage door and slung it open. Catsby leaped up the steps and rubbed against her ankles, back and forth, purring loudly.

"Mom! How did Catsby get into the garage?" she yelled so her mother could hear her from the kitchen.

"I have no idea!" Helena called back.

Mena again decided to let it go. This would only be the first of many battles she would face with her mother living under the same roof, and she had to remind herself to only pick the battles she might actually stand a chance at winning. This was not one of them. She shrugged off her frustration and headed back toward the kitchen.

"Working on any big cases right now, darling?" her mother asked, peering down at her puzzle through her readers.

Mena rummaged through the fridge, gathering the fixings needed for sandwiches. "As a matter of fact, yes." After grabbing what she needed, she shut the fridge door with her hip, walked over to the nook, and set everything down on the small kitchen table. "I don't know if you've heard about Caroline Hanson on the news, but I'm—"

"Oh, yes, yes. Amazing story." Helena set her puzzle down and began helping Mena assemble the sandwiches. "Saw it on the news this morning. Terrible what happened to that poor girl. But thank the good Lord above He brought her home to her parents. They must be thrilled. Can you imagine—"

Helena's face froze, and her eyes widened.

"It's fine, Mom. I'm okay." Suddenly, Mena wasn't hungry anymore.

"Like hell you're okay. I'm so sorry, darling. This must be incredibly hard for you. How on earth are you even working this case? Especially considering..."

"Considering it's probably the same man who killed Sadie?"

Helena winced at the mention of her only granddaughter's name. She shook her head and looked up at Mena, tears welling up in her dark grey eyes. "Yes. Exactly that. How can you work that case? I'd think your boss would want you as far away from it as possible."

"Well, when I got the call from dispatch saying that someone claiming to be Caroline Hanson had shown up in downtown Lexington, I walked straight into my lieutenant's office and told him I wanted the case. After all, I'd been the one assigned to it when she first disappeared."

"I remember. How could I forget? You had only been a detective less than a year, and Caroline disappeared a week after Sadie..."

"I know. And he balked at the idea, at first. But I explained to him that I'd been the only one to work Caroline's abduction case, and that I'd been the only one to work it for the past ten years, albeit to no avail. I told him I needed this case to keep me grounded and that no one knew Caroline's file better than me."

"So he caved?"

"Not until I threatened to quit."

"You didn't." Helena looked impressed by her daughter's moxy.

"I did. And given my clearance rate and job performance, he didn't really have a choice. But he did strongly admonish me that if he got even a whiff of me losing perspective or using questionable judgment, he'd, quote, yank my ass off the case and make sure I was patrolling the streets the next day, end quote."

Helena whistled. "Bet that lit a fire under your ass."

"You bet."

Mena's mother set her readers on the table and turned so she was facing Mena directly. "Listen to me, darling. I know you are strong. I know you've found a way to cope with your loss...with *our* loss. But don't kid yourself, Mena. You're human. You're fallible. You're capable of breaking, just like anyone else."

"Mom..."

"Just, listen." Mena exhaled and sat back in her chair. "If the man who took that girl really is the same man who took Sadie from us, then you have to be careful. And I don't mean about him. You're a good cop. I know that. You can handle him, I'm sure. What you must be careful of is yourself." Helena laid a wrinkled but soft hand on Mena's arm. "Don't forget...I know you, Mena. I know your strengths and I know your weaknesses. Sadie is your weakness. If you're not careful, this investigation...it could break you. And I will not lose anyone else to this monster. Do you understand me?"

Mena nodded her head. "Yes, ma'am."

Mena laid her hand on top of Helena's. Mother and daughter sat there, looking at each other, speaking without words, basking in their unspoken love for one another.

Mena's phone pinged, tearing into their reverie. As much as she hated to look, she was long-past due back in the office, so she stole a quick glance at the screen. It was a text from Felton.

"I'm sorry, Mom. I have to get back to the station."

"Fine, fine. Just...remember what I said. Be careful."

"I will. I promise."

Mena stood, grabbed a sandwich to go, and headed for the

door. When she stopped at the entryway to slip into her coat, she glanced down at her phone. The text from Felton read, *Got three matches on my search criteria. Wanna go bang on some doors?*

Damn right, she did.

19

"So, Caroline," her mother said as they sat at the kitchen table eating pancakes, "what do you want to do today?"

Caroline shrugged as she poked a piece of pancake with her fork and ran it through a river of syrup.

"I know you said you're not ready to go out in public. But your father's at work all day, so it's just us girls. Are you sure you don't want to go for a mani-pedi? I know this great spot in Nicholasville. Small, out of the way. No one would bother you there. What do you say?"

Caroline felt a surge of guilt mixed with discomfort. She knew her mother meant well, but she'd already made it clear she wasn't ready to leave the house. Not yet, anyway. "Thanks, but I really just don't think I'm ready. Maybe in a few days. Is that okay?"

Disappointment played plainly on her mother's face. But she tried to mask it with a small smile and a shake of her head. "I really didn't want to go out, either. It's perfectly fine."

"I really am sorry," Caroline repeated.

"It's fine." Her mom set her fork down, wiped her mouth with a napkin, then tossed it down on top of her plate. "I have a better idea. How about we have a mini spa day, right here in the comfort of our own house?"

Caroline looked at her with a raised brow. "Here? But how…"

"I've got lots of fingernail polish to choose from. And somewhere in the hall closet, I have all the things we need for manicures and pedicures: lotion, clippers, pumice stones, even cuticle cream. How does that sound?"

"I guess so."

"We can pick a movie on Netflix to watch while we paint each other's nails. In fact, I know the perfect movie. You never got to watch the rest of the *Twilight* movies, and they're all on Netflix now. So how about we have a *Twilight* movie marathon?"

"Sounds great." Caroline forced a smile. Sure, she'd love the movies based on Stephanie Meyer's book series, but thinking about all the things she'd missed the past ten years made her heart sink to her knees. Stan and Beverly hadn't allowed Caroline and the girls to even see a television, let alone watch TV shows or movies. Her only indulgence or connection to the outside world had been the books Stan brought her every week. And only rarely were they current books. Mostly, they'd been classics, which Caroline eventually grew to love and appreciate much more than bubble gum and teeny bopper stories like those which included sparkling vampires and werewolves with twelve packs.

"It's settled, then," her mother said, clapping her hands together. "Why don't you clear the dishes and stick 'em in the dishwasher while I go grab all the supplies?"

"Yes, ma'am," Caroline said.

Laura looked at Caroline with sadness in her eyes. "Caroline, honey, you don't have to call me ma'am. You never did that before, and you don't have to start now. Why did you…" Realization must have snuck up and hit her full force because her eyes watered, and she rubbed the back of her neck. "They made you call them sir and ma'am, didn't they?"

Caroline nodded but couldn't look her mother in the eyes.

"Well, okay, then." Laura sighed. "I'm sorry. I didn't know. But Caroline, there's so much I still don't know. You told Detective Kastaros a hell of a lot more than you've told me. You have to trust me. I'm your mother, for God's sake. Don't you know you can trust me?"

"I know," Caroline said. But did she really? She hadn't laid eyes on her mother since she was seven years old. How comfortable was she supposed to feel talking to a near-stranger about the worst thing that ever happened to her? Then again, Laura was her mother. No amount of time away from her should break that bond or call into question the trust and confidence they had once shared. "I'm sorry. What else do you want to know?"

"I'm not going to interrogate you, Caroline. Just...clear those dishes and we'll talk while we have our at-home spa day." Laura took a step forward, and for a moment, Caroline thought she was going to hug her, but she turned and left the kitchen without saying a word.

Twenty minutes later, Caroline and Laura sat on the sofa. Nearly a dozen different shades of nail polish cluttered the coffee table, along with all the other supplies Laura had scrounged up. The first *Twilight* movie played in the background as they took turns painting each other's nails. Caroline had already seen the first movie, of course, but that had been so long ago, and her mother had insisted the series would be best experienced if they started from the beginning – just to refresh Caroline's memory. Laura was painting Caroline's nails black, a color that best represented her current emotional state. When she'd chosen the color, her mother had given her a strange, questioning look, but she relented and never spoke what had gone through her mind.

"So," Laura began as she kept her eyes on Caroline's tiny fingers, which she held in her own hand as she cautiously painted on a second layer. "I do have one question for you about...them."

"Okay."

"Did they...did they ever...hurt you? In any way at all. Did Stan ever..."

"Ew, no!" Caroline's face scrunched up at the mere thought of Stan touching her in that way. "Sorry. It's just, no, he never even tried. At first, I didn't think much about it. I was only seven, too young to really know much about how men think. But as I got older, I did wonder why he never even laid a hand on me. But he told me one time that he liked his girls to be pure. That no one wanted damaged goods. He said his job was to find us a better life, not to...you know." Caroline looked at the work her mother had done and smiled, despite the conversation topic. "Besides, I don't think Beverly would have allowed that."

"Beverly was the wife, right?" Laura set the polish bottle on the coffee table and began blowing air on Caroline's fingernails to dry them.

"Yes. Or his girlfriend, whatever. They seemed to be very much in love, weird as that sounds. He was kind of, what's the word...submissive to her. She clearly wore the pants in the family."

"That's weird. But I guess that happens sometimes." Laura picked up the remote and paused the movie. "Did you ever think about us? Did you miss us?"

"Oh, Mom," Caroline said. She tilted her head, and tears formed in her eyes. "Every day. I thought about you and missed you every day. But I won't lie, he got in my head for a while when I first got there. And I'm sorry about that."

Her mother looked down at her fingernails, and Caroline could tell she was trying to keep her emotions in check. "What do you mean, he got in your head?"

"It's nothing. Forget I said anything."

"Caroline," Laura laid her hand gently on her shoulder. "Remember, you can tell me anything. Nothing is going to make me be upset with you or love you any less. Just tell me. What did you mean by that?"

Caroline looked away from her mother and out the front window. No way could she tell her mother this part and look her in the eye the whole time. "He just told me you guys didn't love me. That if you did, you'd have never let me go. He told me that every time I cried for you, mostly at night. And it didn't take long before I started to believe him. I kept replaying that day – the day he grabbed me at the park – over and over in my mind. Eventually, I saw the whole thing through his eyes, and I convinced myself you weren't looking because you wanted him to take me."

"He actually told you that?" Caroline risked a glance at Laura, and when she did, she saw the exact reaction she'd been afraid of. Anger. Resentment. Hurt. "Damn him! Damn that sonofabitch to hell!"

"Mom, I'm sorry. I swear, I didn't think that way for long. Eventually, I got older and matured, and I came to realize there's no way any parent could ever let their child go on purpose. Especially not you. I'm so sorry. Can you forgive me?"

Laura's head snapped in Caroline's direction. "What? You think I'm mad at you?" Her features softened, and the tension in her body eased noticeably. "Oh, honey, no. No, I could never be mad at you. I'm mad at that asshole for getting in your head like that. What kind of monster…" Laura's cell phone rang, but she clicked the side button and ignored the call. "It's a New York area code. The *Dateline* producer is calling again. But he can wait."

"You can talk to him," Caroline said.

"No. This is so much more important. I need you to understand that my anger at him has nothing to do with you. I could never blame you for anything you experienced, thought, or felt during that time. The man brainwashed you. You are completely blameless in this whole thing."

Caroline smiled at her mother. Her words brought her some level of relief and comfort. "Thanks, Mom. I needed to hear that.

Now, is there anything else you really want to ask me today? Because I'd really like to get back to our spa day and the movie, if that's okay. I get sort of overwhelmed sometimes."

Laura nodded. "Just one more thing. I know you said he didn't hurt you. And I know from Detective Kastaros why he took you and what he was planning to do with you and the other girls. But there's just one thing I need to understand. And I hope you don't take this the wrong way. But as a mother, I just have to know."

"Know what?"

Her mother drew in a deep breath, held it for a beat, then let it out. "I just wonder...if you were so close to home, close enough to escape ten years later, why didn't you try to escape sooner? I know you, Caroline. It didn't surprise me one bit when we learned how you got away from him at the gas station. I told your father, 'that's our Caroline.' But how did he keep you from getting away if you were in the city this whole time? You said he didn't hurt you. And I thank God for that. But did he threaten you? Did he scare you into believing you couldn't get out? Just help me understand what it was like for you."

Suddenly, Caroline didn't want to share anymore. Not even with her mother. She knew her mother had the best of intentions and that she just needed to understand it all. But thinking back on that time with Stan and Beverly and all the years she spent in that basement made her sick to her stomach and scared to death she might one day have to return. It might have been an irrational fear, but she felt it, nonetheless. Caroline hated to shut her mother down, but she simply could not think or talk about Stan one more minute.

"He had his ways," was all she could bring herself to say. "Now, let's get back to the movie. It's just getting to the good part."

Caroline snuck a glance at her mom and saw the disappointment on her face. She hated to make her own mother feel that way, but she was acting out of self-preservation. The social worker lady had been right. Things were becoming a bit over-whelming now that she was back home. The juxtaposition of the happiness she felt at being with her parents again mixed with the sadness she felt every time someone wanted her to talk about the time she'd lost with them while in captivity was just too much for her to process sometimes.

And on top of that, her mother's last question had brought back some of the scariest memories of that time away. She just couldn't think about that anymore. Not today, anyway. Today, she was going to focus on black nail polish and watching Edward and Bella fall in love as she sat next to her mother in the comfort of her own home. Home – somewhere she thought she'd never see again. Especially not those nights in that cold basement when Stan and Beverly made damn sure they could never escape. That they'd never even try.

But that was a conversation for another day.

20

Since they didn't have probable cause for a warrant, Felton and Mena could only knock on doors, show their badges, and ask questions. Anyone could turn them away or slam the door in their face if they wanted, and there'd be nothing they could do about it. They'd met at the precinct first and gone over their strategy for speaking to these three persons of interest and had decided to play it cool so as not to raise any alarms.

The first of the three houses on their list was nestled in an upper-middle-class neighborhood on the south side of Lexington called Copperfield, where most of the houses went for at least a quarter million dollars. Most were brick-framed houses with large front porches and short, well-manicured front lawns. It wasn't completely outside the realm of possibility that Stan was holding young girls in a house like these, but Mena just didn't feel it was the right place in her gut. Too many Nosy Nellies, too quiet, too hard to hide in neighborhoods like these. But the registered owner of the white van was one Stan Jankowsky, who lived at 401 Maplewood Lane, and who owned a plumbing company called Jankowsky Plumbing.

How very creative.

When they arrived at Mr. Jankowsky's front door, Felton rang the doorbell, and as they waited for someone to answer, Mena tried to peek inside the windows. The blinds were drawn, though, so she couldn't see anything. Finally, the door opened, and a tall, heavy-set man with a headful of white hair stood staring at them blankly. He didn't look like the man Caroline had described.

"Yes?" He didn't seem too concerned that two detectives were standing on his front porch, holding up badges.

Mena shot Felton a glance and shook her head slightly.

"My name's Detective Derrick Felton. This is my partner, Detective Mena Kastaros. We just wanted to ask you a couple of questions, if you don't mind."

"Sure. Is everything okay?"

"Yes," Mena answered. She went on to ask him a series of innocuous questions about suspicious activity in his neighborhood, all made up on the fly to avoid spilling even a tidbit of information about Caroline that might wind up on tomorrow's headlines.

Mr. Jankowsky prattled on for about five minutes about some "hoodlums" in the area who rode skateboards up and down the hill and bounced their basketballs at ungodly hours of the evening. When she couldn't stand wasting another minute of precious time, Mena thanked the man and suggested to Felton that they let the gentleman be for now.

"That all you needed?" he asked as they started for Mena's cruiser. "Seems odd for a couple detectives to show up asking about things our neighborhood watch committee should be handling."

Mena and Felton exchanged a "well, shit" glance. Then, without another moment's hesitation, Mena looked at the man and said, "To be honest, sir, we think there might be a burglar working in the area. It's best if you lock your doors and set your alarm regularly. At least for the time being."

Understanding crept across the man's ruddy face, and he nodded. "Thanks, detectives. I'll do that."

He waved once at them, almost a salute, and closed the door.

Once in the cruiser, Felton said, "Well, that was a waste of time. Where's house number two?"

Mena consulted the list. "301 Chestnut Street. A Mr. Stanley Jones."

"Chestnut Street? Isn't that down there near MLK Boulevard?" Felton chuckled softly. "Shit. No way our guy stashed three girls in his house in that neighborhood with no one noticing."

"But how do you know—"

"Trust me, partner. First off, any white person is going to stand out like a sore thumb down that way. Shit, MLK neighborhood's about as close as Lexington gets to having a ghetto. Second off, some white man acting all suspicious like, driving a van, never comin outside...naw, girl. This isn't Stan. No way."

"All right, then. We'll save him for last. The only other man who hit every search criterion is a Mr...." Mena flipped the page. "...a Mr. Stanley Dale Pollard. 404 Smokey Mountain Drive. Over there near Pimlico Shopping Center."

"You got a DMV photo in that packet?" Felton asked.

"Yeah," Mena said, pulling out a print-off of Stanley Dale Pollard's picture from the DMV database. "Here." She handed it to Felton. "Looks about right to me. He's the one who matches Caroline's description the closest."

Felton nodded. "Sure does look like a squirrely little dude. This has to be our guy."

"Well, what are you waiting for, then?"

Less than fifteen minutes later, Mena and Felton walked from the street where they'd parked a couple of doors down and up the driveway of 404 Smokey Mountain Drive. Again, Mena scanned the neighborhood. The houses all appeared to be about forty or so years old and were situated about ten feet apart from one another. Close enough to be neighborly, but not so close they were right on top of one another, as more modern houses tended to be built. The street was quiet, though Mena noticed one young boy riding his red bicycle past them, eyeballing them suspiciously. Yes, this was the perfect neighborhood for blending in and hiding things one wouldn't want those around them to know about.

The driveway was on a steep incline, and when they reached the top, Mena could tell the house had a basement, but the windows were covered from the inside. Once at the front door, Felton banged loudly on the door jamb, announcing themselves as police and insisting the owner come to the door.

A few seconds went by, and no one responded. Felton banged again. "Lexington Police! Come to the door now!" he shouted.

"They're not here," Mena said. "There's no white van or any other cars in the driveway."

"Let's go around back...see what we can see."

Mena nodded and followed Felton around the side of the house. A chain link fence surrounded the backyard, but lo and behold, the gate had not been shut all the way. Both detectives slipped through the gate, walking in an almost crouched stance with their service pistols held up in the ready position. Felton signaled Mena to stay alert. When they made it into the backyard, there was still no signs of anyone being home. Felton pointed to the concrete steps that led upward to a screen door on the back of the house. Mena couldn't believe what she saw when she followed his gesture. The back door was wide open.

"Don't need a search warrant if the door's left open," Mena whispered. She took the lead and climbed the steps slowly, one at a time, her gun still held at eye level.

"Lexington Police!" Mena shouted as she made it to the back door. "We're coming in, and we're armed."

Instincts form her training academy days kicked in as Mena's heart thudded in her chest. Her senses were acute and on high alert. She worried her hands might shake, but a quick glance showed they were steady as ever. It had been almost a year since she'd had to draw her weapon in the suburban town of Lexington, and never before had she faced a situation where she might confront a kidnapper and child murderer, which explained why butterflies did battle inside her stomach.

They surveyed the kitchen first, Felton a few steps behind Mena. They cleared each room on the first floor. There were no signs of life inside the home. In fact, aside from a few small pieces of furniture, there were no personal effects whatsoever.

"They've taken off," she told her partner.

He nodded once.

"There's the door to the basement," Mena said, pointing to her left. "You ready?"

"As I'll ever be."

Mena reached over and unlatched the sliding lock, turned the doorknob, the slowly opened the door. She saw steps plunging into the darkness and immediately stepped onto the first stair.

"Careful," Felton said. "Want me to go first?"

She cast him a look that made it clear she had no intentions of letting him take the lead.

"All right. Just asking."

Slowly and methodically, Mena descended the stairs, one hand holding her gun at eye level, the other feeling along the wall for a light switch. Finally, blessedly, she found what she was searching for and flipped it. Mena continued down the stairs, both hands now on her weapon.

Mena's foot found the concrete floor of the basement, and her brain finally registered what her eyes beheld. The entire basement was set up like a miniature apartment, complete with a living room, a bathroom off in the corner, and even a small kitchenette to the right – exactly how Caroline had described it.

The furnishings were threadbare and eclectic in design, from a yellow shag carpet, to a brown leather sofa, to white plastic end tables. There was no television, she noticed, and wooden boards covered the tiny windows near the top of the walls. Clearly, Stan and Beverly had tried to create a "homey," albeit sheltered existence for the girls.

Then, she spotted a door off to the left. When Felton made it to the bottom of the stairs and stepped up next to Mena, she pointed at the door. "Think that's the bedroom? Where he kept the girls?"

He nodded. "What is this place? Looks like the seventies threw up all over this basement. Creepy, man."

"Yes, it is. Let's go check out that room. You ready?"

"Am I ready? What kind of question is that? Course I'm ready. I was born ready."

Mena rolled her eyes and headed for the last room. Half expecting to find Stan waiting for them behind the door, Mena readied her firearm again, and in four long strides, she stood before it. She raised her handed and used her fingers to silently count down from 3...2...1...

Felton reached out, turned the knob, and slowly parted the door an inch from its frame. Mena kicked the door gently the rest of the way in, and both detectives stood, crouching in a defensive position, just in case their suspect waited for them with a weapon, or worse, yet, a hostage.

There was no Stan. There was no Beverly. Mena found the light switch and flipped it. When the room brightened, she saw three twin beds lined up only a foot apart from one another along the far wall. There was no carpet, no paint on the cement walls, and even less décor than the "living room" had held. In fact, there was nothing in the room other than the beds. Except...

Something caught her eye. Something she hadn't noticed at first. Mena focused and took two steps forward. When what she was seeing connected to each of the beds finally registered in her brain, Mena's stomach roiled, and she leaned forward, placing her hands on her knees, trying hard not to throw up.

"Are those…" Felton began.

Mena nodded, breathing steadily, in and out, in and out. "Yeah," she said between breaths. "Chains. And handcuffs. The fucker chained those girls to their beds."

21

With his eyes on the road ahead, Stan held one hand on the steering wheel. His other hand turned the radio dial as he tried in vain to find a radio station that played some of his favorite classic rock bands like Steely Dan, The Who, and Lynyrd Skynyrd. No such luck. Mostly, he found either top-forty bullshit or that God-awful modern country music that all sounded the same to him. He gave up, settled on an oldies station, and settled into the driver's seat. Might as well get comfortable, he figured. They'd been on the road for seven hours, and they were somewhere between St. Louis and Kansas City. Still almost twenty hours to go.

"Penny for your thoughts?" Stan asked, sneaking a glance at Beverly. She sat in the passenger seat, her elbow on the door and her chin in her hand, staring out the window.

"You don't want to know," Beverly said in a tone that matched her words.

"Yes, I do. Talk to me."

Beverly hmphed and kept staring out at the passing open fields.

Stan waited for her to give in and share her thoughts with him, but she was a vault.

"Bev, darling…"

"Don't 'Bev, darling' me," she said, dropping her arm and turning to face Stan. "You really want to know what I'm thinking? Are you sure?"

"I do."

"Okay, here it is. I don't want to go there. I don't want to see them. I don't want any part of any of that."

"What? I thought you said—"

"Let me finish," she snapped. "It doesn't matter what I said. And it doesn't matter what I want. Does it? It's always going to be The Stan Show. Stan wants to watch football? Fine. We watch football. Stan wants fried catfish for dinner, again? Fine. We eat catfish. Stan wants to start rescuing young girls? Fine. We start rescuing them. I know I may act like I wear the pants in this relationship, but really, it's the other way around."

"Now, Bev. You said you agreed with me. You said you understood. Those girls needed saving. Those girls needed better lives. We do that for them. We take them out of their miserable lives and get them away from their good-for-nothing parents. We find them *better* lives. You said—"

"I know what I said, you arrogant SOB. And, yes, I agreed to join you in this little business. But you also said no one would miss these girls. That we'd never be on the cops' radar because no one would ever report them missing and no one would ever come looking for them. But you didn't consider what might happen if one of those girls got away." Beverly raised her hand to the sky. "Oh, no, wait. She didn't just get away. You let her go! And now, because you did, the police are on our tails as we speak. Oh, no, wait. Not just the police, but the mother of that girl you killed is hunting us down. And to top things off, the only way we can possibly save our hides is by going somewhere even you swore you'd never return."

"Bev, hon, I'm sorry. I really thought you agreed this was for the best."

"Just save it." Beverly folded her arms over her chest, crossed one leg over the other, and lowered her chin so it touched her chest. Clearly, she wasn't ready to hear Stan's explanations or apologies.

Fine. Be that way.

Of course, he didn't say that out loud. No matter how frustrating she was, Beverly was the love of Stan's life, and he wouldn't risk upsetting her any more than she already was. Besides, he could understand why she was so distraught. Aside from everything she'd just leveled at him – all of which was true – she was probably stressed beyond all belief from having to uproot their entire lives and go somewhere even he didn't want to go.

Keeping his eyes on the horizon, Stan's mind replayed the events of the past twelve hours. After their conversation in their bedroom when he'd returned from the detective's house, Stan had convinced Beverly of exactly what they had to do. Knowing they had no time to waste, and despite not having slept a wink since the night before, Stan had gone into autopilot mode. He'd made the appropriate calls while Beverly packed up only their most essential and treasured possessions and loaded them into the van. They'd rented a truck and hauled all their furniture to the local dump. Once the house was empty a few hours later, they'd gathered up the two remaining girls and had stashed them in the back of the van with the few worldly belongings they couldn't part with. After one last look around the house, they'd climbed in, opened the garage door, and made a beeline for I-64 West.

It had been a lot to do, let alone process, in less than a day's time. So he understood Beverly's crankiness and wrote it off as physical and emotional exhaustion. Hell, he didn't even blame her for tearing into him as she had. Maybe he'd had it coming all these years. Lord knew he'd made more than his fair share of mistakes since he'd met her on Match.com fifteen years ago. And the life she'd agreed to share with him, with all the secrets and the hiding…and the kidnapping…would be too much for most women.

But not my Bev.

"Pull off at the next rest area," she said, interrupting his inner monologue. "I gotta use the little girls' room."

"All right," Stan replied. "I think there's one just a few miles up. The girls probably need to stop, too." He'd almost forgotten about them. They were being so quiet back there.

"Look," Beverly said, "I'm sorry I snapped at you. But this is just a lot to digest, you know?"

"Yeah. I know."

"I still believe in what we're doing. I didn't mean to imply that I don't. I just…I'm scared, you know?"

"I know, love. I know. But everything is going to be okay now. We got away from there just in the nick of time. There's no way Detective Kastaros will find us now. Not where we're going."

"That's the only reason I agreed to go there," Beverly said, looking at Stan with a tilt of her head and a sideways grin. "But do you really think we'll be safe? I mean, she's out for blood. If she knows you're the one who—"

"Oh, she knows," Stan said. "If I put it together, so has she. Or at least, she suspects. Either way, you're right. She'll be like a pit bull on a poodle."

A few seconds of silence passed. Then, Beverly cleared her throat and said, "I know you don't want to talk about it. But her daughter. The girl in the picture…"

"You're right. I don't want to talk about it."

"But, Stan, we have never really talked about it. And I know you feel bad about what happened. It's not like you meant to do it, though. You can forgive yourself. Let it go."

"No, I didn't mean to do it," he said, "but it wasn't an exactly an accident, either."

Stan's mind went back to the cold day he'd taken her from the street corner. The young girl, who'd said her name was Sadie, had been walking all by herself alongside a quiet, low-traffic road in the dead of winter. He had known the second he saw her that she was the next one he was going to bring home. He remembered wondering what kind of mother would let their little girl walk all alone down a deserted street in the middle of January. And she'd been so pretty and looked so blissfully ignorant to the dangers surrounding her. She looked frightened. As if she might be lost. And the moment he'd slowed down his van, rolled down his window, and caught a brief glimpse of the scared little girl, he'd known she'd make the perfect addition to the family.

Then, like one of those viewfinders he'd had as a child, the images clicked quickly through his mind. Her, smiling when he'd asked her to help find his lost puppy. Her, chatting away about how her mom never let her have any pets. Her, following him obediently into the house as he introduced her to Beverly. Her, meeting the older girls and talking to them like sisters that first night as they sat around the basement dinner table eating spaghetti with meatballs, her favorite meal.

But then the images began to blur and tilt and spin quickly out of control, just as things had done in the days that followed his first encounter with the girl. After a couple of days, she'd started crying, begging, then demanding Stan take her home to her real mommy. She hadn't been as malleable as the others before her had been. She was willful. Stubborn. Wise beyond her years. She'd refused to believe Stan and Beverly when they told her they'd adopted her from an uncaring mother who'd sent her out alone that cold day knowing full-well Stan was going to pick her up and take her home. She fought, and talked back, and railed against their every command. Stubborn and wise beyond her seven or eight years, there would be no breaking her.

Then came that awful night, a week after she'd come home with Stan, when things had escalated beyond the point of no return. And he'd just...lost it. Lost sight of his mission. Lost his advantage over her. Lost all self-control. He didn't want to hurt her. If only she'd been a good girl, like the others. Then maybe things wouldn't have happened as they had. He wouldn't have had to make the hard decision – the one he always feared he'd have to make but had always prayed he never would. He could still see the fear in the girl's eyes. Still feel the way his two hands wrapped all the way around her tiny neck and squeezed.

"Stan! Watch out!" Beverly shrieked.

He shook his head and blinked rapidly, swerving just in time to avoid clipping the side of a minivan in the next lane. The driver must have seen his dangerous maneuver because she laid on the horn and flipped him off. Stan gave an embarrassed wave and apologized to Beverly.

"You probably scared those girls in the back to death. That rest area is one mile ahead. Where was your head just now, anyway?"

"It's nothing. I'm fine," Stan insisted.

"No, you're not fine. And we were talking about the girl."

"I don't want to talk about her anymore. Not today, anyway. I've got enough on my mind right now as it is."

"Like?"

"Like what the hell we're going to do with these girls," he pointed his thumb toward the back of the van, which he'd partitioned off with a curtain, "when we get where we're going. Like what I'm going to say to him when I see him. Like how the hell I'm going to keep us out of jail...and alive."

"Oh, it's not me that detective is going to want to kill," Beverly sniped, raising the corner of her mouth and twitching her head from side to side in a sarcastic way.

"That's not funny," Stan said. "Anyway, it doesn't really matter."

Beverly looked at Stan and furrowed her brow. "And why, pray tell, does it not matter if some hot-shot detective on a warpath wants to kill you, or me, or both of us?"

Stan gripped the steering wheel with both hands and cast Beverly a sideways glance. "Because...*he* just might kill us first."

22

Mena rested her hands on her hips and watched as uniformed officers and crime scene technicians swarmed the residence, trapesing in and out through the front door. Thankfully, they wore protective gear and booties, so there would be no contamination of the scene. Mena had given a five-minute lecture on how important it was that not one single thing was missed and that there was absolutely no chance of stray prints or DNA being left behind and comingled with anything already in the house.

Felton ambled up the steep driveway, slapped one of the techs on the back as he walked by, and stood next to Mena. "Well, CSU just finished sweeping for prints and DNA. There's no sign of a computer, though he left behind a computer desk and a surge protector. Looks like Pollard took what he could fit in his van, got rid of the rest, and high-tailed it out of here. Doubt we'll turn up any clues as to where he's headed." He sighed and placed his hand on Mena's shoulder. "Sorry, partner. He's in the wind."

"No," Mena said, suddenly overcome with anger that had reached the boiling point. "We'll find him. Can't get too far now that we know who he is. I've already issued a BOLO for him and his van. Plus, Cliff is working on a warrant right now for his IP address and Google search history. We'll be able to find out what sites he visited without his computer. Trust me. We're going to find him."

"What about Beverly? You were going to ask Cliff to dig into her identity. You get a last name on her?"

"Yep," Mena said, pulling out her phone. She swiped the screen and tilted it so Felton could see. "That's Beverly Louise Guthrie. Born June 27, 1956 in Bowling Green. Five foot three, two-hundred-sixty pounds. And that's not a face that blends in with a crowd, if you see what I mean."

"No doubt. Guthrie...so she's not married to Stan? Different last names."

"Kentucky doesn't recognize common-law marriage, but if it did, I'd bet you that's what we're looking at with these two. Cliff found domestic disturbance calls and misdemeanor arrests together for petty theft and cold checks going back to the late nineties."

"But why would any woman help this scumbag abduct young girls and help groom them for what she knew would eventually happen to them once they turned eighteen? I just can't wrap my head around it."

"Plenty of female accomplices have helped their partners abduct young women, and worse. Remember Elizabeth Smart? Her abductor was Brian David Mitchell, but he didn't act alone. His wife Wanda Barzee was right there with him the whole time. And then there was Jaycee Dougard in the nineties. Nancy Garrido even served as the surrogate jailer for Jaycee when Phillip Garrido spent time in prison for violating parole. It's sick, it's twisted, and I'll never understand the psychology behind it, but it happens."

"Both of those girls you mentioned were eventually found and rescued," Felton observed.

"Yep," Mena answered, "and both sets of kidnappers were

arrested and brought to justice. Just like we're going to do with Pollard and Guthrie."

"Roger that."

After two hours of canvassing the neighborhood and interviewing every resident of Smokey Mountain Drive they could, a worn-out Mena climbed into Felton's beige Crown Vic and sank into the passenger seat. Felton joined her seconds later and put the car into drive.

As they crept past the white, wooden barricade and crime scene tape and turned left onto Buckhorn Drive, Felton said, "At least we got statements from several neighbors confirming Pollard and Guthrie were definitely world-class weirdos. And that one on the left – Wanda Jamison – she said she always wondered what those two were up to in that house. They'll make good witnesses at trial."

"If they make it to trial," Mena said, staring out the window and watching the tiny ranch houses float by.

"What do you mean, *if* they make it to trial? You aren't thinking of doing anything stupid, are you, Kastaros?" Mena looked at Felton sideways, one eyebrow raised. "C'mon, now. Don't screw around like that. You know Lieutenant Iverson is just waiting for you to do something reckless in this investigation. And I'm not about to work this thing without you. Promise me you won't go all rogue on me and shit."

"Nah," Mena said. "I mean, yeah, when I finally catch up to these twisted assholes, I'm going to want to kill them both with my bare hands. But what I meant was, what if the prosecutor offers some kind of sweetheart deal and they only have to serve, say, ten or fifteen years? That just wouldn't be right."

"That's exactly why we have to play it by the books and collect as much evidence as we can. We take Bautista a solid case with boxes of bullet-proof evidence, hopefully even a confession, there's no way he's going to bargain with them. Besides, he's up for reelection next year. He's going to want one great big, public guilty verdict in his column before folks head to the ballots. He won't negotiate with them. Mark my words."

Mena's hands clenched into fists as she thought about the prospect of sitting down in a room with Stanley Dale Pollard, facing him one-on-one, and getting him to confess to his crimes, including Sadie's murder. That was, if Lieu would let her conduct the interviews. That was yet to be determined, but unlikely.

When they arrived at the LPD headquarters, Mena and Felton headed straight for Cliff Van Buren's cubicle. Cliff was leaning close to his computer screen, staring at something that must have been of great interest. Either that, or the print was too small for him to read.

"Ever thought about bifocals?" Mena asked as she leaned against the edge of his desk.

Cliff didn't turn his head but instead looked up at her over the tops of his single-vision glasses. "Screw off, Kastaros. Guess you don't want to hear what I've found on your crazy couple, eh?"

"Aw, come on, buddy," Felton said, stepping between them. "Of course we want to hear it. Don't we, partner?"

"Sure thing," Mena said, touching Cliff lightly on the shoulder. "I'm sorry, Cliff. I was only teasing. What do you have for us?"

"For you, then," Cliff said, pointing at Felton. "Not for her. She never laughs at my jokes, anyway."

"Because they're not—"

"She's just serious about the job, Cliff. Don't take it so person-ally. She never laughs at my jokes, either. And I'm one funny mo-fo." Felton chuckled at himself. "Now, what have you got for us?"

The older detective leaned back in his seat, causing it to creak and groan under the pressure. "It took some digging, but I found a website your cuckoo suspect runs on the dark web."

"The dark what?" Felton's face scrunched up in confusion.

Cliff rolled his eyes. "The dark web. The deep web. Same thing. People who are super tech savvy can access parts of the internet folks like us can't find by using regular search engines. Instead, they use TOR – The Onion Routing – to hide things they don't want the rest of us to see. That's exactly what your suspect did with his website. It's called...are you ready for this...*The Rainbow Room*."

Though Felton still looked perplexed, Mena's mind immediately went from the word "rainbow" to remembering Caroline's assertion that Stan had given all the girls he kidnapped names that correlated with colors. It made sense.

"Let me guess," she said. "It's a website where he auctions off girls to the highest bidder."

One of Cliff's eyebrows raised, and he pursed his lips. "Impressive, Kastaros. How the hell did you guess that?"

Understanding colored Felton's face. "Ah, I see. Because Stan named the girls things like Violet and Scarlett and Ebony, etcetera. Hence, *The Rainbow Room*. I get it. Demented, but I get it."

"Yep," Cliff said, turning the computer screen slightly to face Mena. "I'll warn you, it's disturbing, but I've seen much, much worse. In fact, it's not at all what you'd expect from an auction site such as this. The images are subdued, and the girls aren't posing in explicit ways. Just...pictures of girls with descriptions of their personalities listed beneath their photos. It's unsettling, to be sure, but somewhat tame."

Mena focused on the screen. The website looked a lot like other "sex for hire" websites she had seen in her years with the department. Not that she'd seen that many, but she had come across a few in the past decade. The background on this one was black, and the writing was all in white font. She skimmed the words briefly, and her stomach churned as she read about how Pollard offered "quality girls who've been groomed and trained to behave properly and obey…"

Cliff opened another image. "This is what you really need to see."

There, filling the entire screen, was a picture of Caroline, posed somewhat seductively and wearing a tight-fitting blue dress and black stiletto heels. Though her lips smiled, in her amber eyes, Mena saw fear, hatred, and disgust swirling together. The paragraph below her picture described her as "intelligent, obedient, and ready for a new master." Mena swallowed hard as she read the rest of the words which told potential buyers exactly what they could expect out of her. She shook her head and muttered, "Sonofabitch."

Cliff sat back in his chair and crossed his hands behind his head. "As you can see, this bastard hasn't taken Caroline Hanson off the website yet. Probably didn't have time between her escape and boot-scootin it out of town."

"Can you shut it down?" Felton gave voice to the question on Mena's mind.

"Already done," Cliff answered, leaning forward again. "These're just screenshots I took before I shut 'er down."

"What about the other girls?" Mena asked, a sour, bitter taste lingering in her mouth.

"You mean the ones before Caroline?" Mena nodded. "It took some digging, but I found cached images of three girls, which he auctioned to the highest bidder, dating back about six years. There was a Cyan, a Jade, and an Olive." Mena opened her mouth to speak, but Cliff held up his hand. "Already on it, Detective. I've got two techs working to compare their pictures to missing children in the database as we speak. If at all possible, we'll identify those girls."

"How much?" Mena asked.

"What? Oh, you mean the girls? How much did he sell them for?"

Mena drew in a deep breath and crossed her arms over her chest. "Exactly. How much?"

"About one hundred thousand. Per girl."

"Holy shit," Felton said, turning his back, placing his hands on his hips, and lowering his head.

"And what about Caroline?"

"Well, the auction wasn't set to close until midnight tonight, actually. But the highest bid before I shut this virtual shithole down was about one thirty."

"One hundred thirty thousand?" Mena asked, her eyes widening.

"Disturbing, isn't it?" Cliff responded.

"Keep trying to identify those girls, Cliff. Thank you for your hard work," Felton said, facing them once again. Cliff turned on his heel and began walking away, but Mena gently laid her hand on his arm.

"One more thing, Cliff," she said. "We need to do more than identify those girls. We need to find them and bring them home."

"That's a tall order, partner," Felton said.

"I know, but if we can trace the winning bidders' IP addresses…wouldn't that at least be a start?" Mena looked at Cliff, who smiled back at her.

"Already on that, too," he said. "In fact, I have the location of the buyer for the girl just before Caroline Hanson…Scarlett."

Mena and Felton exchanged glances then looked at Cliff, who sat looking like the cat who ate the canary.

"Yep. Sure did. That's how damn good I am. And don't you forget it."

"Well…" Mena said. "Where is this winning bidder?"

Cliff pulled a piece of paper from his printer and held it out to Mena. "Last known location for that IP address. You can thank me later."

"What's it say?" Felton asked, looking over Mena's shoulder. "Where is the sick bastard?"

Mena looked up at her partner and smiled. "Washington, DC. Georgetown, to be exact. IPO address is registered to…get this… Congressman Ward Daviess."

23

F elton stayed behind, talking to Cliff, as Mena made her way down the hallway and to Lieutenant Iverson's office. She hadn't had much facetime with her boss since Caroline showed up, but it was well past time for her to update him on the investigation. Not to mention, she'd dodged three of his calls and numerous text messages in the past twenty-four hours. Mena was already on thin ice, and she'd all but coerced him into allowing her on the case, so she decided, given the recent developments, there was no time like the present.

She knocked on his door. Iverson cleared his throat and told her to open it. Mena stepped inside his office and stood across from where he sat at the only wooden desk on the entire floor. The lieutenant leaned to the side, looking away from his computer screen, and glared at her, his thick, grey eyebrows furrowed, and his lips clenched together.

"Bout time, Kastaros," he said, motioning for her to sit.

"I'm fine," she said, waving him off.

"Sit," he said, gesturing more severely toward the leather-padded chair.

"Okay...I'll sit." Mena did so and leaned forward with her elbows on her knees. "Lieu, I think we need to call in the FBI."

His bushy brows raised. "Oh, really? Why's that?"

Mena knew Lieutenant Mack Iverson did not deign to call in the FBI unless it was absolutely necessary. He came from a certain generation of cops who believed in working the case without interference from federal law enforcement and who believed agencies with three initials served as nothing more than a hindrance to local police. She'd heard him comment on more than one occasion that the FBI, in particular, loved nothing more than to "steal cases" and "take all the credit" for the hard work put in by those who knew the case, the community, and the parties involved better than any suit ever could.

Mena measured her words carefully in making her case for calling the feds. "Three reasons, actually. One, our suspect Stanley Dale Pollard has fled, and, in all likelihood, he's left Kentucky. Two, the website he was running appears to have been accepting bids from and selling these girls to buyers from across the world. And three, we've already identified a potential buyer for the girl he auctioned off a couple of years before Caroline escaped. He's in DC."

"Is that so?" Iverson rested his arms on the desk and leaned forward. "And do you have a name for this buyer in DC? An address? Anything at all we can use to justify trapesing up to our nation's great capital and questioning this buyer?"

"We do. And it's going to require a certain level of...*diplomacy* when we interview this man." Mena clasped her hands together and instinctively looked down to ensure her wrists weren't showing.

"And why is that?"

"Because he's a US congressman."

Iverson leaned back in his chair and whistled, his eyes growing wide as saucers. "Well, shit fire and save matches. Are you sure about this, Kastaros? Because if you're not, you do realize your career—"

Mena held up her hand as if warding off a blow. "Yes, I realize that if we're wrong, it'll mean going back to the beat, or worse. Trust me. I'm fully aware that all eyes are on me during this investigation. But Cliff is one of our best investigators, and he found foolproof evidence that Congressman Ward Daviess bought and paid for a girl we only know as 'Scarlett' from Pollard's website about two years ago. He and the techs traced the IP address to his home office in Georgetown."

The lieutenant smoothed his grey mustache and pursed his lips, apparently in deep thought. After several seconds of uneasy silence, he sat up straight and sniffed. "If what you're saying is true...*if* that IP address can be tied to this congressman definitively..."

"I have no doubt," Mena said.

"If that's true, then you realize this case is about to detonate, right? We've already got national attention, what with *Nancy Grace*, *Dateline*, and other news outlets across the country calling for comments and interviews. If word gets out we're even talking to this congressman in connection with this investigation, it will be twenty-four-seven coverage from New York to Alaska, and beyond. We'll have media from every damn state parked out in front of the precinct day and night. So you'd better be as certain of this as you are your first name before we pick up that phone. There's no unringing this bell, Kastaros."

"I'm aware," Mena said. She stood and planted her hands on the edge of her supervisor's desk, leaning down and matching his gaze. "I want to catch this bastard more than anything, and if it means calling in the FBI and gaining access to resources even better and further reaching than our own, then so be it. I'd stake my career on this, Lieu." She drew in a breath and let it out. "I honestly believe that the path to finding Pollard begins with this congressman. You should make the call."

Iverson reached out and laid his hand on the top of the phone but didn't pick it up. He looked at Mena, and suddenly, the seriousness in his gaze dissolved into something softer, kinder even. "Mena..." He never called her by her first name. Not in all the years he'd been her commanding officer. Mena's stomach tightened. "You also realize...if this turns into the media circus I think it will, every single aspect of this investigation will be fair game." He narrowed his eyes at her. "Every aspect."

At first, Mena didn't understand what he was implying. But a second later, realization hit her like a sledgehammer to the head. "You mean Sadie."

"Yes, I mean Sadie," he said, letting out a deep sigh. "I know you said you can work this case without your personal feelings interfering. And by God, I hope I didn't make a mistake in giving you the chance no other lieutenant would have ever given you. So far, you've held up your end of the bargain." He cleared his throat. "But if this goes national...if this turns into what I think it's going to turn into...those reporters will turn over every damn stone to get all the juicy details. They'll find out about Sadie. They'll find out Pollard is our main suspect in her murder. And you know what will happen next."

"I can handle it." Mena stood with her back straight and her chin held high in defiance. "Don't worry about me, Lieu." But if Mena were being honest with herself, she was slightly worried about herself.

"I appreciate your pride and self-assurance. And I have unwavering confidence in your ability to shove your feelings deep down in some dark hole none of us can ever access. But it could be brutal, Kastaros. I want you to be certain before I make this call." He pointed his finger at her. "Be certain you can keep your word to me. Be certain you can carry on in this investigation no matter what they say or do. Be certain you do your job. And more than that, be certain you can do it without retreating so far into that dark hole that you never come back."

For the first time, Mena's confidence faltered. Lieutenant Iverson had breathed life into her deepest fears with his words of warning. She was not at all certain she would be able to do any of the things he'd just listed. She wasn't even sure she would be able to think like a cop when she finally tracked down Pollard and faced him one on one. And most of all, she wasn't certain she would escape this investigation with her job, let alone her sanity. Despite these misgivings, Mena squared her shoulders, lifted her head, and looked Iverson dead in the eyes.

"If I break my promise to you…if I think, even for a second, that I'm losing objectivity or that I can't handle what's coming next, I'll personally turn over my gun and badge."

"Fair enough," Iverson said with a curt nod.

He picked up the phone, pushed a few buttons, and waited. A few seconds later, as Mena stood watching, he said, "This is Lieutenant Mack Iverson with the Homicide Division at the Lexington Police Department. I need to speak with Supervisory Special Agent Lucinda Jeffries. Yes, that's right. Tell her I need to speak with her about a case. Tell her it's urgent." He waited a beat, then said, "That's fine. I'll hold." He held his hand over the receiver and looked at Mena. "I'll handle this from here. You and Felton go home and get some rest. My guess is, tomorrow we'll have company come lunchtime. The kind who wear navy jackets with yellow letters on the back."

Despite herself, Mena smiled. "Thank you, Lieu."

He waved her off with a flick of his wrist. "Go on. I meant it. Get some rest."

Mena nodded and turned to leave. As she stepped out of the office, Iverson cleared his throat again. She turned around.

"And Kastaros," he hesitated briefly, "you might want to change your bandage."

A tingling sensation swept up the back of Mena's neck, and her chest tightened at the realization of what he'd just said. Her mind told her not to look, but her instincts won out and she glanced down at the bandage on her wrist. There, plain as day, was a bright red rose blossoming through the bandage. She searched her brain for some sort of excuse...a plausible explanation for why her wrist would be bleeding, despite her best efforts to keep her darkest secret hidden from the world. But words failed her, and nothing she came up with sounded anything short of ridiculous.

Mena's shoulders slumped, and she lowered her head like a dog who'd just disappointed his master. In a voice weak as a child's, she said, "Yes, sir. I'll get right on it."

24

When she arrived at the precinct the next morning, Mena saw Lieutenant Iverson talking to two people she didn't recognize in the conference room. Felton had beat her in and was standing in the doorway, leaning against the door jamb. As Mena trudged through the office and made her way toward the conference room, her partner greeted her and handed her a cup of coffee.

"Figured you could use this," he said, glancing at the clock, which read fifteen past eight.

"I know, I know," she said, taking the coffee and giving Felton an apologetic smile. "Late night, as usual."

"Your mom?"

"What else?"

"Figured. Is everything okay? Did you get the new nurse situated?"

"Oh, yeah. Anna's going to be great. Her resume was impressive, and she has a good bedside manner…and patience, which is at the top of the list of job requirements."

Felton sipped his coffee, then said, "And how did Her Ladyship take it?"

"Just as you'd expect. She was adamant she didn't need a babysitter." Mena used air quotes and rolled her eyes. "But I eventually got her calmed down, and by the end of the night, she'd thawed just a smidge to Anna. This morning, I walked into the kitchen and found the two of them working on a puzzle at the table. Wonders never cease."

"You two done chatting like schoolgirls over there?" Iverson called from across the room.

Mena took a step away from Felton and gave her boss a thin-lipped smile. "Sorry, Lieu."

"Whatever. Come over here. I want to introduce you."

To Iverson's right stood a man and to his left, a woman. Both of whom Mena assumed were with the FBI, as she'd never met either of them before. They'd made it to the precinct even sooner than expected.

The man was shorter than Iverson, maybe five-foot-seven, at best. His brown hair receded all the way to the apex of his head, and like Iverson, he wore an unfashionable mustache, though his was thinner and brown. Pockmarks covered his face, and his eyes reminded her of a crow's – dark and beady. Also contrary to her expectations, he did not look fit at all. In fact, his belly strained against his white button-down shirt and hung over the waistband of his dark green slacks.

In stark contrast, the woman on the lieutenant's left was tall and beautiful with strawberry blonde hair and a fair complexion. She stood a good two inches taller than Mena, but only because of her sensible black pumps. The woman's eyes were aquamarine, and she reminded Mena of a ballerina with her straight posture and delicate features. She smiled and was the first to extend her slender, elegant hand toward Mena.

"Special Agent Celine Rousseau," the beautiful woman said as Mena shook her hand.

"Detective Mena Kostaros." Mena tried to fight off the feelings of insecurity this lovely creature stirred inside her, but it wasn't working. "You're from the Frankfort field office, I presume?"

"That's right. Lieutenant Iverson called our SAIC late last night, and we came first thing this morning. It's a pleasure to meet you."

"And this is Special Agent Irvin Riggs," her boss said.

The squatty man held out a chubby hand, and Mena shook it firmly. "Pleasure," he said with a curt nod.

Iverson introduced the pair to Felton, and he shook their hands, as well. Their boss straightened his back and cleared his throat. "Now that we're all in the same room, I think we can agree we've got a proper task force on our hands."

Mena scratched her temple and narrowed her eyes at her boss. "Task force?" She didn't want to seem ignorant or ungrateful for the help. Of course it made sense in to create a task force to find Pollard and the girls he likely still had with him, as well as those he'd already sold. But Mena had never worked with the FBI before. Though Lexington was the second biggest city in Kentucky, there'd been no reason during her ten years as a detective to form a task force for any of her cases. And she'd heard horror stories about jurisdictional pissing matches and arguments over who claims credit for closing the case.

"Yes," Iverson said. "SA Riggs was the investigator in charge of the Wayne Blackburn case last year, which, as you know, led to a first-degree murder conviction."

Mena knew the case well. Wayne Blackburn was the man eventually identified, arrested, and convicted for the murder of a Centre College freshman who had disappeared on her walk home from a football game. There had initially been no suspects and little evidence, but the FBI had been brought into the case by Danville PD, and within two months, they'd arrested Blackburn.

"And SA Rousseau was first in her graduating class at the Academy. She's earned a stellar reputation and quite an impressive case closure rate during her time with the FBI. She's investigated hundreds of cases in her distinguished career. We're quite thrilled to have her on board."

Mena gave the impressive woman her most gracious smile.

"So," the lieutenant said, clapping his hands together. "Let's get started, shall we?"

"No time like the present," Riggs said.

Everyone took their seats around the small conference room table. Mena sat next to Felton, Iverson sat at the head, naturally, and the two newest members of the task force sat opposite her.

"If you don't mind," Rousseau said before they had even settled into their chairs, "I think the best thing to do is to divide the task force into two sections." She spread her hands apart and laid them palm-down on the table. "Lieutenant Iverson brought Riggs and me up to speed before you arrived, and it occurs to me there are two main areas of focus for this investigation. One is trying to locate and apprehend Stanley Dale Pollard. The other is locating the girls he's already auctioned."

"I agree," Iverson said before anyone else had a chance to respond. "To that end, I want Rousseau and Felton to work on finding the girls. And Kastaros," he turned his head to face Mena, "you will work with Riggs to track down Pollard."

"So," Mena began, "you're splitting us up? On one hand, that makes sense, considering the girls were likely sold to people in varying states. But..." She tried not to look directly at Riggs. "... but we've already identified one buyer – a US congressman, for God's sake. He's in DC. Felton is from DC and I think —"

"Actually," Riggs interrupted. "I have several contacts in DC. I have a cousin who is a lobbyist, and his wife works at the Russian embassy. I've led a couple of investigations with connections in the capital, so I think it's a splendid idea."

Splendid? Who ever says splendid in the twenty-first century?

"And," Iverson said, "SA Riggs has headed up more than his fair share of cases like this one. In fact, he worked on the Serena

McKinney case in 05, and that was a very similar set of circumstances."

Riggs nodded. "Mm hm. Selena McKinney was kidnapped by a stranger from a shopping mall parking lot, as you recall. Made national news. White, upper-class, pretty, young girl goes missing from an upscale male in Cincinnati? Of course the sharks came out on that one. Anyway, our lead suspect was Kenny Wayne Hopkins, a known grifter with two prior convictions for sexual assault. Knew it was him from a witness description and video footage of his vehicle fleeing the scene. Long story short, two weeks later, we found him just across the state line in Pennsylvania. He'd been hiding out with an old Army buddy he'd kept in contact with over the years. He's serving a life sentence at Mahanoy. Third strike and the bastard was out."

"If I recall," Felton spoke up, "they never recovered Selena McKinney's body."

Mena forced herself not to smile.

Riggs grimaced. "True, but we caught Hopkins. Tracked him down through good old-fashioned investigative skills. That's the point."

An awkward silence fell over the room until Rousseau spoke up. "I'm anxious to get started, Lieutenant."

"Good," Iverson said with a nod. "Felton, take Agent Rousseau to the other conference room. You guys can set up shop in there. Kastaros, you and Riggs can use this one as a war room. There's a whiteboard and plenty of room for boxes once we start building the case file. Let's get this ball rolling, shall we?"

Everyone around the table stood, and the sounds of chairs screeching across the linoleum floor echoed in the air. Felton, Iverson, and Rousseau filed out of the conference room, leaving Mena alone with Riggs.

"Well," he said after a beat, "guess we'd better get started. Why don't you bring me up to speed with what you know about Pollard so far, and I'll see if any ideas jump out at me. Then I think we need to speak with this congressman for ourselves. The other two will need to talk to him, of course, but he may have a way to contact Pollard." He heaved his pants up by the waistband. "And don't worry, Detective Kastaros. I know how to play well with others. I won't hog *all* the glory. Hell, I might even let you drive the car...even though you're a lady. How's that sound?" He chuckled, amused at his own wit.

Mena smiled, stifling the words she really wanted to let fly.

And I might even let you finish this investigation with your manhood intact. How's that sound?

25

Mena's new partner, Special Agent Riggs, decided to drive his car on their trip to DC, after all. Turned out, he really didn't trust a woman behind the wheel. She'd chosen to ignore his comments about how women don't know how to drive defensively and how they drive too slowly, and so on. Mena did this by biting the inside of her cheek every time Riggs opened his mouth. It was a painful, but effective way of preventing herself from saying something that might get her into trouble. Unfair as it was, she knew he could make all the chauvinistic remarks he wanted, but God forbid she stand up to him and give him the verbal beat-down he really deserved. Sadly, she was used to it by now.

After leaving Lexington, Mena listened as Riggs regaled her with stories of his glory days, including every major investigation he'd been a part of and all the times he'd testified at the trials of the men and women he'd apprehended over the years. The stories were interesting, to be sure, but the way he bragged about himself and his accomplishments as if he were the best darn FBI agent ever to come out of Quantico made the first two hours of the trip seem like days.

Blessedly, Mena's cell rang, forcing Riggs to stop speaking...at least for now.

"Detective Kastaros," Mena said, holding a finger up to apologize to Riggs for interrupting his trip down memory lane.

"Detective?" the voice on the other end was soft, but instantly recognizable.

"Caroline? Is everything okay?"

"Yes, well, sort of."

"What's wrong? Did something happen?"

"No, it's just...Mom talked to the producers of *Dateline* today, and they really want me to come for an interview. They're offering to fly us to their studio in New York in two days to record it."

"But you're not ready," Mena guessed.

"I don't think I am. But Mom and Dad are insisting. They say the money the producer is offering the pay us would help our family. They really need the money. My dad's not working much because of the cold weather, and my mom hurt her back at work a few years ago so she can't help now."

"And you feel it's up to you to help out," Mena balanced the phone between her ear and her shoulder.

"I guess so," Caroline replied. "But...I don't know if I'm ready to talk about it. Not yet, anyway."

"Do you want me to talk to them? Because I don't mind one bit. I agree with you. It's too early. And with Pollard...I mean, Stan...out there somewhere...until we catch him, it could hurt the investigation."

"Would you mind? They might listen to you."

"I'll call them right now."

"Thank, Detective Kastaros," Caroline replied.

"Please, Caroline. Call me Mena."

When the line disconnected, Mena started dialing the Hansons' house phone.

"Was that the victim? Caroline Hanson?" Riggs asked, seeming genuinely concerned.

"It was. It's a long story, but—"

"Sounds to me like her parents are hungry for their fifteen minutes of fame," he grumbled.

"I don't think it's that," Mena said. "They're just down on their luck, and I think they're genuinely trying to do their best for Caroline. Besides, they had their fifteen minutes, as you put it, back when Caroline first disappeared."

"I remember," Riggs said with a nod, his eyes still on the road ahead. "Seems like their faces were everywhere. Hey, didn't they get a decent amount of money from their interviews the first time around?"

"It's not like that. Sure, they were paid for their interviews, and I think some local car dealership had a fundraiser for them, but I can't remember how much they got from that. Couldn't have been that much. You've got them all wrong, Agent Riggs. They're decent, honest, hard-working people who have been on an emotional roller coaster ride for over a decade. Not to mention, they thought they'd suffered the worst possible thing a parent could ever experience—the loss of a child."

"Oh, yeah," Riggs said, shifting in the driver's seat. "I heard about your daughter. Sorry about that. I didn't mean…"

"Don't worry about it. I'm fine." But she wasn't really. Every time she thought about Sadie, a big black hole opened up in the earth, and Mena was tempted to jump right in and let it swallow her whole. This moment was no different.

After a couple minutes of uncomfortable silence, Mena pushed CALL on her cell. Laura Hanson answered on the first ring. After exchanging pleasantries and giving Laura a brief update on the status of the investigation, Mena got right down to the reason for her call.

"I'll be honest, Laura," she said as Riggs quickly whipped his car into the next lane. Mena grabbed the oh-shit bar tightly.

"Now really is not a good time for Caroline to be on national television. It's too soon. She's only been home less than a week."

"How did you know about the interview offer?" Laura asked, her frustration ringing loud and clear.

"Caroline called me. But don't be upset with her, Laura. She's frightened, and she's right to be scared. Stanley Dale Pollard is still out there somewhere, and until we catch him, she needs to keep a low profile and be very careful of her surroundings. Why do you think we've still got a patrol unit parked in front of your house twenty-four-seven?"

"Detective," Laura paused, "I am sure you mean well, but this family is struggling. We have no way to pay the bills, and the network is offering us quite a sum of money for the interview. I can't see any logic behind canceling. And no offense, but Caroline is our daughter, not yours, so I..."

A pregnant pause ensued. It was clear to Mena that Mrs. Hanson realized she'd inadvertently invoked Sadie's memory to make her point. It was the second time in five minutes someone had brought up her daughter's death.

"I'm sorry," Laura said. "I really am. I only meant..."

"I know what you meant, Laura. It's okay. Just please, at least consider doing the interview without Caroline. I'm sure the producers would understand. It would still be a good story, even without her there."

"But what would I do with Caroline? If you don't want her to leave home, but we really can't cancel the interview. What then? She's too old for a babysitter."

Without thinking, the words slipped out of Mena's mouth. "She can stay with me."

"I don't know," Laura said. "Would that even be allowed?"

"It's only for a couple days, right? Besides, as long as you and Mark give your permission, I can see the harm."

"Oh, well, if you insist."

"I do. If that's what it takes to keep Caroline safe and out of the public eye, then by all means, call me before you leave tomorrow, and I'll come get her. I'm out of town today, but I should be back by tomorrow night."

"Thank you, Detective. It means a lot."

They arrived at the Capital Complex in DC shortly after 2 PM. It took several laps around the quad, but Riggs finally found a place to park along Independence Avenue. Mena had only ever been to DC once – for her sixth-grade field trip. The hustle and bustle of Metropolitan DC was nearly overwhelming, but Mena was determined not to appear fazed, especially in front of her well-seasoned new partner. As they crossed the street and headed for the Congressional Offices, Mena couldn't help but admire the architecture of the Cannon House. The building was faced with white marble and limestone and each side of the structure, which took up an entire city block, was lined with dozens of tall, white columns. The white stone steps that led to the front door, which faced the corner of Independence and Jersey Avenue SE, led straight up to a large wooden door. When they made their way to it, Riggs grabbed the brass handle and held the door open for Mena.

After showing their badges and sidestepping the metal detectors, a short black woman with long, thick, red dreadlocks checked their names against the pre-approved visitors' list and gestured for them to follow her.

"Welcome to the Cannon Building," she said as she walked fast paced down the corridor. "It was built in 1908, making it the oldest of our congressional office buildings. But by 1913, overcrowding of the offices led the architects to add fifty-one rooms and a fifth floor, which you can only see from right here at the inner court."

She stopped and pointed upward. Mena's gaze followed her

finger and sure enough, there was an additional level she had not noticed from the outside.

"Let's move along, shall we? The Congressman is waiting for you."

Riggs stepped ahead of Mena, not bothering to use manners or common courtesy.

This man is such a chauvinist.

A few steps later, they walked under an archway and stepped out into the floor of a grand, white rotunda. Bright sunlight shone in through the oculus in the very center of the dome above them, brightening the entire grand room and making the marble archways sparkle. But their guide didn't comment on the rotunda or the dome. Instead, she ushered them quickly across the shiny floor, under another archway, and down yet another corridor.

On the elevator ride to the third floor, the guide explained how an underground tunnel connected the office building to the capitol. This, she said, was how the congressional members made it from their offices to the house and senate without being bothered by pedestrians and political extremists, as well as avoiding the harsh, inclement weather of DC winters.

Finally, they arrived at an office at the end of a long hallway with an opaque glass door that had CONGRESSMAN WARD DAVIESS painted in gold across the front. The guide knocked, held her finger up at Mena and Riggs, and poked her head into the room when a voice responded. Muffled voices went back and forth before their guide stepped back outside and said, "The Congressman is ready for you."

"Well," Riggs scoffed, "glad the congressman has made time out of his busy day to speak with law enforcement about a very important investigation."

The guide fixed Riggs with a glare full of contempt. Then, a second later, her face softened, and she turned to face Mena. "Have a nice day, Detective."

"You, too. And thank you for escorting us. We'll find our way out when we're done."

The guide smiled, tucked her chin to her chest, turned, and walked away.

Once again, without letting Mena go first, Riggs stepped into Congressman Daviess's office. Mena sighed and stepped in behind him.

"Congressman Daviess, I presume?" Riggs asked, holding up his badge.

The politician smiled and gestured for them to sit in the two maroon leather seats in front of his large, highly polished mahogany desk. Just as Mena was about to take him up on the offer, Riggs cleared his throat.

"No, thank you, but we'll stand."

"Suit yourself," Daviess said, but not unkindly.

Mena spoke up before Riggs could assert his control over the entire interview. "Congressman Daviess, my name is Detective Mena Kastaros with the Lexington Police Department out of Kentucky, and this is Special Agent Irvin Riggs with the FBI." Riggs glared at her for a fraction of a second, then shifted his eyes back to the man before them. "As I'm sure my office told you when they set up this meeting, we're here to talk to you about an ongoing investigation into the kidnapping of a young lady named Caroline Hanson."

"Yes," Daviess said as he unbuttoned his suit coat and sat in the tall wing-backed chair behind his desk. "But as I told your office, I'm not sure I can be of much assistance. You see, I've seen this case mentioned in the news the last couple days. Quite a story, I'll admit. I'm just not sure what the reappearance of a missing girl has to do with me, as wonderful as the news may be."

"You see—"

"Actually, what Detective Kastaros was about to say is that we're here to question you about the suspect in this case. One Stanley Dale Pollard. Ring any bells?"

The congressman pursed his lips, furrowed his brow, and shook his head. "No. Can't say that it does."

"Really?" Riggs said. "That's quite interesting."

Mena clenched her jaw, drew in a deep breath, and let it out. "You may not know him by that name, necessarily. But I believe you have heard of his website."

Daviess held up a hand. "Listen, detective. As I am often forced to remind folks, I can't control which businesses make campaign contributions. My staff members always try to check and recheck these companies, but you see, we can't all be investigators, so some...shall we say...unsavory business sometimes slip through the cracks. Sad, but true."

Mena nodded. "I see. Then you have never heard of a website called the Rainbow Room?"

The congressman's face turned ashen, he blinked rapidly, and Mena swore she saw the slightest trembling in the man's hands.

"That's what I thought," Mena said. "Now, let's start over from the beginning, shall we?"

Daviess nodded once.

"Do you know Stanley Dale Pollard?"

"Please," the man said, "have a seat."

26

"Who were you on the phone with earlier?" Laura asked as she breezed into Caroline's room carrying a basket of laundry. She set it on the floor by the foot of the bed and planted her hands on her hips.

Caroline was sitting at the head of her bed, reading one of her favorite books which she'd found sitting on her bookshelf – *A Wrinkle in Time*. "Detective Kastaros," she answered honestly. She wasn't sure why she felt slightly guilty. Probably because she had all but ratted her mother out to the detective over the whole Dateline interview situation.

"Mm hm. That's what I thought. Well, I'm not going to tell you not to talk to her. She's a nice enough person. And it's important for you to help in the investigation, I guess." Laura sat down next to Caroline and folded her hands in her lap. "But just be careful."

Caroline looked at her mother with one brow arched. "Careful? She's a cop."

"I know that, sweetheart. I'm not saying anything bad about her. I'm just saying I don't want them to use you, that's all. They don't really need you to find...*that man*. You've already spoken to her twice and told her everything you know, right?"

Caroline nodded. "As much as I can remember. But sometimes, I don't really think of certain details unless she asks me a specific question. And I don't mind helping. Besides, I want them to find Stan. What he did was wrong. No, he never really hurt me, but he took me from you guys and kept me hidden away from the world for ten years. He stole my life from me. I want her to catch him, and if that means talking to her about everything that happened, I'm fine with that."

She watched her mother, trying to read her expression, but couldn't figure out what she was thinking. Then, after a few quiet seconds, her mother patted her leg.

"I understand. Now, there's something I've been meaning to tell you. It's good news, actually. You know how I've been getting dozens of calls since you come home?"

Caroline nodded. "Yeah."

"You already know about the TV interview. But I got a couple more I think you should know about. One came from someone from the law firm that represents the University of Kentucky." Caroline watched her mother, whose eyes lit up like Christmas. "They are offering you a full scholarship! Can you believe it?"

"But how...I mean, I haven't even..."

Laura waved her hand through the air. "Psh, don't worry about that. They said all you have to do is pass your GED and then you get to go all four years for free. Isn't that amazing?"

"But I didn't even finish third grade. There's no way I'll pass the—"

"Don't worry about that right now. They said it's a lifetime offer. There's no rush. Anyway, we also got a call from that big Chevy dealership on the north side of town. They want to give us a new car. A brand-new Equinox! They said we can pick out the color and everything. It's so exciting, right?"

"But I..."

"But what, Caroline? These people want to help. This whole town has been looking for you for ten years, and you finally came home. People just want to do what they can, that's all. Why are you being so weird about all this?"

"It just doesn't feel right...taking things for free just because of what happened to me." Caroline shrugged. "It makes me feel—"

"Feel what? Thankful? Blessed? Because that's how your father and I feel. You know we've suffered since you went away. I had to stop working because of my bad back, and your father's business only brings in money eight months out of the year. People just want to help. The least you could do is be grateful."

If her mother had slapped her, it would have stung less. Of course she was grateful. It wasn't that. It just didn't feel right, taking money from complete strangers when she hadn't exactly earned it. Regardless of what she'd been through, she didn't feel like she deserved all these free things.

"Besides," her mother continued, ignoring Caroline's obvious distress, "you're not the only one who suffered. I'm sorry, but it's true. I'm not downplaying what you went through. I'm sure it was horrible. And I have thanked God every minute since you came home to us that you returned safe and unhurt. Remember, your father and I thought we'd lost our only child. We tried to hold out hope, and we did, but there were times, dark times, when we had to admit to ourselves you might never come home." Laura stood and paced the floor. "You don't know this, but after you first...*left*, the same thing happened. People gave us things, they donated money, we did interviews all over the place. But after a while, everyone disappeared. They stopped calling. They stopped checking in. The money from the fundraisers dried up. And just like that," Laura opened her hands wide, "we were broke again and on our own. Now, people want to help once again. And why shouldn't we let them? Hm? We've earned it."

"You mean, *I've* earned it." Caroline's hand flew to her mouth, and instantly, she regretted her words.

"I see," her mother spat. "So the fact that your father and I spent ten years of our lives thinking we'd lost our only child... damn near lost everything—the house, our savings, the truck—it means nothing? Now not only do we have you back, but we have a chance to get back on our feet, and you want us to turn it all down. Why? Some misplaced sense of pride?"

This stung Caroline to the core. Pride was the last thing she felt when it came to this entire situation. "Mom, I didn't mean—"

"Let me guess," Laura continued, "Detective Kastaros told you not to take the money and things, too, didn't she? I know she talked you out of the Dateline interview, too."

"No," Caroline said. "She didn't say anything like that."

"Oh, so I suppose it's just a coincidence that you called her and now your father and I are going to New York alone. I guess if it's up to her, you'd have us turn it all down, right?"

"I'm sorry," Caroline said as tears streamed down her face. "I'm really sorry, Mom. I know how much you guys need the money. I do. And I want to help if I can. But I'm not sure I'm ready for all this attention. I wish you could understand."

Laura looked at Caroline briefly, then her features softened. She took two steps and sat back down on the edge of the bed. "I'm sorry, sweetheart. I really am. I shouldn't have snapped at you like that. I feel awful. It's just...your father and I, we really are struggling. We could use the help is all. The car, the tuition, the fundraisers, the interview money...it could really dig us out of the deep hole we're in financially." She reached out and smoothed a piece of Caroline's hair behind her ear. "But, honey, you're more important to me than all of that. You coming home to us after all these years, safe and sound, is what matters most. If you want us to turn it all down, then that's what we'll do. We won't be mad. I promise. And we'll find another way to—"

"No," Caroline said. "No, don't do that. I want to help if I can.

If that means taking the money and things, then do it. But as far as the interview goes…I'm just not ready. Can you understand that?"

Laura tilted her head and ran her hand down Caroline's back. "Of course, sweetheart. You don't have to go. You can stay with Detective Kastaros as we planned. But I hope you understand why your father and I still have to go. Do you?"

"I do," Caroline said with a nod. "And maybe one day soon I'll be ready to face the world. But right now, the thought of Stan and Beverly being out there somewhere, watching me through the television, just creeps me out."

"I understand, sweetie. I do. Now, get some rest. We'll talk more tomorrow."

Laura pulled back the covers and Caroline slid her legs underneath. Her mother then wrapped the comforter up around her and tucked it underneath her chin, just as she had when she was little.

"Snug as a bug in a rug," she said.

Caroline smiled.

Laura bent down, kissed her on her forehead, told her goodnight, then switched off the bedside lamp and exited her room, leaving the door partially cracked on her way out.

As Caroline lay there, staring up at the fluorescent stars that twinkled from her ceiling, she remembered what it was like to stare at the ceiling of the basement at Stan's house. Why did her mind always have to go there? How long would it be before she could look up at these stars and just enjoy them instead of thinking back to those awful, lonely nights when she lay there in that tiny, uncomfortable bed dreaming of her parents and her home? Sure, she had the two other girls to keep her company, so she wasn't completely alone. But it wasn't the same. She could still feel the iron clamps around her ankles which Beverly would clasp tightly shut every night before tucking the girls into bed. Caroline rubbed her ankles together once just to make sure there were no iron shackles this time. Nope. They were gone. She was definitely not in that basement anymore.

Still…that didn't mean she felt all the way home yet either. She knew logically that she was in her childhood bedroom, safely tucked into the bed she'd slept in for almost eight years. And her mother's routine of tucking her into bed was comforting in its way. But the conversation she'd just had with her mother – *argument*, really – felt like taking a step backward. Caroline wanted to please her parents, and she knew their intentions were pure and that they only wanted what was best for her and their family. It was just as clear to Caroline now that, while she had her parents again and she was no longer being held captive by a couple of lunatics who intended to sell her to the highest bidder, she was caught somewhere between the two places.

Strangely, she found herself wishing she could talk to Detective Kastaros again. Mena was the only one who didn't push her. The only one who seemed to understand that coming home again was a process and that there were monsters out there who took things from you that you could never get back. Maybe it was because she'd lost her own daughter. Or maybe it was because she had worked with victims her whole life. Or both. Whatever it was, Caroline realized as she lay there staring at those silly starts that no one understood her the way Detective Kastaros did. And suddenly, she was anxious to stay with her, even if it was only for a couple of days.

27

This time, Mena agreed to sit in the chair across from Congressman Ward Daviess. Reluctantly, Agent Riggs followed suit. She sat with a straight back in the comfortable leather seat, crossed her right leg over her left, and stared directly at the man before her. He rubbed the back of his neck and Mena noticed tiny beads of sweat appearing around his hairline. She wanted to let the dust settle for a few moments and see if Daviess would offer anything voluntarily. This was an investigation tactic she'd learned over the years since most suspects would eventually crack under pressure and spew details they might not have otherwise offered, if only to break the awkward silence. But Riggs apparently had not learned this maneuver during his illustrious career.

"You'd best start by telling us the truth. Right here and now," he said, focusing his beady eyes on the congressman.

"My wife can't find out. Or my kids. And what about my career? I was just re-elected two weeks ago. I can't let my constituents—"

"I'd say that bird has long since flown the coop," Riggs interjected.

"What Agent Riggs means is that your career should be the least of your worries at this point. Please keep in mind that we wouldn't be here if we hadn't already connected you to the Rainbow Room. And, we never ask a question we don't already know the answer to." Mena leaned forward. "So, let's start again, shall we? Tell us where to find Stanley Dale Pollard."

"I swear I don't...it doesn't work like that," Daviess said, dabbing his forehead with a handkerchief he'd retrieved from his inner coat pocket.

"Enlighten us," Riggs said.

The congressman slumped back into his chair and sighed. "I'm going to prison, aren't I?"

"I'd say that's a pretty safe assumption." Riggs looked like he was enjoying this way too much. "But first, tell us what we want to know. And don't leave out the part about where to find Scarlett."

"Who?"

"Congressman Daviess," Mena said. "You know perfectly well who we're referring to. But the only way you're going to have a snowball's chance in hell at ever seeing your kids again is if you are honest with us right here and right now. First, tell us where we can find Scarlett. Then we're going to get back to the matter of your auctioneer and where to find him. Now...start talking, or I'm going to let Agent Riggs here run things his way and trust me, my way is better."

Riggs gave Mena a look that could freeze an Eskimo to the bones, but Mena turned her attention back to her subject and waited for him to cooperate.

"All right. All right. Scarlett is in an apartment I rented for her in Georgetown. It's at the corner of Wisconsin and O Street. She's perfectly fine, and I take good care of her there. And, by the way, she is eighteen. I made sure of that before I...well, you know. There's nothing illegal about..."

"Nothing illegal about purchasing a young girl from a website on the dark web so that she will do your bidding?" Mena tried to keep her temper in check, but this weasel was testing her patience. She glared at him as he looked back at her, slack jawed. "Yeah, that's right. We know everything about Pollard and his website, and don't even pretend you didn't know, or at least assume, that these girls were taken against their will! You knew full well you were purchasing another human being for your own sick, twisted gratification."

Daviess looked at her with wide eyes and shook his head. "I swear, I didn't know…"

"You mean to tell me you truly believed the young *girls* on this website you had to go out of your way to find on the dark web were being sold of their own free will? That these barely legal *girls* were just waiting with bated breath for you to buy them from this scumbag? That these *girls* wanted nothing more in life than to be sold to the highest bidder and then used as a sex-slave by men like you who think they are entitled to have and do whatever they want with no consequences whatsoever?"

Heat flushed through Mena's body. Congressman Daviess stared at her with eyes wide as two moons. From her peripheral vision, she could tell Riggs was enjoying her little outburst. Mena had never, not in ten years on the force, let an interviewee get to her the way this man did. But she was self-aware enough to know that while, yes, he was a criminal who deserved what she'd said and so much more, her temper came from knowing Daviess was connected to Pollard – the man who'd ruined her life. Unwilling to let Riggs think she condoned his style of interrogation, she drew in a deep breath then let it out and changed tactics.

"Listen, you're right. Your career is over. And quite possibly your marriage. But the amount of time you spend behind bars for your crimes will depend on your cooperation with us. Do you understand what I'm saying to you?"

"Yes."

"Then, for the love of God and all things holy, help us find

Pollard and I will personally talk to the federal prosecutor and tell them how you helped us put an end to this nightmare. That you brought home at least two innocent young girls who were snatched away from their parents, including Scarlett. That you realized how horrible your decision was and that you were willing to do anything in your power to stop the man who is peddling young girls to men like you."

"Can't hardly argue with that, can you, Daviess?" Riggs smirked, tilted his head, and looked at the congressman under a furrowed brow.

"No. I cannot," Daviess said, staring down at his shaking hands.

"Right. Now, where can we find Stanley Dale Pollard?" Riggs asked.

Mena scooted forward on the edge of her seat and gave the man an encouraging nod. "Any little bit of information might help. No matter how small. Just think. In all your communications with him, did he ever mention anything that might help us find him?"

"He has a brother," he finally said, though it looked as if it pained him physically to help the detectives.

"Yeah, well," Riggs scoffed, "so do I. Your point?"

"I don't know. I'm trying to help here," Daviess added. "I just... I think I remember him talking about a brother who helped him with his business from time to time. Sent him girls if he had trouble...you know..."

"Kidnapping them?" Mena said flatly.

"Uh, yeah. I guess. He said something about his brother having access to all kinds of young girls. But that's literally all I know. He never went into any details. I swear."

Mena looked at Riggs but couldn't read his expression. He just sat there staring at the congressman without blinking. After a few seconds, he slapped his hands down on the desk.

"All right. Guess our work here is done."

Riggs and Mena stood at the same time, but Riggs beat her to the door and opened it. Standing right on the other side were two uniformed DC officers. Riggs motioned for them to enter the room.

"Congressman Ward Daviess, these fine officers are going to read you your rights. You're under arrest for accessory to kidnapping, rape in the first degree, human trafficking, and I'm sure many other charges which will be sorted out in good time."

"Right now?"

"What," Riggs said with a laugh, "did you think we were going to just stroll out of here and let you go home? Kiss your pretty wife and kids goodbye before you were arrested for multiple federal offenses?"

"Well…I…." Daviess stood as the officers surrounded him and gently forced him to turn so they could handcuff him.

"I've heard some good ones in my day. I'll grant you that. But Mr. Daviess…I guess I can call you that now that you're no longer a congressman…that's about the funniest thing I've heard in ages." Riggs lifted his hand and waved. "See you in court, you low-life piece of—"

"All right," Mena said, motioning for Riggs to follow her out of the office. "I think he gets the point."

Riggs fixed Mena with another icy glare, but she ignored him and stepped out of the office and into the hallway. Riggs shook his head and joined her. They walked in silence down the corridor, through the rotunda, down another corridor, through the front door, and out into the cold November air.

When they climbed to relative warmth inside Riggs's parked vehicle, Riggs sat still in his seat without putting the key in the ignition. He just stared out the window, frowning.

"Can we get going?" Mena asked. "It's freezing. At least turn on the heat if you have something you want to say to me."

Riggs turned in his seat at stared straight into Mena's eyes.

"I'd appreciate it if you'd never again patronize me. Especially not in front of a suspect like that. Can I get a 'Roger that?'"

Mena's jaw dropped, and her eyes widened. "Excuse me? Am I hearing you right?"

"Damn skippy, young lady. I don't much care for—"

"Young lady? Now who's patronizing whom?"

Riggs held his hand up between them. "Wait just a minute. I can't abide—"

"What? A woman standing up to you? A woman being a good detective? A woman knowing how to drive a damn car? What exactly can't you abide, Agent? Because from where I'm sitting, you are the one who has been patronizing to me since the moment we first met. I don't know how they do things up in Frankfort, or how they did them back in your day…"

"Oh, now, hold on there," Riggs said with a huff.

"No, you hold on. I'm not quite done. I wasn't going to say anything to you about the way you started that interview with Daviess, but since you've opened this can of worms, let me enlighten you. I've been a detective for ten years. I've worked hundreds of cases, and my closure rate is unparalleled in our department. I've won three commendations and two awards in the past five years alone. And I've put dozens of hardened, violent criminals behind prison walls. I did that. Me. A woman." Mena pointed at her chest. "You had better get used to working with me, female parts and all. Because we've only just started this investigation and I will exhaust all possible resources to find this sonofabitch and lock him away, too." She paused and looked out her side window. "Or better yet, watch them plunge the needle into his vein." She turned her attention back to Riggs. "But what I can't have is you trying to manhandle me and talk down to me just because you're a grumpy, old, chauvinistic cop who's ready for retirement. I will be treated as your equal because I *am* your equal. We are partners, like it or not. Get over it, or get used to it, I don't care. But right now, we have to call Detective Felton and

Agent Rousseau, as well as the DC police and let them know where to find Scarlett."

Riggs just stared at Mena, his jaw twitching and his lips pursed. He appeared to be going over every snappy comeback he could muster and deciding which one to launch at her. But she was ready for it. She was fed up. And she was determined not to let this old asshole get in the way of her doing her job. She sat there glaring right back at him, willing him to fire back at her.

Instead, after several drawn-out seconds, he turned to face the front, shoved the keys into the ignition, put the car into drive, and pulled out of the parking place. Silently, he flipped his turn signal and merged into traffic. Then, as they sat at a stoplight staring through the front windshield, he broke the awkward silence.

"Good for you," he said. "No one's ever called me on my shit like that. So good for you. Now, why don't we call your partner and the DC police and update them? Thanks to us, Scarlett, or whatever her real name is, will be going home very soon."

Mena was dumbstruck. But rather than making the situation any more uncomfortable for them both, she simply smiled, pulled out her phone, and dialed Felton's contact. She'd never stood up to anyone like that in her entire life. But damn, if it didn't feel good.

28

R iggs dropped Mena off at the precinct, and she immediately got into her own vehicle. She was ready to get home and relieve her mother's nurse, who'd agreed to stay a few extra hours. She'd already talked to Felton and Lieutenant Iverson several times during the drive back from DC. Through the back and forth communications, Mena had learned that Ward Daviess was sitting in a holding cell and that local police had found Scarlett, alive and well, just where the disgraced congressman had said she'd be. Felton and Agent Rousseau were on their way to Washington to debrief the young girl, whose name turned out to be Molly Dotson from Versailles, Kentucky. So much had happened in the past twelve hours, but Mena was still no closer to finding Pollard. Her eyes were dry and heavy, and her muscles ached, and the image of a straight razor danced before her eyes – something to relieve the pressure building inside her. But she had one more stop to make before she could find her release again.

Fifteen minutes later, Mena knocked on the Hansons' door. Laura answered, holding back their massive barking dog.

"Detective Kastaros," she said as she wrestled with the beast.

"Please come in. I'll just put Zeus in his cage." She grabbed the collar by both hands, pulled him across the living room, and shoved him into a black metal cage. "Caroline!" she yelled once she'd secured the lock.

Mena stood and watched Laura as she scuttled about, trying to clean the living room and make room on the couch for them to sit. When she gestured toward an empty spot on the sofa, Mena politely held up her hand and shook her head.

Caroline appeared moments later, carrying a small, pink duffle bag with her name in silver glitter lettering on the side. She must have seen Mena looking at it because she instantly said, "It's from when I was little. Mom kept it for me all these years. Just in case…"

Mena smiled and nodded. "We'd better get going."

Laura walked between Mena and Caroline and put her hands on the girl's shoulder. "You be good for the detective, you hear?"

"I'm not a child," Caroline said with kind eyes. "But I'll be fine. Besides, you'll be back tomorrow, right?"

"Actually," Mark said as he stepped into the room. "Your mother and I are thinking of making a little mini-vacation out of the trip."

Laura's gaze darted over to Mena. "It's just one more day than we had planned. We'll be back on Friday. I hope it's okay. I just…we just never had a vacation before and with all the stress…"

"It's okay," Mena said, trying to put Laura at ease. I have to work during the days, but I'll be home and night. And my mother is living at home with me now so she and Caroline can keep each other company while I work."

"It's very kind of you to offer this, Detective," Mark said. "We appreciate it more than you know. Of course, we wish Caroline could go with us. But you said—"

"You don't have to explain yourself to me. I'd be glad to help out in any way I can."

Laura's shoulders relaxed and her facial features relaxed. "It's mighty nice of you, all the same."

"Are you ready, Caroline? We'd better get going."

After Caroline hugged her parents goodbye, she followed Mena out to her waiting car. Mena waved at the patrol officer parked across the street and he waved back.

Just as Mena was sliding the key to her brownstone into the lock, Caroline looked at her and said, "Are you really sure it's okay for me to stay here? Like, you're not going to get in any trouble or anything, are you?"

Mena pushed the door open but turned to face Caroline. "It's not illegal if that's what you're asking. But I'm not going to tell anyone…are you?"

Caroline smiled. "Okay. I just don't want you to get in trouble for me."

"You let me worry about that," Mena said. "You just worry about how you're going to survive the next two days with my mother."

The girl arched an eyebrow, and she looked at Mena curiously. "Why? What's wrong with your mother?"

"Oh, she'd harmless, really. But just don't say I didn't warn you."

They stepped into the foyer. Caroline looked around, assessing her surroundings, and her eyes landed on the wall next to the staircase leading up to the second level. "That must be your daughter," Caroline said, pointing to the neatly arranged array of photographs, whose frames varied in size and color.

Mena's heart sank, and she swallowed a lump that formed in her throat. "Yes, um, yes. Those are all pictures of my Sadie."

"She was really pretty," Caroline said. She smiled, but it did nothing to hide her discomfort.

"Yes," Mena said. "She was."

Mena looked at the largest of the pictures in the center of the display. The frame was made of dark red wood and in the middle was a snapshot of a day she recalled vividly. Sadie stood to Mena's right, smiling bigger than she'd ever smiled before. Both wore goofy Mickey Mouse hats and, in the background, the iconic castle which told anyone looking at the photo that the pair were in Disney World. It was Mena's favorite picture and one of her fondest memories. She couldn't remember Sadie ever being happier than she had been that day.

"Where's her dad?" Caroline's quiet voice broke the spell cast by the memory.

"He...uh...he died. I was pregnant with Sadie and he was hit by a drunk driver on the way home from a high school football game." Thinking about that God-awful night stirred up emotions Mena had shoved down deep for nearly twenty years. But Caroline meant no harm with her questions and besides, it was sort of nice to think about Brent again.

"I'm sorry. You've been through a lot. Is that why you..." Caroline pointed at Mena's wrist.

"Mena! Is that you?" Helena shouted from the living room, breaking the uncomfortable silence.

"We'd better go in," Mena said. "Trust me, we don't want to start off on the wrong foot with Helena Kastaros."

In the living room, Mena and Caroline were greeted by Anna, who was already in her winter coat and mittens. She slid her purse up onto her shoulder and grabbed her keys. Mena noticed bags under the redhead's eyes and wondered if Helena was already wearing her out. "She's eaten dinner. About eight o' clock. She took a bath right after and we have watched two episodes of *Castle*. I think she's pretty tired. But it was an uneventful day."

"Thank you, Anna," Mena said. "I'll see you in the morning."

Anna nodded and said her goodbyes. Then a minute later, she was gone.

"Mom, there's someone I would like for you to meet," Mena said as she gently guided Caroline further into the living room until they stood before Helena. Her mother was in her armchair with a crocheted blanket over her legs, staring at the television. "Mom?"

"Hm? Oh, yes, hello there, darling," Helena said when she finally took her eyes off the screen at glanced at Caroline. "My, my, aren't you a skinny little thing. But pretty. Look at those eyes. You look familiar. Do I know you?"

"Mom, this is Caroline Hanson."

A second or two went by when Helena's expression was blank. But then, the corners of her mouth turned downward, and she looked at the young girl over the top of her glasses. "Oh, my. You're that poor dear who just showed up at the Christmas tree lighting last week." Then Helena looked at Mena. "I thought you were working on her case. Is she allowed to be here?"

"Yes, Mom. She's allowed to be here. And I'm still working on her case. But her parents had to go out of town, and she is not quite ready to be alone, so I said she could come stay here with us for a day or two. Just until her parents get back."

"Well, yes, of course you can stay here," Helena said. "You're more than welcome. And we'll have lots of fun together, you and me, while Detective Mena goes to work tomorrow. We've got puzzles and games and, oh, I just learned how to use this thing called a Netflix on the television. We could watch movies and—"

"Mom, don't overwhelm her. I'm sure there'll be plenty for you to do tomorrow. Right now, I'm just going to show her to the guest bedroom, then I'll come help you to bed, too."

Helena flicked her wrist. "Oh, poo. You're no fun. But that's fine. You get some rest, dear. We'll talk more tomorrow. It was a pleasure to meet you."

"You, too, Ms. Kastaros," Caroline said with a small wave. "Goodnight."

"Let's go upstairs," Mena said. "I've got a spare bedroom you can stay in. Mother, I'll be back in a bit. You just stay put."

"Oh, I don't know," Helena said with a smirk. "I was thinking about doing some gymnastics while you're away." She winked at Caroline, who giggled despite herself.

Mena shook her head and gestured for Caroline to follow her. When they reached the top of the stairs, Mena showed the girl the bathroom, the closet where she kept towels and extra blankets, and finally, the guest bedroom. Caroline set her pink duffle bag down on the floor and sat down on the edge of the bed, which was covered with a white and yellow duvet. She bounced slightly.

"This is comfy," Caroline said. "A lot more comfortable than my bed."

"Well, you just get changed and get some sleep. Remember there are extra blankets in that closet if you get cold. This room can get a little drafty. And there are several books on the shelf over there." Mena pointed to the other side of the room where she kept a variety of books from JD Salinger to Janet Evanovich and a few in between. "Just help yourself. It always helps me to read when I have trouble going to sleep."

"Thanks, Det—I mean, Mena. Thanks for letting me stay with you."

"It's no problem at all."

"Can I ask you something?" Caroline wrapped her arms around her waist.

"Sure," Mena said. "Ask away."

"You said you found out Stan's real name and where he lived. That he escaped with Beverly and the girls and they're on the run."

Mena sighed, walked over to the bed, and sat down on the bed next to Caroline. "Yes, that's true. Why? What are you thinking?"

"It's just...I'm worried about the other girls. The two younger ones. Ebony and Hazel. What if we don't find them? He must have taken them with him. Do you think he'll get spooked and maybe do something like…" Caroline's hand flew to her mouth and she shook her head. "I'm so sorry. I wasn't thinking. Your little girl, Sadie. I'm so stupid."

Mena placed her hand on Caroline's arm and gently lowered it from her face. "Caroline, it's okay. Really. Am I sad about what happened to my daughter? Absolutely. Does it hurt whenever I think about her? Like a bitch. But what matters most to me is finding those girls and stopping Stan from hurting anyone else. And you have helped us so much already. So, no, you're definitely not stupid. In fact, I think you're very smart. And brave."

"Thanks, Mena," Caroline said as squeezed her hand. "That means a lot."

"But now that you mention it, I did want to ask you…do you recall Pollard ever talking about a brother? Maybe something about him helping find girls or bringing girls to him and Beverly?"

Caroline stared at the floor as she pondered Mena's question. After a moment, she nodded her head slowly. "Yeah, I do remember Stan talking on the phone to some man every now and then. I didn't know for sure it was his brother, but now that I think about it, I do remember him saying something about 'dad.'"

"This is important, Caroline. Do you remember the man's name? Or did they ever mention where he was from? We did some digging but so far, we haven't been able to confirm anything about Pollard's family, so any little piece of information would help. Take your time."

She didn't have to think this time. Instead, she perked up and looked at Mena with hopeful eyes. "I do remember something else now that you mention it. His name was Walter. And one time I heard Stan and Walter arguing about their home."

"Their home?" Mena raised an eyebrow.

"Yeah, they were arguing about their family and Stan kept

saying things like it was all his fault and that he knew he'd broken their family's hearts."

"Did he say how or why?"

"Something about a place called The Ranch. He kept saying The Ranch and it sounded like Stan had done something to upset his family. It sounded like Walter was tired of helping Stan because he didn't want their family to find out. And then one time, he said the strangest thing."

Mena was now all-ears and quite literally sitting on the edge of her seat. "Go on."

"He said, 'I can never go home. The prophet will never accept me back into the fold.' But I don't know what a prophet is exactly, so I don't know if that helps or anything."

Mena's mind was reeling, and the room spun around her. Suddenly all thoughts of going to the bathroom and cutting her wrist completely disappeared, and in their place were a bunch of words jumbling together but starting to slowly formulate a cohesive thought that was just beyond her reach.

Young girls.

Home.

The Ranch.

Family.

The Prophet.

If a Mac truck had slammed into her, the impact couldn't have been any greater. Suddenly, she was sure she had pieced together the first real clue that just might lead them to Pollard, Beverly, and the girls. It might be a longshot, but something was better than nothing. And if her hunch was right, she may be able to find the bastard sooner rather than later because, after all, how many polygamous cults were there in the United States?

29

One thousand, six hundred and seventy-two miles from home, Stan directed his van down the final dirt road on his destination. Beverly seemed surprised the van had made it that far, but being a mechanic, Stan wasn't. He'd kept the old jalopy in as good a shape as possible, including putting a new engine in less than two years ago. What was the point in dropping money on a brand-new van anyway? Not only would it draw unwanted attention since his on-paper income wouldn't support such a purchase, but Stan had become attached to the vehicle. Plus, it was about as nondescript as one could get. And when on the run from the law, nondescript was exactly the adjective he wanted to describe his mode of transportation. He'd even switched out the license plates three times along the way.

When he turned into the gravel driveway of the last house on the left at the end of Old Delaney Road, he put the van in park and turned to face Beverly.

"We're here," he said.

"I can see that."

"There's no turning back now. Nowhere else to go."

"Mm hm." Beverly gazed out the windshield and refused to turn and face Stan.

"Listen, love," Stan began, "I know this isn't ideal. Hell, I'm not sure what to expect out here, either. But Walter has been a good brother to me, and he's the only one we can trust right now. Besides, he's not like our father. Never has been. That's why he's kept in touch. Why he's helped us out all these years."

Finally, Beverly turned halfway in her seat and looked at Stan. "Okay, but how do you know he hasn't already called you father and tipped him off? How do you know we're not walking into an ambush?"

"Think about it, Bev, darling. If Dad were here, we'd know it. That man doesn't go anywhere without an entourage. There'd be a fleet of cars and guys in suits walking the perimeter of the house. We'd have been spotted and stopped before we even turned on this street."

"Then you think Walter actually kept his word and didn't tell your father about us coming out here?"

"I do."

"That's good," Beverly said. "But it won't be long before he finds out. We're in his territory now. This is his land. Nothing goes on around here without him finding out. Are you ready to face him when the time comes? It's been—"

"I know how long it's been," Stan said. "Damn near thirty years. And yeah, if it comes to it, I'll be ready to face the old fucker. Besides, he's in his early eighties by now. How harmful could he possibly be?"

"Are you seriously asking me that? This is your father we're talking about. Need I remind you what he did to you all those years ago?"

Stan held up a hand to ward off whatever she was about to say next. "No. No need. I remember it well. We'd better get in there. Walter's probably wondering what the hell we're doing sitting out here in his driveway. Hell, he's so paranoid, he's probably got a shotgun trained on our heads as we speak."

"What about them?" Beverly gestured toward the girls in the back of the van.

"Hm. Good point. You stay here with them. I'll go talk to Walter. Gauge his mood. I'll explain about the girls, then I'll motion out the window for you to come in once it's all clear."

Beverly nodded. "All right, then. Be careful. You don't really know where his loyalties lie. Your father may not be here, but Walter may change his mind and call him at any second. I don't like this. Not one bit."

"Me, neither, Bev. But—"

"I know. I know. We have no other choice."

Stan nodded, turned off the engine, and stepped out of the van. He walked slowly, one foot in front of the other, looking all around him for any sign of danger, as he made his way up the sidewalk and to Walter's front door. Two steps up, he stood before the front door, his hand poised to knock. But before he could, the door opened slightly, and his brother's profile appeared in the crack.

"That you, Stanley?" A voice whispered through the screen door.

"Yes, Walter. It's me. Stanley."

"You see any cars out there? Any sign of Father?"

"No, Walter. He's not here. He didn't see us, either. I can promise you that. It's seven o'clock in the morning. Bright as hell and not a cloud in the sky. I think I'd have seen Father's army coming if he was here."

Walter stared at Stan for a good few seconds, then shut the door. Stan thought at first his brother was turning him away until he heard several locks disengage and saw the door open all the way.

"Hurry. Come on in."

Stan opened the screen door and stepped over the threshold.

Walter waved him further into the living room. Looking around, Stan noticed all the blinds were drawn, blocking out the sun's rays. It might as well have been nighttime inside his brother's house. The air was musty, dank, and humid, and it was obvious the place hadn't been aired out in God only knew how long. When his gaze landed back on his brother, he saw that Walter was leaning his shotgun against the wall by the front door.

"Where's Beverly?" Walter asked.

"That's what I need to talk to you about," Stan said, his hands on his hips and his feet planted wide apart.

"Don't tell me you let that woman go," Walter said. "She's about the only damn good thing you've had in your life ever since you left here."

"Don't I know it," Stan agreed. "No, she's here. But we're not alone."

Walter's eyes bulged, and he took a step toward the shotgun again. "Stanley...what have you done? Did the police follow you out here? Damnit, brother. I told you to be careful. Why did you let them..."

Stan held his hands up between them. "No, Walter. Just stop and listen. I told you. No one followed us out here. Not Father. Not the police. No one has any clue we're here." He lowered his hands to his sides. "Hell, I doubt the police even know I have a brother. I use Mom's maiden name. Have ever since I went to Kentucky."

"Then who? Who's with you?"

Stan ran his hand over his balding head and paused before answering. "I had to bring two of the girls with me. They're in the back of the van."

"Aw, hell, Stanley," Walter said, shaking his head and clapping Stan on the shoulder, "you scared me. If that's all it is, we can work that out. Mind you, they can't stay here long. Can't take that kind of risk. But we'll figure something out. For now, bring 'em in here. Beverly, too. The girls can stay in the back bedroom.

I got all the things we need to keep 'em secured. As for you and Beverly, you can share my room. I'll take the couch."

"Walter, I can't let you do that."

"Like hell. I ain't seen you face to face in damn near three decades. Least I can do is show my baby brother some hospitality."

"Well, thanks, brother," Stan said, patting his brother's hand.

"But we do need to talk about Father," Walter said.

"Do we really have to?" Stan asked. The tiny hairs on the back of his neck prickled at the mere thought of facing his father again. "I mean, I've been driving for two days straight. Can't we rest a little before we decide how to handle the old man?"

"'Fraid not, man. It won't be long before he finds out you're here. It's only a matter of time. And we've got to decide how to play this. Now, I can handle him on my end. But, brother, you were kicked out. By our own father. The Prophet himself shunned you and forbade you from ever returning to The Ranch. Now, Father surely knows I talk to you from time to time. We just don't talk about it."

"About me, you mean."

"Yup. That's true. We're not even allowed to mention your name. Now, Mom won't be as hard to get through to. I know she misses you. It's the old man and the other wives we have to worry about. And of course, all the men. Our brothers and the other members of the Righteous United Brethren you have to worry about. They're devoted to The Prophet. If Bernard Lee James says to jump, they don't ask how high, they just throw themselves off the damn cliff. You remember how it was."

Stan nodded. "I do."

"Well, nothing's changed. If anything, it's gotten worse. Father has seven wives now. Twenty-four children. Lord only knows how many grandchildren. The Righteous United Brethren are now the biggest fundamentalist sect in Utah. Warren Jeffs had nothing on our beloved father."

"Aw, hell," Stan said. He'd figured old Bernard was still running things as The Prophet. And he was under no delusions that much had changed. But to hear he'd only grown more powerful in the past thirty years sent a shiver down Stan's spine.

"If Father finds out you're here...no, *when* Father finds out you're here, he'll demand to see you."

Stan shook his head and shifted his weight from one foot to the other. "But I've been shunned. I'd think he would want nothing to do with me. Why would he summon me?"

"That, my brother, is something we don't want to find out. I've been thinking. It might be best if we beat him to it. Tell him you're here and ask him to let you go to The Ranch. It'd be better if he found out directly from me than if he found out from someone else, if he hasn't already."

Stan paced the room and ran his hand over his balding head again. He'd been hoping he could hide out with Walter long enough to figure out what to do next. But the idea of facing his father head-on and confronting him after all these years was not something he was ready for. He recalled clearly the day he'd left The Ranch for the last time. The day he'd been cast out. As much as he'd railed against his father's fundamentalist views and rebelled against the teaching of The Prophet, it had still pained him deeply when his own father had turned his back on him. And the words his father had spoken to him that last day when he'd expelled him from the sect were still etched in his memory like a bad tattoo.

Stan turned to face Walter. "He said he'd kill me."

"He what?"

"I never told you that. Didn't want to put you anymore in the middle." Stan sighed heavily before continuing. "But that day he sent me away, he said if I ever returned, he'd kill me with his own bare hands."

"Shit, Stanley. Surely, he didn't mean it. The old man can be mean as a snake sometimes. That's true. And Lord knows I've even been on the receiving end of his verbal lashings from time to time. But ain't no way he'd kill his own son. Ain't no way."

Stan shook his head. "No, Walter. He meant it. He told me if I ever set foot on The Ranch property again, he'd take me out back, shoot me square between the eyes, and bury me with a bag of lye, like some lame cow. Those were his exact words. Said no one would ever find my body. I left and never came back. So don't tell me he didn't mean it. Sick old fuck."

"He's an old man now, Stanley. You should see him. He's eighty-two. Sure, people still fear him, but he just sits there in his office all day, pretending to go over paperwork and barking orders. He won't hurt you. Not if we go to him first. He may say some hurtful things. Best be prepared for that. But I won't let him hurt you. You have my word." Walter stepped closer to Stan, placed his hands on his shoulders, and looked him square in the eye. "Trust me on this, brother. Best to take the bull by the horns. Get it over with. Maybe the old guy will let you stay here, after all."

"What, you mean, if I ask nicely?" Stanley scoffed.

"Well, maybe not that easily, no." Walter dropped his hands and folded them across his chest. "But I think I know a way to save your ass from the police and get back in Father's good graces all at the same time."

Stanley titled his head and arched an eyebrow at Walter. "Oh, yeah? You think I can just stroll in there and get his blessing? Just like that?"

"Hell, no," Walter said with a chuckle. "Won't be that easy. It's going to take something big on your part. Something he couldn't say no to."

"You're not saying…"

"Yep. Sure am. You're going to convert back. Repent of your sins. Throw yourself at his feet and beg for mercy. The prodigal son returns, and so on."

Stan shook his head. "I don't know, Walter. I promised myself years ago I'd never go back to his way of life."

"You want protection from the law? You want to stay alive?"

"Well, of course I do."

"Then swallow your pride and get ready to grovel. That's your only option."

"All right," Stan said. "Let's say I was willing to consider this plan of yours. Let's say I was willing to repent and ask to be let back into the fold. What about Bev? What about the girls we still have?"

Walter smiled. "He'll let Bev in, too. Of course, you'll have to take on another wife, or three, but let's deal with one thing at a time. As far as the girls go, well, there's really only one choice to be made there, brother."

"And what's that?"

The corner of his father's mouth twitched up into a half-smile, and he folded his arms over his chest. "You'll have to get rid of them. Permanently."

30

The first thing Mena did when she walked into the precinct the next morning was to make a beeline for Felton's desk. He'd texted her last night upon returning home from DC, and she was anxious to talk to him about her theory. She found him sitting at his desk, leaning in toward his computer screen, and staring at it intently.

"What's so interesting?" she asked.

Felton flinched and looked at Mena. "You scared the shit out of me." He turned his attention back to the screen. "Just doing some research to see if I can find any communications on Ward Daviess's cell phones that might lead us to Pollard, or at least maybe some of the other men who've bought girls from him. So far, zilch."

"I'm sure something will turn up," Mena responded. "Do you have a minute? I have an idea I'd like to bounce off you."

"Sure," Felton said, turning his chair so he was facing her. "What's up, partner? You look pretty, by the way."

Mena opened her mouth to reply but couldn't thank of what to say. Her partner had never commented on her looks before, and she'd not made any special effort in the looks department this morning. Ultimately, she decided to ignore it.

"I was talking to Caroline last night…"

"Oh, did she call you?" Felton asked.

"No, she, um…I was talking to her and she thought of something else that hadn't occurred to her until last night. Remember how I told you yesterday that Daviess told me and Riggs that Pollard has a brother?"

"Yeah."

"Well, Caroline remembers overhearing Pollard talking to his brother on the phone several times. She remembers them arguing, and when I asked her what they were arguing about, she said it sounded like they were arguing about home or family and something Stan had done wrong to upset his family."

"Okay, so he had a falling out with his family. Doesn't surprise me, especially considering he's a creep."

"But there's more," Mena said. "She distinctly remembers him talking about a specific place several times. She referred to it as The Ranch."

Felton looked at her with a flat affect and raised his shoulders. "I don't understand the significance. Maybe his family lived on a horse ranch or something."

"I don't think so. It gets better. When they talked about The Ranch, they also talked about how Stan had upset The Prophet. So I started thinking…maybe, and I know this sounds kind of crazy, but maybe Pollard's family is some sort of polygamous cult?"

"You mean like Mormons?" Felton sat back in his chair and steepled his fingers. "I guess that makes sense. It would explain his propensity toward young girls. Those Mormons love to marry them young. That and marry fifteen women at the same time."

"Actually," Mena held up a finger, "it's not all Mormons. Joseph Smith publicly disavowed the tenant of polygamy back in

1904. It's only the fundamentalists who still practice multiple marriages and all that comes with it, and the Mormon church itself denounces anyone who practices it."

"Like Warren Jeffs, that famous polygamous leader who was arrested a few years back. How do you know all this? What did you do last night, watch a marathon of *Big Love?*"

Mena rolled her eyes at Felton. "No, smartass. But I just might have stayed up until three a.m. doing some basic research on Mormonism and polygamy. It may be a longshot, but I have a feeling there may be something to this, Felton. It feels right."

He sat forward in his chair again and looked up at Mena. "You may be right. There is an underlying theme of the exploitation of young woman that would tie Pollard together with fundamentalist Mormons. It makes sense."

"You agree with me?" Mena asked.

"I think it's worth looking into. But how on earth would we know where to start looking?"

"That's what we need to figure out next. We don't have much to go on."

"Just the brother's first name, right? Walter, was it? Hang on." He turned around to face his computer.

Mena smiled as she watched her partner peck at the keyboard with his pointer fingers, one key at a time. She'd tried to encourage him to take an online typing course, but he'd just laughed her off.

"There is a Walter Pollard in Cynthiana," Felton said after a few seconds.

Mena frowned. "No. If Pollard took off to hide out with some long-lost brother, he went further than forty miles."

"Well, yeah," Felton said with a laugh. "His picture just popped up. He's African American. Six foot four. Definitely not our guy. So, what now?"

"Let me think," Mena said, chewing on her fingernail as she concentrated.

"Go think at your desk," her partner said. "I can't concentrate with you looming over me like that."

"Screw you, Felton," Mena said, punching him lightly on the shoulder.

Mena waved him off and headed to her desk. She glanced at the picture of Caroline tacked to the corkboard on the wall and shook her head.

I just can't get there. I can see it, but it's just out of reach.

She pulled out her chair, sat down, and scooted in closer. With a jiggle of her wireless mouse, the screensaver blinked away and her desktop showing the LPD logo appeared. Mena opened a new Google page and sat there, strumming her fingers on the top of her desk.

Where are you, you weasely bastard?

She was certain she was barking up the right tree. It just made sense. She decided to go over the facts, as she knew them so far, in her mind.

1. Pollard and his common-law wife had packed up all their belongings and moved out of the house where they'd been living and holding the girls hostage.
2. He'd probably taken the remaining girls, Hazel and Olive, with him. Or at least, she hoped that's what he'd done. So he was likely traveling with at least three other people.
3. He had at least left in his white van, but he may have changed cars along the way. At least the license plates, if he had any sense in him whatsoever. They'd never track him down by his tags.
4. He had a brother named Walter to whom Caroline had overheard him talking, sometimes arguing, about coming home, disappointing the family, The Ranch, and The Prophet. All of these details led Mena to

believe in her gut that Pollard's family were some sort of fundamentalist Mormon cult.

It worked. Going through the details one at a time made the pieces all fall into place. Where else would you find a polygamous cult other than Utah? Sure, there might be smaller sects in other surrounding states, but from her research the night before, she'd learned that most stayed close to the "Mecca" for Mormons – Salt Lake City, Utah. But Utah is not a small state. It was a large, hexagon-shaped, land-locked territory that covered almost ninety-thousand miles of land. More information she'd learned from her research last night. Finding one man hiding in one of hundreds of polygamist families would be harder than finding a needle in a haystack.

But...

The idea that hit her was the most inspired one she'd had in years. She typed her search terms into the search bar and a second later, the results displayed. Five million, nine-hundred results, to be exact. Article after article touted headlines about women who'd escaped the Fundamentalist Church of Jesus Christ of Latter-Day Saints—FLDS, for short—and how they'd braved the secular world and started over. Most went on to have normal lives living out of the eye of the public, even marrying again and starting nuclear families. But the search result that got Mena's attention, the one she clicked on, was exactly what she'd been hoping to find.

The website, onetruelove.org, was colored in soft, muted tones and had a very welcoming aesthetic to it. The mission statement, printed in italic, bold font next to a picture of a smiling woman with long, blonde hair draped over her shoulders, said it all. Their purpose was to provide a "safe, non-judgmental community for survivors of the polygamous lifestyle."

It only took a minute or two to find the forum she was looking for. After creating an account under the pseudonym

"Rachel Jenson," Mena was able to access all the topic and even post questions or comments of her own. After scrolling through two pages of topics, she found exactly the one she needed for her mission. It was entitled: "Survivors Seeking Family Members." She drew in a deep breath, let it out, and started her own post under the thread. It read:

My name is Rachel. I'm seeking my long-lost sister, and I hope someone here can help me. She ran away from home when she was only fifteen. Last I heard from her, all she would tell me was that she had married a nice man in Utah, and she had eight kids. She didn't come right out and say it, but putting it all together, I'm convinced she's trapped in a polygamous marriage. That was two years ago, and I have not heard from her since. I only want to find her so I can at least know she is okay and maybe, just maybe, try to save her from this harmful and deceiving lifestyle. The only other thing I know is that she mentioned a place called The Ranch. If anyone has any information about this place – where it might be, who is in charge, etc. – it would mean the world to me if you passed it along. I just need to know she's alive. Thank you.

Pleased with herself, Mena sat back in her chair and re-read her post just to make sure it sounded genuine and believable. Once she was convinced that members would have a hard time not responding, she reached out for her mouse and clicked SUBMIT.

31

That morning, Mena had told Caroline she'd be home in time to relieve Anna and cook dinner for them all, but she'd just phoned to say she would be later than she'd anticipated. She'd asked Caroline if she felt comfortable sending the nurse home and hanging out with Helena until she could get away for the night, and Caroline had assured her they'd be just fine.

Now, Caroline and Mena's mother sat at the kitchen table working on a new puzzle. This one was a thousand pieces, and when they finished, it would be a picture of the coast of Santorini, according to the colorful picture on the box, which showed a blue ocean in the upper left-hand corner and all-white houses with blue roofs on the right. Caroline had no idea where Santorini was until Helena had explained it was her family's hometown in Greece and that they had moved to America when she'd been only two years old.

"You hungry?" Caroline asked, mostly to break the silence. She didn't know how to cook anything at all, and there wasn't much in the fridge they could heat up.

Helena shook her head but kept her gaze fixed on a particularly tricky section of the puzzle where all the white pieces looked the same. "I can wait for Mena if you can," was all she said.

"Yeah," Caroline said, picking up a piece and turning it this way and that to imagine where it might go.

"Listen," Helena said. She took off her readers and set them on the table, folded her arms, and looked directly at Caroline. "Let's talk about the proverbial elephant in the room, shall we?"

Caroline gave Helena a quizzical look. She had no idea what Helena was talking about. "Okay…"

"I know your story and what you went through. I think it's mighty brave what you did. I can't imagine the courage it would take to escape the kind of situation you found yourself in for so long." Caroline sensed a "but" coming down the line. Sure enough, Helena did not disappoint. "But I'm worried about my daughter. This case is either going to make her or break her. And I'm afraid it's going to be the latter. I've seen the way she copes with stress, and she's doing it again now that the investigation has gotten more intense."

"You know about the cutting?" Caroline asked.

Helena nodded. "She thinks I don't know. Thinks she hides it so well. But I'd have to be blind not to see the scars and bandages peeking out from underneath her shirt sleeves. I even know where she hides her razor."

"But how…"

"She's been doing it off and on since adolescence. Mena's never admitted it to me, and I've never asked. But I knew. I still know. I should have taken her to get help. I should have insisted she talk about whatever was driving her to do such a drastic thing. It's my biggest regret in life. The past is the past, and I can't change that now, but I'm worried about her now."

"You love her a lot, don't you?"

Helena sighed. "Mena and I don't always see eye to eye. I

raised her all alone, you see. I was forty when she was born, and I never married, so she never had a father figure. It was always just the two of us. Maybe I spoiled her a bit. She's very independent and strong-willed, just like her mother. But she's all I have in this world. All I've ever had. That's why it hurts me so much to see her in pain."

Caroline's heart sank. "I don't want to make things worse for her."

"Oh, no, child. It's not your fault. Not at all. That's not what I meant. All I meant was that I see what this case is doing to her. It's bringing out ghosts from the past and opening old wounds. You know about Sadie?"

Caroline nodded. "Her daughter. She told me she thinks Stan killed her."

"And he probably did. Can't be a coincidence that we lost our little angel only a week before you..."

"Before he kidnapped me."

Helena nodded once. "So now, she's not just trying to find the man who abducted you and took you away from your family, but he's the same man who stole her baby from her in a violent way. On top of that, I've come home to stay with her, and let's just say I'm not the easiest person to get along with sometimes."

Despite herself, Caroline giggled. While Helena had been nothing but gracious and kind to her, she could see the stubbornness that would make living with her every day a bit of a struggle. Her thoughts turned to her own mother and she found she could relate to their struggles. Though Caroline's own mother had been wonderful when she'd first returned home, something had shifted when the offers for interviews and charitable donations had started rolling in. Despite it all, she was grateful that her mother was back in her life again.

"Anyway, I've noticed that Mena really cares about you. Sometimes I wonder if she sees a bit of Sadie when she looks at you. But that's normal, I guess. I just worry that if she doesn't find that bastard, and soon, she may take unhealthy risks and spiral even deeper into that dark place she goes to where even I can't reach her. It's just…"

A loud, crashing sound reverberated through the house, and both Caroline and Helena jumped in their seats. They looked at one another with wide eyes and open mouths.

"Call 911," Helena said.

Caroline grabbed her phone and did as instructed. When the dispatcher answered on the first ring, she hurriedly told him where she was and that they'd just heard a loud crash inside the house somewhere. The dispatcher told her to find a secure place to hide and to lock the door and that police would be there as soon as possible. She instructed Caroline to keep the line open. Caroline slid the phone into her back pocket without hanging up and looked at Helena, who was trying to push herself up to standing.

"Here," Caroline said as she moved to get behind her. "Let me help you. They said to hide in a room and lock the door."

"The hell with that," Helena said. "My daughter is a detective. There are at least three guns in this house that I know of. Run to the kitchen."

Caroline went as fast as she could. Her heart raced, and her stomach was in knots. What if someone was inside the house? What if Stan had tracked her down here and was here to take her back to the basement? She couldn't let that happen. Not again.

"Now, open the drawer next to the refrigerator. Do you see it?"

Caroline yelled back, "Yes!"

"Good. Now open it up. There should be a pistol in there. Fully loaded."

Caroline slid open the drawer and, sure enough, a black, metal handgun lie there cockeyed with a box of bullets next to it. She reached in and pulled it out gingerly. Caroline had never handled a gun in her life. Part of her was afraid it would go off on its own, though she knew deep down that was impossible.

"What do I do now?" Caroline called out.

"Bring it here."

She was about to take the gun to Helena, but then it dawned on her. The woman was seventy-something years old and feeble. The gun would be of no use in her hands, no matter what kind of crack-shot she might have been in her youth. In an instant, Caroline made a decision she prayed she wouldn't regret.

"I got this," she said to Helena. "Go to the bathroom and lock the door."

Mena's mother looked at Caroline as if she had lost her mind. But Caroline stood her ground and did her best impression of a girl on a mission who was not afraid and was willing to do anything to protect them both. After a second or two passed, Helena's face softened, and she waved her hand in front of her face.

"Oh, all right. You can move quicker than I can, anyway. Just be careful. If you see anybody in the house, shoot first, ask questions later."

"Okay. I'm just going to take a quick look."

Helena reached her hand out toward Caroline, even though they were far apart. "Be careful."

Caroline nodded and took her first step toward the living room, from where the noise had come. They hadn't heard a sound since the crash. But that didn't mean the person or persons who caused it weren't inside, waiting for her to come into view just so they could grab her and drag her out of the protection of Mena's house. Slowly, she crept out of the kitchen, passed the dining room, and toward potential danger. Whoever or whatever it was, Caroline was not going to just cower in the corner and wait for them to snatch her. No, this time, she was armed and ready. This time, she wouldn't go without a fight. Hell, this time, she wouldn't be taken alive.

Caroline heard the bathroom door close, letting her know Helena was safe inside and out of harm's way as she stopped at the end of the hall where it opened up to the living room. She stood with her back against the wall and the gun raised at eye level. She had no idea how to hold a gun, exactly, but she gripped it with both hands in a way that felt natural and which gave her more control over it. Her index finger rested gently on the trigger. Caroline drew in a deep breath, let it out, then stepped around the corner and held the gun out in front of her, prepared to pull the trigger, if that's what it came to.

But to her surprise and relief, the living room was empty. The TV was still turned on and the classic game show Helena had been watching earlier still played in the background, but the volume had been turned all the way down so they could concentrate on their puzzle. Now, all Caroline could hear was the wind howling, car doors slamming, and dogs barking. She looked at the front of the house and noticed the curtains were dancing on a breeze. It took a few seconds for her mind to register the fact that the window on the right was shattered and that there was glass all over the hardwood flooring.

Lying near the window amidst the shards of window glass, was a brick with a piece of white paper tied around it with twine.

What the hell?

Caroline tiptoed across the oriental carpet that covered most of the room with the gun still poised to shoot, just in case her instincts were wrong, and someone *was* in the house. But she felt certain the only thing she was going to find was the note someone had clearly tossed into Mena's house by means of a large red brick. When she made it to the object, she bent over and used two fingers to pull the twine loose. With that out of the way, she picked up the paper, stood, and stared at it for a few seconds, trying to decide whether to open it or wait for the police to arrive. In the end, curiosity got the best of her, and she slowly unfolded the note, as if she were somehow delaying the inevitable.

When Caroline read the words scrawled across the page in large block letters, all the air seemed to be sucked out of the room, which started to spin all around her as she tried to calm her breathing.

I knew he'd never let me go.

32

I t was late, and Mena felt guilty about missing dinner with her mother and Caroline. But she'd been researching her theory online and checking the polygamy survivors' forum throughout the day, waiting for someone to respond to her post. And just as she was about to give up for the day and leave, Lieutenant Iverson had stopped by her desk and announced a task force meeting at 7 PM. Apparently, there'd been some developments regarding some of the girls that had already been sold by Pollard, and Agent Rousseau and Mena's partner Felton were going to brief the team on the status of that part of the investigation.

Mena looked at the clock on her phone. She had less than half an hour until she had to meet the others in the conference room, so she decided to check the OneTrueLove forum one last time, just in case. She clicked on the website, which she'd saved on her favorites bar, and watched while the department's spotty wi-fi tried to connect to the page. It normally ran pretty fast, but since their computers ran on a secure cloud server, sometimes the network got jammed by high traffic, especially if someone was downloading or uploading large files. This must have been one of those times.

Finally, the page appeared on the screen, and she clicked on the forum link and scrolled to her new topic. To her delight, she noticed she had three new replies.

The first was from happymommy87. Mena tried to contain her excitement as she read the short post.

Sounds to me like your sister may be in a polygamist marriage, as you suspect. This forum is a great place to find help for you and for your sister. I don't know anything about a place called The Ranch, but I'm in Colorado, not Utah. The best advice I can give is to be patient but consistent in your support of your sister. Tell her you love her and miss her and that you don't judge her for her lifestyle choice. Hopefully, she'll eventually come around and see that you're only trying to help. Sorry I can't offer anymore. Best of luck!

Feeling frustrated with the lack of information, Mena clicked on the second response, posted by lifeafterpoly, and when she read the first few words, her heart leaped in her chest.

I believe The Ranch you are referring to is the one in Poplar Creek just outside Provo, Utah. All I know is what I've heard, and I've heard some crazy things. They follow the original teachings of John Taylor, and they believe that plural marriage is essential to reaching the "highest degree of exaltation in the celestial kingdom." But they dislike the term "polygamy" and instead refer to plural marriage as "living the principle." Your sister has likely been brainwashed, I'm sad to say, and it'll be next to impossible to convince her to leave her family, especially if there are kids involved. But as the first poster said, this is a great place for community and support and there are lots of resources for you to access. Good luck!

Now, she had a bit more information. She jotted down "Poplar Creek" on a notepad so she'd remember to Google that next, but first, she needed to read the last reply. The poster's handle was bensmommy123, and it read:

I know exactly which sect your sister is likely a member of. It's called the Righteous United Brethren, and yes, they're in Poplar Creek outside Provo. Their leader is a man named Bernard Lee James, and the people on the compound they call "The Ranch" all believe he is The Prophet. Last I heard, he had thirteen wives and forty-three children. But who knows what's true and what's rumor? He's an old man now, but he runs Poplar Creek as if he's some sort of king, and if your sister is, indeed, part of that cult, you need to do everything in your power to rescue her. Not only do they practice polygamy, but they exploit the young girls and The Prophet assigns them as wives to much older men called "brethren" who he deems worthy of the celestial kingdom and who are living the principle. In reality, they're forcing themselves on pre-teen girls. But you should be careful when dealing with Poplar Creek and The Prophet. I hear that even though he's an old man, he's powerful and scary as hell. In fact, rumor has it he cast his oldest son out of the family years ago when he found out the son was stealing some of the young wives and helping them escape the compound. After that, James became a paranoid dictator, and he closed the sect off from the outside world. If that's where your sister is, I will say a prayer for both of you. But I suggest that if you're serious about helping her, you contact the local authorities or the federal prosecutor in Utah since I know they're working to try to shut down the compound, and they're looking for any reason they can find to indict him. Keep us posted.

. . .

Mena sat back in her chair and let out a breath she hadn't realized she'd been holding in. She'd hoped her little ploy might help her glean a trickle of information, but this was more like an avalanche. Her little hunch had paid off in spades. Now, not only did she have the name of the compound – Poplar Creek – but she also had the approximate location and the name of its leader. Beyond that, this post confirmed all of Mena's theories and everything fell into place neatly.

Pollard was definitely part of a polygamous cult, and he had fallen out with his family. And the bit about him funneling young girls out of the compound made sense when she thought about The Rainbow Room. There was no excuse for what he had done. It was despicable and unjustifiable to sell young girls to the highest bidder. But Mena was willing to bet he had convinced himself he was finding them better lives and that his desire to do so had morphed into a sick, twisted "mission" to sell these girls to rich men who would give them the lives they couldn't have otherwise, at least, in his mind.

But one thing didn't make sense. If Stan had started his criminal career by sneaking innocent victims off the compound, holding them until they turned eighteen, and then finding them "better" lives, why Caroline? Why Sadie? Mena didn't know the backgrounds of the other girls yet, but neither Caroline nor Sadie came from troubled homes. Why did he take them? Perhaps he just spiraled out of control and lost touch with reality at some point and convinced himself that all young girls needed saving. God only knew what went on in the minds of demented men like Stanley Dale Pollard.

Mena's concentration was broken when she felt the presence of her partner looming to her left.

"You look like you've got the weight of the world on your shoulders," Felton said.

"I think I might have found Pollard," she said, fully aware of the uncertainty in her own voice. "Not sure, but I've got a lead."

"That's great. But hold your horses. Lieu is waiting for us in the conference room with Beauty and the Beast from the FBI. Tell us all about it in the briefing."

Mena nodded, stood, grabbed her notepad, and followed Felton down the hallway toward the conference room.

Waiting for them both on the other side of the door, Iverson sat at the head of the long, wooden, highly polished table. Riggs and Rousseau sat on either side. Felton walked around the table and sat down next to Rousseau. As he scooted up to the table, he leaned over and started chatting away at the beautiful agent, who indulged him with a polite but disinterested gaze. Mena smiled.

Could he be any more obvious?

Iverson clapped loudly, startling Mena, and called the meeting to order.

"Gang's all here," he said as he placed his palms face down on the table and spread them wide. "Let's get down to it, shall we? Agent Rousseau, I hear you have made some progress in finding some of the girls Pollard's sold over the years. But first, give us a quick update on young Scarlett."

"First," the agent said, "her name is Molly Dotson. But she's doing as well as can be expected. She's been reunited with her family, and we've put her in touch with a therapist to help her. Of course, we'll follow up in a couple days and check in on her, but I think she's going to be just fine."

"Excellent news," Iverson said with a wide grin. "Now, what about the other girls. What have you found so far?"

Rousseau opened a leather portfolio and flipped the first page of her notepad. She pointed down at her notes with a fancy silver pen. "So far, we have identified six girls by comparing their photos from The Rainbow Room to information we found on NCIC. We've only been able to locate two of them so far. Their abductors were both men of wealthy means and/or high social standing, and so far, it appears both girls are alive and relatively healthy. Of course, they're traumatized by their experiences, but it seems the men who purchased them were keeping them as second wives, almost. Both were living in luxury apartments, much like Molly Dotson, and both were well taken care of. Physically, anyway. Emotionally, now, that's a whole different story." She flipped to another page. "Now, as for the other four girls, I have some ideas—"

The door opened so unexpectedly, everyone turned to see who had dared to interrupt such an important meeting without knocking. A rookie, whose first name Mena still hadn't learned, stood there breathing heavily and staring directly at Mena.

"Sanders," Iverson said, "is there something we can do to help you?" His frustration was thinly veiled.

"I...uh...Kastaros...a call just came into dispatch and, uh..."

"Spit it out, rookie," Iverson commanded.

"Dispatch just received a call. It came from your house, Kastaros. Someone called from a cellphone but said they were at your house and that there's an intruder. Should I..."

Mena bolted out of her seat, nearly knocking the heavy chair over in the process. She shot a quick, pleading glance at her lieutenant.

"Go, go," he said, waving her off. "But take Felton with you."

Felton jumped up out of his seat and was at Mena's side in a split second. She turned to the rookie detective. "What else do you know? Tell me now!"

The poor guy looked like he was about to wet himself. He was virtually shaking in his boots. "I..uh...that's literally all I know. It just came in like, a minute ago. Patrol cars are en route."

Mena pushed past the young man and made a beeline for her desk. She grabbed her coat, her wallet, and her keys, and shoved her gun into its holster. As she sped silently across the precinct toward her waiting car, her mind ran over all the worst-case scenarios and what on earth could be happening to her mother and Caroline while they waited for uniforms to arrive.

Once inside her cruiser, she barely waited for Felton to get his leg inside and shut the door before she screeched out of the parking lot and barreled down Main Street toward her brownstone.

"I'm sure it's fine," Felton said after a couple quiet, uncomfortable moments. "City police are probably already there, and we'd have heard by now if—"

Mena shot Felton an icy glance. "You mean if one or both of them are dead?"

Her partner raised his hand in surrender and looked out his side window. "Just sayin."

She sighed. "I'm sorry, Felton. I didn't mean to snap at you. But if something happens to my mother or Caroline because I wasn't there to protect them—"

"Don't think the worst until we know all the facts. We'll be there in five minutes. Until then, just try to stay calm, and remember, I'm here, no matter what happens."

"I know. Thank you," Mena felt even worse now for barking at him. "It just doesn't make any sense, though. We know Pollard skipped town. Who could possibly want to hurt me directly or hurt someone I care about to get to me?"

"I don't know," Felton admitted. "It makes no sense. It could just be a random act. Maybe some druggie just breaking into houses looking to score. Maybe it's just a coincidence."

Mena flipped on her cruiser's lights as they approached a red light. "You don't believe in coincidence. Neither to do. We've both been doing this job long enough to realize that nothing just happens in life. I want you to look me in the eye and tell me that you truly believe someone breaking into my house right now has absolutely nothing to do with the fact that we're only days away from finding Pollard and shutting down his whole operation."

"You're right. You're right."

Mena didn't voice the next words that filtered through her mind.

If something has happened to either one of them, I will put a bullet between that sonofabitch's eyes, even if it means the end of my career. I will not lose anyone else.

She put her foot to the accelerator and sped down the road, blowing through every stoplight they encountered and praying the entire time that she wouldn't have to view the body of yet another person she loved.

Not again. Never, ever again.

33

An empty feeling had settled in the pit of Stan's stomach, and he rubbed the back of his neck as he sat next to Walter in a row of metal chairs just outside his father's office. He was surprised he had been granted an audience with The Prophet. He had not been surprised, however, by the security measures taken when he was being escorted from Walter's house to The Ranch. After sleeping most of the day, Walter had awoken Stan around two in the afternoon to tell him their father had agreed to see him, but that they had to take precautions and follow the instructions given to them to a T.

Around 6 PM, Stan had looked out the front window of Walter's house and had seen a row of black Town Cars coming down the lane. All the vehicles were parked in different positions surrounding the house and several men in cheap, dark suits and wearing sunglasses, despite the setting sun, walked up the lawn to the front door. Once Walter had let them all inside, they'd frisked both brothers, patted them down, and secured all of Walter's weapons without saying a single word. Then one man, apparently their father's head of security, stepped up to Stan and rattled off the protocol and what to expect during his brief visit with The Prophet. Walter and Stan had been escorted to one of the waiting cars, and less than five minutes after their arrival at Walter's house, Stan was on his way to see his father for the first time in thirty years.

Now, he sat in the cold, hard chair next to Walter, bent forward with his elbows resting on twitching legs. No one else was waiting for their turn to be heard, and as far as Stan could tell, no one was inside the office with The Prophet. He wondered what the hell was taking so long. But then again, he wasn't entirely sure he was ready for this meeting, so the wait was both welcome and excruciating at the same time.

After another ten minutes had passed, the door to the office opened, and one of his father's henchmen pointed at Stan. "The Prophet will see you now." Both Stan and Walter stood, but the somber man shook his head. "No. Just you."

Walter sat back down and looked up at Stan with apologetic eyes. Stan straightened his back, lifted his chin, and stepped forward. At the doorway, he caught the first glimpse of Bernard, who sat behind a large mahogany desk, covered in stacks of papers, with his back turned to the door. All Stan could see was the white Stetson hat peeking out over the back of a tall, maroon, wing backed chair. Once inside the office, Stan stood a few feet from the desk. The guard shut the door without a word, and suddenly, Stan was all alone in a small room with the man he feared most in this world.

"Do you recall the parable of the Prodigal Son?" His father's voice was shaky and sounded much older than he recalled, but no less frightening.

"Yes," Stan said to the back of the chair.

"Do you recall the verses?"

Stan cleared his throat. "Luke 15: 11-32. *'Jesus continued. There was a man who had two sons. The younger one said to the father: father, give me...'*"

The chair slowly turned around, and when he was finally face to face again with his father, the sight of him stuck Stan to his core. The Stetson rested low on his father's head, so Stan couldn't tell if he'd lost his hair, but the skin on his face was spotted, wrinkled, and droopy. His lips appeared thinner than he recalled, but his prominent nose was the same, as were his beady, black eyes. Bernard Lee James wore a blue and white checkered dress shirt, mostly covered by a brown, tweed suit coat, and a bolo tie. He narrowed his gaze at Stan.

"After all these years away from here, you still know the Good Word?"

Stan nodded, trying to appear braver than he really was. "How could I forget? You had us all memorize the Bible, front to back. That's how I learned to read."

Bernard nodded once and pursed his lips. "Walter tells me you are the Prodigal Son, returned home to his father. That you seek absolution for your sins and that you are prepared to pay penance for dishonoring this family. Is that true?"

Stan faltered, only briefly. He'd known Walter's plan to get Stan back into The Prophet's good graces so he could be once again in his protection, but now that the moment was here, he wasn't sure he could go through with the charade. But it only took a split second for him to remember he was out of options and that this place was the only sanctuary available to him. He knew he had to make the sacrifice.

"It's true," Stan said finally.

"You hesitated."

"Only because I'm not sure if you'll accept my apology. I'm not sure I'm worthy of your forgiveness."

The Prophet steepled his fingers and touched them to his lips as he appeared to ponder Stan's words. "And this unexpected visit and show of attrition would have nothing to do with your legal troubles in Kentucky?"

Stan was so unprepared for this, he took half a step back

without even realizing it. But he recovered quickly. "Walter told you."

"Walter told me nothing, other than you are sorry and wish to return to the fold. But I'm not a regular man. God spoke to me in a dream. He told me everything and that you would return to me on bended knee, begging for forgiveness."

Stan knew what had really happened was that some of his father's far-reaching connections had kept him informed of Stan's activities over the years, and that someone had filled him in on every detail of his current predicament. But calling him out would not only be pointless, but dangerous, so he went along with the pretense.

"Of course. You are The Prophet, after all."

Bernard leaned forward with one elbow on his desk. "And you want to return to the brotherhood? You want to be part of the flock again? An obedient sheep who will do as he's told, when he's told?"

Stan nodded. "Yes. If you'll have me."

His father placed his other elbow on the desk and clasped his hands together. "You realize all that entails? What will be asked of you?"

Stan assented with a nod.

"You'd be assigned a second wife, of my choosing, as soon as can possibly be arranged. That mistress of yours would have to become a legal wife. She'd have to submit and toe the line. Will she be obedient?"

"She knows what will be asked of her. She will obey."

"Mm-hm. Right." His father picked up a pen and clicked the end of it repeatedly as he pondered Stan's fate. "And if I decide to forgive you, to absolve you of your past transgressions, there'd be no more sneaking your brethren's wives off into the night? No more stealing brides? Have you rid yourself of those silly ideas you once possessed?"

"I have seen the light," Stan said. "I know the wrongs I

committed against you. Against the church. Against God. And I repent."

Bernard sat motionless in his chair for a long, drawn-out moment. "If I absolve you, if I let you return, you must immerse yourself in the Good Word again. You must live the principle and seek redemption in the celestial kingdom. You will obey me, and you will obey God's direction through me. If I say you shall have ten young brides, so it shall pass. Anything I ask of you, so it shall pass. If you can agree to those terms, I believe I can be persuaded to receive you again into this family. You would have my protection and you would be safe from the vindictive, unscrupulous arm of the law. You'd be safe. Do you accept?"

Stan didn't have to think about it. Did he want to want to be back under his father's thumb? No. Did he want any woman in his life or bed other than Bev? No. But as he'd explained to her, any second, third, or subsequent marriages would merely be formalities, and the rest, they'd get through together. It was their only hope for freedom. It was *his* only hope for survival. So, without blinking, without another moment's hesitation, he replied with a nod of his head.

"Good," The Prophet said. "Accepted. Now, all that remains is for you to say the words."

With a sigh, Stan took one step closer to the desk. He knew what was expected of him. He also knew that this formal meeting and verbal agreement were all he'd ever get from his father. Bernard Lee James was not a man who smiled, shook hands, or God forbid, hugged anyone. He didn't have to do any of those things. He was The Prophet. The words he spoke came from God above directly, so breaking a vow made with him was tantamount to a self-imposed sentence of eternal damnation.

Stan drew in a breath, let it out, and said the words he knew his father wanted to hear.

"'*Father, I have sinned against Heaven and against you. I am no longer worthy to be called your son.*'"

The Prophet stood and extended his arms in a welcoming gesture. "*Let us have a feast and celebrate. For this son of mine was dead and is alive again; he was lost and is found.*"

And with the recitation of those verses, Stan knew he had accomplished his goal. What it would cost him, only time would tell. But with those words he'd bought himself a reprieve and, quite possibly a longer life.

34

Caroline stood in the middle of the living room, talking to Officer McKee, when Mena burst through the front door and rushed over to her. The detective gripped her shoulders, looked at her intently for a moment, then exhaled and pulled her into a tight embrace. She squeezed Caroline so tightly, she could barely breathe, but it felt good.

"I'm so glad you're okay," Mena said. "I was freaking out. And Mom!" She pulled back from Caroline and took two steps over to where Helena sat on the recliner with a quilt wrapped around her shoulders. She bent over and enveloped her mother in her arms. Caroline could hear her sniffling the whole time. When she stood upright again, she grabbed her mother's hand and reached out for Caroline's. "You guys have no idea how worried I was when I heard about the 911 call." She turned to Officer McKee. "What the hell happened here, officer?"

McKee had closely cropped, dark hair and a double chin. His belly protruded over his belt, and it looked as if the buttons on his uniform top might pop off any second. He grabbed the walkie on his shoulder, spoke rapidly into it, then faced Mena. "Got a call from dispatch about a possible intruder. Officer Jenkins and I arrived about four minutes after the call came in. We were just down the road, wrapping up a domestic. Anyway, when we arrived, we saw the broken glass and proceeded to enter the house with our service weapons drawn. The front door was open, and when we entered, we encountered Miss Hanson and your mom...I mean, Ms. Kastaros, sitting in the living room. We first ascertained that they were both physically unharmed, then Jenkins and I swept the house and quickly determined it was all clear."

"Thank God," Mena said. She shifted her focus back to Caroline. "Did you ever see anyone inside the house?"

"No," Caroline answered. "Someone just threw that brick through the window. That's all."

"Also," Officer McKee said, "when we arrived, young Miss Hanson here was holding one of your guns. We've secured it and checked to make sure no rounds were fired. Clip's full and there's still one in the chamber."

Mena's eyes widened as she looked back at Caroline, whose heart sank when she realized for the first time she might get in trouble for brandishing a detective's service weapon. But whatever emotion Caroline first saw flash across Mena's face quickly faded into a softer one.

"I'm just glad you didn't have to use it," she said with a smile. "But most of all, I'm glad you two weren't hurt. I thought for sure..."

Caroline watched as Mena bit her tongue to keep from speaking aloud the fear they'd all likely shared – that the intruder had come to take Caroline away again. "I'm fine," she said. "Really. I'm fine." She turned to Helena. "Your mom's a real trooper. She wasn't afraid at all. She wanted to face off with them herself."

"Pssh." Helena waved off Caroline's words with a flick of her wrist. "Me? I'm not the one who faced the threat head-on, ready to shoot anyone she encountered. And I'm three times her age and then some." She pointed at Caroline. "She reminds me of you."

"There is one other thing," Caroline said, hardly believing she'd almost forgotten the most important part of the story. "There's a note."

"A note? What note?" Mena looked at Caroline, then Helena, then Officer McKee.

The officer turned and called for Jenkins, who walked over with a large Ziploc baggie in his hand. Inside was the note that had so unnerved Caroline. Mena would find out about it eventually. She might as well know about it now.

Jenkins handed the baggie to Mena, who examined it. But the note was folded over inside the bag, so all that showed was a white piece of paper. Caroline could see the confusion on Mena's face.

"What does it say?" she asked.

"It says, '*C, You belong to me. I'm coming back for you soon. S.*'"

"But that doesn't make sense," Mena said.

"It's obviously from him," Caroline replied. "Who else would do this? Besides, it has my first initial and his on it. It has to be him."

"It can't be," Mena said. "I haven't had a chance to tell anyone this yet, but…hang on…" Mena turned and called for her partner, Derrick Felton, to join their group in the living room.

When he stood next to Mena, he greeted Caroline and Helena each with a firm handshake, then turned to Mena. "Sup, partner? I hear your mom and Miss Caroline had quite a scare tonight."

"Yeah. And there's a note, too. It says Pollard's coming back for her, but I know it's not from him."

"Oh, yeah? And how do you know that?" Felton crossed his arms over his chest.

"I was going to tell you and the rest of the task force during the meeting earlier, but then this happened. I know where we can find Stan. He'd not here, so there's no way he could have thrown this brick."

"He's not here?" Caroline was confused. She had just assumed he was still lurking around town, waiting for the perfect opportunity to take her back. "But I don't understand."

Mena looked at her apologetically. "I haven't really had much time to explain. But you might as well hear it all now. And you need to hear this, too, Felton. Matter of fact…" Mena pulled her cell from her back pocket, dialed a number, and waited while it rang.

After the second ring, a gruff voice came over the speaker phone. "Riggs."

"Agent Riggs," Mena said. "This is Detective Kastaros. Detective Felton is with me. I know where we can find Pollard."

"I'm here with Rousseau and your lieutenant in the conference room still. We were waiting to hear from you about whatever the hell happened at your house. Is everyone okay?"

"Yeah, yeah. Hi, Lieu. Just someone pulling a prank, I think. Everyone is fine. But while I have everyone's attention, I need to fill you in on what I've learned."

"What have you got for us, Kastaros?" another man shouted louder than he needed to. Caroline figured that must have been Mena's boss.

"I did some research online and, long story short, I am confident I've found him."

"How confident? How do you know?" This voice was feminine, softer.

"I'll explain all the details later, but I've tracked him to a place called Poplar Creek just outside Provo, Utah. That's where his family lives. He's hiding out with them at a polygamist compound called The Ranch."

"I'll be damned," her boss said. "A polygamist compound? How on earth did you figure that out?"

Mena winked at Caroline. "Caroline gave me a lot of good

information, and I just investigated based on what she told me. I couldn't have figured it out without her."

Caroline's spirits soared and a sense of pride swelled inside her.

"Well, then, let's go get the sonofabitch," the lieutenant said.

"That's what I was hoping you'd say," Mena said with a nod. "But, of course, we need the FBI's resources and cooperation from local law enforcement in Provo first."

"You just let me handle that," the lieutenant said. "Riggs, Rousseau, you two do what you need to do to get us out to Utah, pronto. As for the locals, let me handle them. Great work, Kastaros. And Miss Hanson? Thank you for helping. You're one brave young girl."

Caroline didn't know what to say. She was overcome with emotion as she'd never felt as much love and appreciation in her life. She choked back tears and replied with a simple, "Thank you."

"I can have a plane ready at the local airport in under an hour." The other male voice apparently belonged to one of the FBI agents. "And we'll have a federal warrant in hand when we arrive."

Mena said, "Thanks, Riggs. We'll meet you there. We're leaving now."

"Great work, team. Let's go get this SOB and bring him back here. I want to be there when they plunge that needle into his arm."

Mena pushed a button on the phone and the call ended. She turned and looked at Helena. "Mom, I hate to ask, but…"

"Of course she can stay with me while you fly off to Utah to bring that monster home." When Mena fixed her with a quizzical look, Helena said, "I may be old as dirt, but I heard every word. Now, go. Get this thing done and over with, then come home to me safe and sound. Caroline and I will be just fine, won't we, child?"

"Yes, ma'am," Caroline replied.

A few minutes later, after the uniformed officers had left and the mess had been cleaned up, Mena and her partner were saying goodbye before leaving for the airport. Caroline was worried about Mena, but she knew the detective was tough and could take care of herself. She was anxious for the whole ordeal to be over.

"Please be careful," she said as Mena hugged her goodbye.

"Always," Mena answered. "Now that you know where I keep my guns, if anything else happens while I'm away, shoot first and ask questions later, you hear?"

Caroline snickered but nodded her head.

"I'm serious. I'll make sure there's at least one patrol officer parked outside now, but be vigilant and lock all the doors after we leave. I'll call you as soon as it's over. In the meantime, you might want to check in with your parents. Have you heard from them?"

"No," Caroline said. "Not since this morning. They taped the interview yesterday. It's supposed to air in two days. They were going to spend the day sightseeing in Manhattan. I'll call them before bed."

"All right. Be safe." Mena turned and looked at her partner. "You ready?"

"Let's do this thing," he said.

Mena stepped out onto the porch but turned to face Caroline one last time. "Hey," she said. "I'm really glad you're okay. I can't tell you how worried I was when I heard about the call. You're like…"

Caroline threw her arms around Mena and squeezed her tightly. Tears poured down her cheeks because she knew exactly what Mena was having trouble saying. "I know," she said. "I feel the same way."

35

At The Ranch, Mena watched from the side of the porch as Riggs and Rousseau stood on either side of the door, their backs flat against the front of the house. She watched as they looked at one another and nodded. FBI agents surrounded the main house, ready to storm the compound on Riggs's cue. Felton was to her left, his weapon drawn and aimed at the front door.

Riggs did a quarter-turn and pounded on the door. "FBI! Open up!"

A second later, the house was lit up on the inside and out. Mena waited by the porch, trying to steady her breathing as she watched the front door. When it opened, a woman in a white nightgown with a long, silver braid trailing down over her right shoulder stood there looking dumbfounded.

"What's this all about? It's one o'clock in the morning! Where's your warrant?"

Riggs reached into his pocket, produced a folded piece of blue paper, and held it up in front of her. "Right here, ma'am. We're here for Stanley Dale Pollard. Now open the door and let us through or we are more than willing to take more of you with us tonight."

"That's my son," the woman said. "What's he done wrong? Why does the FBI want him?"

"We'll discuss that with your son. Where is he?"

She planted her hands on her hips and huffed. "I don't know."

"Fine," Rousseau said. "Play it that way, if you want. But step aside, or we'll arrest you for obstruction of justice."

The old woman stared the agents down for a moment but sighed and stepped to the right. "He's upstairs. Second bedroom on the left."

As the agents filed into the house, Mena and Felton quick-stepped up the porch with their guns drawn and followed them inside. She could hear women shouting and children crying as she looked around the interior of the home, half hoping it would be her who spotted Pollard first. She was disappointed that the law wouldn't allow her to be the one to arrest him, but as a concession, Riggs had agreed to let Mena be the first one to talk to Pollard after he was arrested. She could hardly wait to look him in the eye and tell him it was all over. It'd take every ounce of strength she had inside not to spit in his face, but it was going to be worth it.

A shot rang out, bringing Mena back to the moment. She and Felton exchanged a split-second glance and said "shit" in unison as they bounded up the stairs. Mena beat him by a hair. Her heart beating rapidly as she reached the top of the stairs and heard a struggle. Mena rounded the corner, stepped inside the room, and raised her weapon, ready to fire.

Inside, she found a man she assumed was Pollard from the thinning red hair on the back of his head, laying face down on the hardwood floor, wearing nothing but a pair of white under-wear. Riggs had his knee in his back and was cuffing him tightly while reading him his rights. Next to Pollard on the floor was a heavy-set woman, likely Beverly, also laying on her stomach.

Agent Rousseau's knee was in her back. But a Smith & Wesson revolver was on the ground, inches away from her hand, which a third agent had stepped on. Rousseau bent down, picked up the weapon, and held it up for all to see.

"Well, Ms. Beverly Louise Guthrie, looks like you're under arrest for the attempted murder of a federal agent. And here we thought we might go easy on you," Rousseau said with a wicked grin.

"What happened?" Mena asked as she holstered her firearm.

"Bonnie Parker here tried to protect her Clyde by trying to kill us," Riggs said.

Mena pointed to the half-naked man on the ground. "Is that…"

Riggs nodded. "That's your guy."

"Stand him up," Mena commanded, more harshly than she intended. But she didn't apologize.

"You got it," Riggs said. He huffed as he leaned over, grabbed Pollard by the cuffed wrists, and hauled him to his feet.

His head hung low. Mena took a step forward. Her pulse was racing. "Look at me," she said. Pollard just shook his head. "I said, look at me."

Slowly, Pollard raised his head until he finally met her gaze. "You must be Detective Kastaros. We meet at last."

Mena's hands clenched into fists, but she kept them down at her sides, just to be safe. "You know who I am? Good. Then you know I've been looking for you for over ten years. Even before Caroline Hanson. And you know why."

Pollard slowly nodded. "I do. And we have lots to catch up on, you and me. But first, I'd like my clothes."

An hour later, Mena walked down the aisle of the airplane and took the seat opposite Pollard, who sat with his hands cuffed in his lap, staring out the window.

"All right, Pollard," Mena said. "You promised me answers, let's have them. What did you mean when you said I don't know the whole story?"

"Ask me what you really want to know first," he said, still staring off into the dark night sky.

Mena raised an eyebrow. "What exactly might that be?"

Pollard turned his head slowly and fixed his gaze on her. "You want to know why I killed your daughter. Am I right?"

Every one of Mena's muscles tensed. She gripped the armrests on either side of her to keep herself from lunging at him. "Fine," she said. "Have it your way. Let's talk about my daughter. Her name was Sadie Kastaros. But I don't ever want to hear her name cross your lips. Are we understood?"

"Loud and clear," Pollard replied. "Now ask me."

Mena drew in a deep breath and counted to five, something one of her therapists had taught her to avoid lashing out verbally. "All right, why did you kill Sadie?" She hated to let him dictate the conversation, but if he was willing to admit to murdering her daughter after already having been mirandized at The Ranch, she was willing to play his little game…for the time being.

He leaned in across the aisle and whispered, "I'll never tell. You'll never have the answers you want. Live with that."

The world around Mena spun out of control and she had to fight against every instinct coursing through her, telling her to lunge across his seat and choke the life out of him. But she kept her composure when an idea came to mind. She knew exactly how she could get him to tell her everything she needed to know. But pulling it off would be the key.

She stood from her seat, stared coldly down Pollard, then brushed past him and walked back to where Riggs sat a few rows back. He was leanings his head back against the headrest and his eyes were closed. It was nearly four in the morning and, clearly, with the excitement of the evening past, Riggs was taking the plane ride home to catch up on some much-needed rest.

"Riggs," she said, gently nudging him with her finger.

The agent startled and opened his eyes, and for a second, he seemed to be unaware of his surroundings and who was standing inches away from him. But recognition then hit him, and he smiled at Mena and sat up straight in his seat. "Detective Kastaros. Sorry about that. Just counting sheep. Been a long couple of days."

"It has," Mena agreed. "Hey, I need a favor. And before you say no, hear me out. That's all I ask."

"I'm not sure I like the sound of that, but all right. I'm all ears."

"I want to be the one to drive Pollard to the station when we touch down."

"No. Absolutely not."

"You said you'd hear me out," Mena reminded him.

Riggs rolled his eyes and his head bobbed around on his thick neck. "All right. All right. Go ahead. But this better be good."

"I know what you're thinking, but I swear I'm not going to do anything stupid. It's not worth it. I wouldn't risk my badge, and I'm not going to prison for that shit stain. But, Riggs, this man killed my daughter."

"Which is exactly why I can't let you…"

Mena raised an eyebrow and titled her head toward him. He waved his hand for her to proceed.

"I just want to hear him say it. Maybe he's so arrogant and so eager to brag to me about what he did that he'll confess. I tried just now, but there's so many people around. I think if I can get him alone on the car ride to the station, I can get him to confess to everything, including my daughter's murder."

"Go on."

"I've been looking for him for ten years, Riggs. And now I finally have him. If this man doesn't confess, not only to his activities with the girls, but also to killing my little girl, he could possibly go free. And I can't let that happen. Please. Just let me try. You have my word. No harm will come to him."

Riggs seemed to contemplate this briefly, then heaved a big sigh and said, "Oh, all right. I guess I do owe you one after the way I treated you when I first got here. But do you think your lieutenant would be okay with that? I don't want you getting in trouble over this."

"Just let me handle Lieu."

"Fine." Mena oddly found herself wanting to hug the rotund little weasel but held back.

"But you have to swear on your badge he'll make it to the station…alive and unharmed. Do I have your word?"

Mena nodded. "I swear. I just want to talk to him. Thank you."

As she turned and headed back to her seat, a pit grew in Mena's stomach as she realized she'd just made a promise she wasn't sure she could keep.

36

Mena's cruiser slowed to a stop, far enough onto the shoulder that she and Pollard could safely exit the vehicle without being run over by cars and tractor trailers barreling down I-75. The second she put it in park, Pollard began stammering.

"N-n-no. No. No. No! Why here? Why the fuck did you bring me here?"

Mena's eyes shifted up to the rearview mirror and she looked Stan right in his rapidly blinking eyes. "You know why."

She opened the driver's side door, slammed it shut, and walked over to the back-passenger's side and opened the door. Pollard leaned away from Mena when she reached in and tried to grab his arm, but she snatched his arm up anyway and jerked him toward the open car door.

"I don't have to go with you. Help! Somebody! Help!" He looked back at Mena as she stood there with her hands on her hips, smiling at the futility of his screams.

"No one is going to hear you, Pollard. Do you really think anyone is going to stop here anyway? Good Lord. I'm not going to hurt you, but we need to talk. Humor me and get your ass out of the vehicle. I think you owe me that much. Don't you?"

Pollard seemed to ponder his options, which were severely limited at this point. After a few seconds, he shook his head. "Aw, hell. Fine. But if you try to hurt me in any way, I'll…I'll…" He must have realized there really was nothing he could do and that he was at Mena's mercy because he hung his head and sighed heavily. Then, Pollard looked up at Mena and said, "You swear you just want to talk?"

"I swear. Now, get the hell out of the car and come with me."

Reluctantly, Pollard shimmied out of the back of the cruiser. Mena steadied him by holding on to his elbow. When he was completely out of the vehicle, she shut his door and began marching him down the dirt and gravel path toward Clays Ferry Bridge.

"Watch your step," Mena said as they began side stepping down a steep incline covered in dirt and rocks and little tufts of dead grass. The sun had already peeked out over the horizon and was shining brightly on their path, so Mena could easily see where they were stepping as she guided Pollard by the handcuffs down the hill.

Mena had thought her anger toward this man would far outweigh any other emotions that might threaten to wash over her being in this place for the first time ever, but she was surprised by the deep feeling of grief that sank in her belly like a heavy stone. Her hands trembled as she fought back the tears forming in her eyes. Mena had never been to this place for this very reason. She wasn't sure she could handle her emotions. But she tried to focus on the anger and hatred she felt for Stanley Dale Pollard instead, and it helped. Somewhat.

She urged him forward, ducking his head and hers to avoid tree branches along the way until the trees opened and they had to slide-step down a dirt slope.

"Careful," Mena warned Pollard.

"Why are you doing this?" he asked in a whinier voice than any sixty-year-old man should ever use.

"Almost there," she said. "Just up ahead. You know the place."

Once they reached the bottom of the dirt-covered hill, Mena stopped, and when Pollard took another step forward, she yanked him back by his handcuffs. She jerked him around by his shirt sleeve until he was facing her and shoved him backward a bit so he was far enough not to be in her face, but still close enough for her to reach him.

"You know this place. Don't pretend you don't," she spat.

Pollard was more out of breath than Mena, and he heaved as he hung his head low. "Yeah. I know. But it's fucked up that you'd bring me here. Say what you gotta say."

"I don't want to say anything. I want to listen," Mena replied.

"Listen? What do you want me to say? I done told you—"

"Lies. You told me lies. Sadie's death wasn't some 'accident.' I want you to tell me right here and right now. What. Happened. To. My. Little. Girl?"

Pollard rolled his head back and let out a deep breath. "It was an accident. I didn't mean to—"

"Bullshit. You don't accidentally strangle a little girl, Pollard. Tell me what happened. And I want the truth. You dumped my baby right here," she pointed at the ground, "like she was garbage. Did you kill her here? Or was this just the best place you could think of to dispose of her...her..."

She couldn't bring herself to say "body." The roar of the river water rushing furiously by nearly drowned out every sound, but Mena could hear birds chirping as they flitted around above their heads, oblivious to the scene playing out below them. She waited, her hands on her hips, for Pollard to start talking. He knew what she wanted, no *needed*, to hear. So she used her tried and true technique of waiting patiently for him to grow uncomfortable in the silence and respond.

After an interminable pause, he growled and said, "Naw. Hell naw. I am not going to tell you. What's the point anyway? I'm going to prison. I can't bring her back. You're never going to believe anything I tell you anyway, so, no. Take me to jail. I ain't sayin shit."

She could feel every muscle in her body tensing as heat flushed through her from her head to her feet. Images of her little girl laying on the riverbank with her arms and legs splayed out in the snow flashed through her mind. Her nostrils flared, and she clenched her teeth. She wasn't leaving here without an answer, and she'd known for years this moment was coming. Now that they were there, he refused to give her the answers she needed to move on. There was no way in hell she was letting him leave without telling the truth. She deserved to know what had happened to Sadie. And he was the only one who could give her the answers she sought.

Mena reached behind her back, pulled out her gun, and aimed it right at his center mass. "Tell me what you did to my baby."

Pollard stumbled backward, and his eyes bugged out like demented some cartoon character. "Whoa. Whoa. Whoa. You can't do that. You can't shoot me. You're a cop. And I'm hand-cuffed, for Christ's sake!"

"Don't care. Talk." Mena cocked her gun.

"Jesus! Okay. Okay. Fine. I'll tell you."

"I'm listening." She shifted her weight from one foot to the other and tilted her head to the side. "Talk."

Pollard dropped his chin to his chest and shook his head. After a few drawn-out seconds, he lifted his head again and looked right at Mena. "I really didn't mean to hurt her. But after a few days, she just wouldn't listen. She wasn't like the other girls. She fought me at every turn. I've never seen anything like it."

Pride welled up in Mena's chest at the thought of her little girl standing up to this monster. Of course she had fought him. It's exactly the way Mena had taught her to handle herself if someone ever tried to hurt her. She held back the tears that threatened to spill, lest Pollard see them and think he'd gotten to her.

"What happened to her?" Mena demanded, taking one step forward.

"All right. Jesus." He glanced up at the sun, which was now well above the horizon, and squinted. "Aw, hell. One day, about a week after she came home with us, she just demanded we take her home...to you. I tried to reason with her. Tried to—"

"Feed her lies about me. Go on."

"They weren't lies. I really thought...oh, fuck. Never mind. Anyway, she got belligerent and was screaming in my face that she wanted to go home. I tried to check my anger, but she started yelling and screaming, and I was afraid one of the neighbors would hear. Then she stomped on my foot and I just...I just...I didn't think. I grabbed her by the throat and started squeezing. I didn't think I squeezed that hard, but I guess I did because when I let go, she fell to the ground." Mena's stomach roiled, and her heart raced as Pollard breathed heavily before finishing. "We tried to help her. God knows we tried. But it was too late."

"So you dumped her body here?" Mena pointed the gun at the ground. "You left her laying here in the snow all by herself beside the river like some animal?"

"I'm sorry, okay? I've regretted it every day since it happened. I'd never taken a life before, and I haven't since. I never will again."

"And you think somehow that makes it all okay?" Mena shouted through gritted teeth.

The temptation to pull the trigger and watch the life drain from Pollard's eyes was growing exponentially by the second. Mena knew if she didn't check her anger and get him back to the station soon, she might give into temptation and then where would she be? She still wouldn't have Sadie, but she'd also be without her career, and quite possibly, her freedom. But just walking him back to the car as if nothing had happened didn't seem quite right, either.

"I mean it. I'm really sorry about your little girl."

Mena pointed the gun back at Stan's chest. "It's not just my Sadie. Maybe she's the only one you killed. Not that I believe that. But you ruined the lives of God knows how many other young girls and their families. What gave you the right to take those girls from their parents? Why? Was it out of some twisted sense of moral superiority? You think somehow you could give them better lives?"

Pollard looked at Mena with narrowed eyes. "How did you know that?"

"It's the only thing that makes sense. But you got it wrong, Pollard. So far, we've not been able to find any evidence that any of these girls' parents are unfit in any way. You were making judgment calls that weren't even based on the truth. It was all for nothing."

"That's not true." Pollard shook his head vehemently. "Not true at all. Okay, so maybe I got it wrong with Sadie, but—"

"I told you. Do not speak her name. You have no right."

He flinched, likely afraid he'd pushed her one step too far. "Sorry. Sorry. But maybe I did get it wrong with your daughter. Clearly, I misunderstood what I saw that day. But you don't know the half of it. These parents are far from saints. They leave their children alone, they abandon them, they put their own selfish needs above their own flesh and blood, and they…"

Pollard stopped and gave Mena a look she couldn't read. She stared into his eyes, and only after holding his gaze for longer than was comfortable did she realize he was holding something back. "They what, Pollard? What are you not telling me?"

"Nothing. Just what I said. They're selfish, and they neglected their kids. That's all. I want to go to jail now."

Mena took two steps forward until she was standing closer to Pollard than she ever cared to be. She could smell the stinking sweat and fear rolling off him in waves. When she pressed the gun flush against his chest, he flinched.

"Tell me whatever it is you're holding back. Now."

"You're not going to shoot me," Pollard said as a sardonic smile spread across his face. "You love that badge too much to risk it. And the power that comes with it. No, I don't think I will tell you. Besides, you wouldn't believe me anyway. I told you how I killed your little girl, and you didn't shoot me. You're certainly not going to shoot me just because I won't tell you—"

Mena's free hand shot up and wrapped around his throat, and she shoved the gun up to his left temple. Pollard's eyes bulged, and his face turned beet red. He sputtered, and unpleasant choking sounds escaped through his clenched teeth.

"Tell me what I want to know. Now. Or I will shoot you right here, and I'll toss your body into the muddy river. No one will ever find you, so help me God. And if you don't think I can come up with a believable explanation as to how you got the best of me and escaped after you convinced me to let you stop for a piss break, then you're stupider than I ever gave you credit for. Now…tell me what you're hiding."

"Okay," he choked out. "Just…stop. Let go. Please."

She didn't let go right away. It took her a minute to contemplate her options and the odds that she could actually make anyone believe the escape story. God, it would feel great to watch Pollard die a slow and painful death. It was the moment she'd dreamed of and waited for longer than she could even remember. It was the promise she'd made herself and Sadie – that she'd find the monster who had taken her away and that she'd make him suffer the way her baby had. Mena held back the cries that threatened to escape as good and evil battled within her. She might be justified in killing Pollard in most people's eyes. But that didn't mean it was something she could bear for the rest of her life. And when it all came down to it, she imagined little

Sadie telling her to let him go because she wouldn't want her Mama to be responsible for taking another life like this.

Mena lowered her weapon and loosened her grip on Stan's throat. "Fine, then. Tell me everything."

Pollard spat at the dirt and coughed for several seconds until his breathing normalized and his face returned to its normal pale, freckly shade. "God, you're one crazy bitch. You know that?"

"Yes. Now, talk."

He inhaled and exhaled deeply several times then squared his shoulders and looked right at Mena. "They weren't all my idea. The girls. All of them except one were my idea."

"What on earth does that mean? No more riddles."

"It means, I was paid to take one of them. The one that got away."

"Caroline? Someone paid you to take Caroline?" Pollard nodded. "But who would pay you to take a young girl from her parents? Is someone behind all of this? If so, Pollard, you had better give me a name. Right now."

Pollard leaned forward, and Mena recoiled on instinct until she realized he was trying to whisper something in her ear. It was ridiculous, considering there was no one around for miles to hear whatever name he was about to give her, but she humored him and kept her finger on the trigger, just in case.

When he whispered the name she'd asked for, Mena touched her fingertips to her parted lips as a sudden chill hit her to the core. Then, in an instant, her heart sank as she realized what this meant, and that Caroline would never be the same again.

37

Caroline followed the uniformed officer into the police station, down the hallway, and through a set of double wooden doors to the detective's section of the building. After passing the receptionist desk where a young girl not much older than herself set down her phone as they walked by, Caroline saw to her right the interview room where she'd spent hours waiting and talking to Mena only a week ago. The detective stood at the end of the hallway in front of another interview room, apparently waiting for Caroline to arrive.

His duty done, the officer who had led her in nodded at Caroline, turned on the thick heel of his black boot, and headed back the way they'd come, leaving her standing before Mena, who looked somewhat uncomfortable, or nervous, or some other emotion Caroline couldn't quite read.

"Is everything okay?" she asked Mena as a million thoughts flitted through her mind as to what could have gone wrong now.

"Caroline," Mena began, "we need to talk. Let's sit in here where we can have some privacy." She gestured to the open door that led to the interview room Caroline had never been in before.

Butterflies did battle in Caroline's stomach, and her pulse beat at her temples. "Sure. Okay."

Mena was the first to enter the room, and she offered the empty seat closest to the door to Caroline, who reluctantly sat and scooted closer to the table. She expected Mena to sit in the chair across from her. Instead, the detective slid the chair around from the other side of the table and drug it over in front of Caroline. Mena sat in the chair, crossed her leg, reached out, and patted Caroline's knee.

"You doing okay today?" she asked.

Caroline nodded. "Mm. Hm. How about you? You never made it home last night. I got your text that you were working late, but I still worried about you. Then when you sent the officer to pick me up this morning, I *really* got worried."

Mena sat back in her chair and brushed a loose strand of hair back behind her ear then laid her hands in her lap. "Yes. We arrested Stanley Dale Pollard last night. That's why I couldn't come home."

Relief washed over Caroline, and she let out a deep breath she had been holding in ever since entering the room. "Seriously? Where? I mean, you said he'd fled Kentucky, so where did you find him?"

"Utah. He was hiding out at a polygamist cult's ranch. We arrested both him and Beverly without much resistance."

Caroline couldn't help but notice the knowing smile on Mena's face when she said the words "without much resistance." Something told her one or both of them had put up a futile fight. She wouldn't put it past either of them, especially not Beverly. That woman was a hellcat if ever Caroline had seen one. She recalled the way she'd clearly worn the pants when it came to Stan and the way she controlled nearly every situation, despite Stan's attempts to pretend he was in the driver's seat.

"That's good," Caroline said. "But then, if they were in Utah, who threw the brick through your window last night?" She gulped down a breath, and it felt like a large boulder had dropped into her stomach. The only other rational explanation was that someone else was after her. But the note had clearly been intended for her alone, and there was no mistaking the author at least wanted her to believe it was from Stan. So, who then?

"That's why I brought you here. There's more."

"More? What else could there be? Stan or Beverly clearly wrote the note attached to that brick."

"Sort of." Mena pursed her lips and drummed her fingers on her knees. She was clearly uncomfortable with telling Caroline whatever was about to leave her mouth. "The note was written by an associate of Stan's. Some Japanese guy he knew somehow. We haven't made all the connections yet, but it wasn't Stan who ordered the brick be thrown through my window. It was someone else."

Caroline wrapped her arms around her chest. Suddenly, the room felt even colder than it had moments ago. "Who?"

"Caroline," Mena leaned forward and grabbed her hands, holding them gently between the two of them, "someone hired the Japanese guy to deliver the message, just like they hired Stan and Beverly to kidnap you ten years ago."

It felt as if someone had mainlined ice water through Caroline's veins. She just knew her face had gone ashen because it felt like all color had drained from her cheeks. "Who?" she repeated.

"Caroline, I'm not sure how to tell you this. I feel horrible about it all. It's not going to be easy to hear, but…"

"Please," Caroline said, "just tell me. I can handle it. Who hired him?"

Mena sighed. "Your parents."

She felt disoriented. Like the earth around her was spinning on its axis. She shot Mena an incredulous glare. "My…parents? But…how? Why?"

Mena hung her head as if she were the one who should feel shame in this moment. "It appears they knew Stan through his mechanic business. Your father fixed the driveway for him and Beverly that summer, and Stan started doing repairs on your dad's equipment. When your mother hurt her back and couldn't work anymore, they fell on hard times, and...I don't really know the how or why of it all, but it seems they concocted a scheme to sell you to Stan and Beverly for a sum of money. Stan paid them twenty-thousand dollars for you, and the plan was to auction you through the Rainbow Room when you reached the age of eighteen. Caroline, I'm so sorry to be the one to tell you this."

Caroline shot up out of her chair, knocking it to the ground with a loud crash. "It's not true. My parents love me! There's no way they'd ever—"

Mena stood and reached out to Caroline, who jerked away and turned her back. Sobs threatened to rack her entire body, but she held them at bay because if she gave into the grief she was feeling and cried, it meant she accepted what Mena was telling her, which she didn't. Caroline knew Mena cared about her, and she knew she would never make up such lies just to hurt her, but she had to have it wrong. If Stan told Mena these horrible lies, he did it in a last-ditch effort to spare himself or to hurt Caroline in the worst way imaginable out of spite for leaving him.

"Caroline, listen. I know this is a lot to hear. And I know it hurts to know your parents would do such a thing, but I believe Pollard. He has no reason to lie."

"He does!" Caroline spun back around and spat the words back in Mena's face. "He's probably hoping for some kind of deal or something. Or he's just trying to mess with me! He's been screwing with my mind from the beginning. He told me my parents didn't want me the day he kidnapped me. And now he's lying about this just to...I don't know why, but he's lying. He has to be."

"No," Mena said. "I'm sorry, Caroline, but we've already picked up your parents early this morning. There here. In the other interview room. I spoke with them myself, and they admitted everything. It's all true. But I want you to know, you're not alone in this. I'm here for you. We'll get through this. Together."

Caroline wanted to continue fighting. She wanted to rail against Mena and prevent reality from sinking in, but no matter how badly she wanted it all to be a lie, something inside of her told her it was true. She'd only known this detective a few short days, but she knew in her heart of hearts that Mena would not lie to her, and if Mena said her parents had confessed, then denying the truth just to keep the pain at bay would be futile. Besides, it all made sense now. Memories came flooding back of all the times her mother and father had screamed and thrown things in front of her as a child, all because they were fighting over money problems. Then, there was the overly sensitive reaction her mother had had over all the donations and interview money since her return home. And now that she thought about it, her mother did seem insistent that Caroline not talk as much to Detective Kastaros and stay out of the investigation. Had she been afraid of being discovered?

Mena reached over, picked up the chair, and set it back on its legs. Caroline slumped down into it and cradled her head in her hands with her elbows on her knees. The grief she'd been trying not to give into finally overwhelmed her, and she began to cry. Loudly and consumingly. Mena ran her hand over Caroline's back and just sat there in silence until Caroline's sobs began to subside.

Then, like lightning on a clear day, another thought struck Caroline, and she sat bolt upright, looking right into Mena's kind, sympathetic eyes, which also brimmed with tears. "But he let me go."

Mena's brow furrowed, and she looked at Caroline quizzically. "Yes."

"I mean, if my parents sold me to him, why did he let me go ten years later? That makes no sense. Why would he do that?"

The detective's shoulders slumped, and it was clear there was still more painful revelations on the horizon. She sighed. "According to your mother, when all the money from the…the first time he paid them ran out, they tried to make do for a while, but eventually, they needed more money, so they contacted Pollard and…" Caroline could see that it was paining Mena to relay this last part to her. "…so they came up with a plan for Pollard to let you go, and your parents agreed to split any money they earned this time around with him fifty-fifty."

"Oh, God," Caroline said as she doubled over. "Oh, God. No." Caroline cried again. This time it felt like she cried for hours, though only a couple of minutes had likely passed. When she recovered enough to sit upright again and speak, she looked at Mena with pleading eyes. "What am I going to do? How am I ever supposed to go on knowing my parents sold me to that…beast?"

"Shhhhh," Mena said as she scooted forward and enveloped a sobbing Caroline in her arms. "I told you. We'll get through this together. I promise. I'm not going anywhere, and you'll never be alone again. One day at a time. We'll get through it."

Caroline pulled away from Mena and looked into her eyes. In those eyes, Caroline saw the kind of motherly love she thought she'd found again in Laura Hanson. A love that was unconditional and asked for nothing in return. A love that would guard and protect Caroline come what may. A love that was looking for a place to call home. Maybe Mena Kastaros would never be Caroline's real mother. Maybe she'd lost her one chance at maternal security. But maybe in Mena, she had found a safe haven. Someone she could look up to as she matured and went through life's challenges. Maybe they were exactly what one another needed at exactly the right time. Mena had lost her daughter, and Caroline had basically never had a mother. Maybe they really could create their own family. Just Caroline, Mena, and Helena.

But before she could move on and start her new life and her

new family, there was one thing left to do. It wouldn't be easy, but it was necessary for her to accept the truth and put the past behind her.

"I want to talk to Mark and Laura. One last time. I want to say goodbye."

38

M ena leaned against the wall of the second interview room as Caroline took the empty seat across the table from where her parents sat side by side. She had already conducted separate, formal interrogations of both Laura and Mark Hanson, but Caroline had asked to speak to both of her parents at the same time. There was no rule against this kind of situation. But even if there had been, Mena would still have made the exception for Caroline and let this happen. The girl had been through enough. Of course she had more than earned the right to confront the parents who had abandoned her. No. What they had done was worse than abandonment. Caroline deserved this opportunity to look them in the eye and say whatever it was she needed to say.

Laura Hanson leaned forward and reached her hands out toward Caroline, who recoiled a if it were a rattlesnake making its way across the table. "Caroline, honey."

"Don't." Caroline snapped.

Mark looked up at Mena. "You told her?"

"Sure did." Mena smiled despite herself. "Your daughter has a right to know what you did to her. If it were up to me, you two would have already been booked and carted off to jail. But she wanted one last chance to talk to you. This is for her, not for you."

He glared at Mena as if he could see straight through her, and for the first time, she saw how completely devoid of human decency the man was. But she would not let him get to her. She stared right back and tried not to bat an eyelash. Eventually, he rolled his eyes then turned his focus back toward Caroline.

"Why?" she asked.

Mark looked taken aback. But he quickly recovered. "Baby, listen. I want you to know…it was only because we couldn't afford to take care of you the way you deserved. The system is rigged against people like us. We work and we work and look where that got us. Broke and struggling to make ends meet. We knew we couldn't raise you and give you everything a child should have. We did it because we love you. We did it because—"

"You did it because you are heartless and you have no idea what love really is," Caroline said, cutting him off before he could ramble on anymore about how noble their reasons were for selling their daughter to a stranger.

Mena felt a sense of pride rise inside her watching Caroline sit there, her back straight and her eyes focused on her parents without betraying the depths of the pain they had put her through. She reminded Mena once again of Sadie – strong-willed and prepared to stand up for what was right. She wanted to wrap her arms around the girl, but her desire to let her have her moment eclipsed her need to comfort her.

"Caroline," Laura said, breaking the silence that had ensued, "you should know we struggled with this so much it nearly tore us apart, and we lost more sleep over this than you can even imagine. We loved you. I know you don't believe that now, but it's true. We did what we thought was best for you."

"No, you did what was best for you both. Plenty of parents struggle with money. But they find a way to make it work. You, on the other hand, were more concerned with your big pay day than you were with what might happen to me with Stan. Did you ever even stop to think about what might happen?" Caroline stood and looked down at her parents. "Do you know what my life was like for ten whole years? Do you know what he was about to do to me? What he did to countless girls before me?"

"Baby, he promised us he'd find you a good home with people who would love you and give you everything you ever dreamed of. He told us you'd never want for anything again. We thought..."

"Even if I could believe that you didn't know what he was doing, which I don't, you still knew you were selling me for a profit to some strange man who fixed your lawnmowers. If you really thought you couldn't take care of me, you could have found a family member. Or for God's sake, you could have even put me in foster care."

"We didn't want that kind of life for you," Mark said, keeping his eyes focused on his calloused, dirty hands, which were clasped before him on the table.

"Oh," Caroline scoffed, "so you thought living in a basement, chained to the bed every night so I couldn't escape, and being groomed for auction on my eighteenth birthday would be a better life than foster care? What is wrong with you two?"

Mena pushed herself away from the wall, walked over to Caroline, and rested her hand on her shoulder. "Caroline, I don't think they have anything else left to say that you need to hear. Let's go."

Caroline held up her hand. "I will. Just one last question, then we can go, and these two can go rot in a prison cell for the rest of their lives for all I care."

After patting Caroline lightly on the shoulder, Mena returned to the side of the room and leaned against the wall again. She wanted this to be over for Caroline, was ready for her to get away from these two pieces of shit and start her life free from everyone who had ever hurt her, but she wanted her to leave feeling like she'd said everything she needed to say. As Mena watched Caroline standing before her birth parents, a deep, all-encompassing love for the girl swept over her, and she vowed to herself in that moment that she would watch over Caroline for the rest of her life, whatever shape that required of Mena.

Caroline returned to her seat and smoothed the front of her sundress then looked up at her parents one last time. "What would you have done if the money from the kidnapping ten years ago had been enough, or if you had somehow started making more money? Would you have ever come to look for me? If you didn't need the money again, would you have gone the rest of your life never knowing, or caring, where I was or what had happened to me? Could you have lived the rest of your lives without ever knowing what happened to your daughter?"

Laura Hanson raised her eyebrows and her shoulders lifted as she sat back against her chair. Clearly, she had never even entertained this idea. She looked to Mark, who just shrugged.

"Sure," he said, "we'd have done anything to find you. If we didn't need the money."

"Baby, don't you see?" Laura quickly interjected. "It doesn't matter. We did tell Stan to let you go. We just couldn't bear it anymore. We didn't know what he was planning until we contacted him the second time." She sighed heavily. "The truth is, when we told him we wanted you back—"

"You mean, when you ran out of money and realized you could make more from donations and interviews again if I suddenly returned after ten years," Caroline said, staring blankly at her parents.

But Laura Hanson ignored this and continued with her story. "He said he could make more money off you by selling you on that website. We couldn't offer him as much as he wanted, but when we threatened to tip off the police about his activities, he agreed to let you go. We still had to pay him half of anything we earned from the interviews and such."

Caroline slammed her hand down on the table. "But you still did it all for money! It had nothing to do with missing me or doing the right thing!"

Like a shadow moving across the sun, a darkness took over Laura, and her eyes narrowed at Caroline. She leaned forward. "Now, listen here, young lady. You just be grateful we made that call in the first place. If it weren't for us, you'd be God knows where by now."

"And there you have it," Mena said, taking two steps away from the wall. She placed her palms face down on the table and leaned in close to the Hansons. "You two lowlives will never hurt Caroline again. Do you hear me? You're going to prison for the rest of your natural lives. Caroline will live a happy and full life without either of you in it. You don't deserve her. She deserves—"

"Who? You?" Mark Hanson chuckled. "What? Are you going to step in and be her mommy now?"

"I'm almost eighteen," Caroline said.

"Yeah?" Laura spoke up. "But until then, you got no home, no place to go…Mark's right. What are you going to do? Live with this detective and play house together? That'll be rich."

Mena tried to steady her breathing, which was a feat in and of itself. "I'll do whatever it takes to keep Caroline safe. So, yes, if she wants to stay with me, she can. I'll protect her from people who would take advantage of her. Neglect her. Abuse her. She'll be safe with me. Safer than she ever was with two rat pieces of shit like you."

Laura threw her head back and cackled. "Oh, that's just funny. I see what you're doing, Detective. You're going to use my little girl to replace the one you lost because you couldn't hold on to her."

Mena's pulse began to race, and she clenched her fists at her sides in an effort to keep from pummeling Laura Hanson's smug face.

"That's right," Mark spoke up. "Stan told us all about how he had to take your little girl, too because you let her roam the streets all by herself when she was too little to—"

"Enough!" Caroline shouted. "I hate you both. I hope you rot in your jail cells. Never, ever try to contact me. You're dead to me." Laura shook her head, crossed her arms, and laughed under her breath. "Go ahead. Laugh all you want. You two showed your true colors just now, and that's exactly what I was hoping you'd do. It's exactly what I needed to see so I could leave this room and ever think of you ever again. And, yeah. Mena will take care of me. I trust her. She's a good mother. Something you would know nothing about." Caroline looked at Mena. "Can we leave now?"

Mena wrapped her arm around Caroline's shoulder and squeezed her closer. "I thought you'd never ask." She turned to face the Hansons, who, rather than looking sad that they were losing their only child once and for all, both wore expressions of hatred and rage. "And you two…sit here and wait until an officer arrives to take you to booking. You're both under arrest for kidnapping and child abuse. And when I talk to the prosecutor, I'm sure we will come up with a whole slew of other charges, so get used to the view you sick, twisted fucks. You'll never see the light of day again if I have anything to do with it."

She guided Caroline out of the interview room and into the hallway and slammed the door behind her.

Just as she did this, Lieutenant Iverson appeared around the corner, curling his finger at Mena. "My office. We need to talk."

Mena nodded in his direction. "I'll be right there. Just let me get Caroline situated, and I'll meet you in your office."

Iverson didn't budge at first. He was likely contemplating forcing her to march into his office immediately, but he shot

Caroline a quick glance, muttered something under his breath, and said, "Fine. Five minutes."

Mena waved at him politely and guided Caroline to the other interview room. When they approached the open door, Mena turned Caroline around and gripped her gently by the shoulders. "I'm so proud of you. I know that was difficult, but I hope now you can find some peace."

"I think with you by my side, I can do anything," Caroline said with a smile. "Thank you, Mena. For everything."

"Don't mention it. Now, go have a seat in this room. I have a feeling I'm being called to the principal's office."

"Are you going to get in trouble for letting me see my parents?" Caroline's eyes were wet and full of worry.

"Oh, no. Not that, anyway. And everything is going to be okay. Just wait for me in here, and when I'm done, we'll leave here. I'll take the rest of the day off, and you and I will go do whatever it is you want to do. Ice cream? You got it. Shopping? Of course. You name it."

Caroline seemed to ponder her options briefly, then looked back at Mena and said, "Can we just go back to your house and hang out with your mom? Maybe watch a movie and make some popcorn?"

"How about we binge watch some Netflix? Weatherman is calling for rain today, anyway. It'll be a perfect day to stay inside and forget about everything."

This seemed to make Caroline happy. A huge grin played across her face, and she wrapped her arms around Mena. "Thank you, Mena. I love you."

"I love you, too, kiddo. I love you, too."

39

Mena rapped lightly on Lieutenant Iverson's office door.

"Come on in," his voice boomed from inside.

Mena turned the knob and pushed the door inward. She stepped into his office and stood in front of his desk. "You wanted to see me?"

He gestured for her to sit in the chair opposite his desk. She obliged. "I'll get right to the point, Kastaros. I don't believe in beating around the bush. Your conduct with Pollard on the ride home from the airport was unacceptable. Did you truly think it wouldn't get back to me that you tried to choke the life out of a handcuffed suspect in federal custody?"

Mena's mouth opened, then closed. There really wasn't anything she could say to dispute the truth.

"Now, I understand how difficult this case was for you. Hell, I probably shouldn't have let you twist my arm into allowing you to lead the investigation. But that's on me. I should have thought long and hard about how this might impact you."

"Lieu, I—"

He held up a hand. "Save it. I hate to bring up a sensitive subject, but last time we were in here talking, I hinted that I knew about your little bad habit." He pointed to her wrists, and Mena could see a bit of bandage poking out from under her sleeve. "That's another thing that's on me. I should have pulled you from the case the minute I realized how hard this was on you."

"It's something I've struggled with for a long time," Mena admitted. "Since I was a teenager. I'll get help, I promise."

"Yes, you will," Iverson said. "You'll see a department shrink starting tomorrow and you'll go as long as I deem necessary. But that's a whole nother matter. What happened this morning was inexcusable. What if you'd actually hurt him? Or God forbid, killed him? What would I do with you then?"

Mena shrugged. "I just wasn't thinking. He was talking about Sadie and how he killed her and I just…saw red."

"I'm not saying I don't understand it, or that I wouldn't even be tempted to do the same thing if I were in your shoes. But our ability to control our urges and impulses is what separates us from animals. I simply can't have one of my best detectives going half-cocked and trying to kill a handcuffed suspect, even if he deserves it."

"So, I'm fired," Mena guessed.

"No, I don't think we have to take it to that extreme," Iverson said. "But there have to be consequences. If I don't find a way to discipline you publicly, it'll appear I run a rogue unit and that I don't have control over my detectives. Surely you can understand that."

Mena let out a breath she'd been holding. Relief washed over her but was quickly replaced with a sense of dread as to what her punishment might be. "What do I have to do? I'm sorry about everything. But please don't demote me. I worked years to earn my badge and one mistake shouldn't—"

"I'm not demoting you. Not technically." Iverson sat back in his chair and leveled his gaze on Mena. "I'm starting a cold case unit, and I'm assigning you as the lead investigator."

Mena was confused. While she wasn't thrilled about the assignment, she wondered how being made lead investigator for a new unit qualified as a demotion. Her face must have registered her curiosity, as her lieutenant smiled and continued.

"Well, we don't necessarily have the office space for the unit, just yet. So you'll be relegated to the basement where we keep all the cold case files in boxes. I'll get you a desk, a phone, and a computer, but I think once you see your accommodations, you'll understand how it's a demotion."

"But I…what about Felton? We've been partners for five years. He doesn't deserve to be—"

"And he's not. Felton will stay up here and run homicide once he passes the sergeant's exam. If and when you can prove that you need and deserve another detective in the unit, if Felton agrees to have you back on his team, you can come back. But for now, it's just you. Flying solo, so to speak."

Mena had been in the basement where the old cases were kept. It was musty and dank and dark. She could just feel the humiliation start to rise inside her, and the thought of facing her co-workers after this was not a welcome one. But if it was what she had to do to keep her job, she wasn't about to fight her boss over it. At least she got to keep her gun and her shield. She'd spent the past several hours practicing her speech as she turned them over, but now…now there was hope.

"About the counseling," Iverson said, breaking her reverie. "That starts effective immediately. You'll report to this doctor first thing tomorrow morning. Here's her card." He reached across his desk and handed her a white business card. She grabbed it and flipped it over. On the front was the Lexington Police Department's shield, embossed in blue. In bold, black letters in the middle was the name: EVELYN SAUNDERS,

PSYCHD, MD. "You'll like her. She's been the in-house shrink for a couple months. Just getting started in her new office, but everyone seems to really respond to her. She's got a real...motherly way about her."

"Lieu, I really don't want—"

"Doesn't matter what you want. This is non-negotiable. It was frankly the only way I could convince the brass to let you keep your shield."

These words cut Mena to her core. To think that the higher-ups had wanted to strip her of everything she'd worked so hard to achieve made her stomach flip in on itself. But knowing that her lieutenant had gone to bat for her softened the blow a smidge.

"Ever heard of lingchi, Kastaros?" Iverson leaned forward on his desk.

Mena shook her head. "Ling what?"

"Lingchi. It's the ancient Chinese practice of causing the lingering death of an opponent by making little slices in their skin until they slowly and methodically die from their wounds. Felton actually told me about it. He learned it from—"

"An Army buddy," Mena finished.

They both chuckled softly.

"Loosely translated, it means 'death by a thousand tiny cuts.' I think that's what you're suffering from right now. But Dr. Saunders can help you with that."

"I'm suffering from the death by a thousand tiny cuts? How is that?"

"First Sadie was taken from you. Then Caroline Hanson disappeared, and you busted your ass for years to make detective so you could find and stop the man responsible for both. Then your mother got sick and went to a nursing home only to be neglected and mistreated there, so you had to bring her home. And all that happened right about the time that Caroline resurfaced, and you began hunting down Pollard. Hence, a slow, painful death. You're dying on the inside, my friend. And I don't want to see you sustain that final cut that ends it all for you. So, I'm stepping in and I'm throwing you a lifeline. It may not feel like it now, but I am." He smoothed his mustache. "This new assignment combined with therapy may be exactly what the doctor ordered, no pun intended. I'm hoping the cold case unit will allow you the time you need to work on your anger and your issues and get the help you need so I can have my star detective back. What do you say? Will you work with me here?"

Mena knew she had no choice in the matter. And hearing how much Lieutenant Iverson actually cared about her touched her deeply. She wasn't thrilled about this new assignment or the idea of being banished to the basement, but if that's what it took to climb out of the hole she'd dug for herself, so be it. And if she could get help for her issues in the process, no matter how much she loathed the idea of sitting with a shrink three or four hours per week, then she'd just have to bite the bullet.

"Okay," Mena said finally. "I'll do it. When do I start?"

"Right now," he said. Lieutenant Iverson stood, bent over behind his desk, and produced a large brown bankers' box. He set it on top of his desk with a thud. "This is your first assignment. Solve it. Impress me. Show me I made the right decision."

"I won't let you down, sir."

Mena grabbed the box, hoisted it up under her right arm, and walked out of her boss's office. As she walked down the hallway, her first cold case assignment on her hip, she decided to look at the glass as half full rather than half empty. Sure, she'd been demoted. Sure, she'd disappointed the higher-ups and her lieu-tenant. Sure, she had demons that needed to be exercised, driven into pigs, and forced off the side of a cliff. But at least she still had her job. She still had her life. And most importantly of all, she had Caroline. She wasn't going to stop until she got it all back and one day, she'd look back on this day and see it as the day her life started over again.

~THE END~

ACKNOWLEDGMENTS

For this book, I'd like to acknowledge all the readers, fans, and followers who have supported me over the years. Without you all, I wouldn't have a reason to write. Aside from the usual suspects (mom, dad, sister, daughters, and extended family), there are too many people to name who have been there from the beginning, encouraging me to write when I didn't feel like it, and urging me to never give up. So, if you've ever read any of my work in beta form, or if you have supported me with encouraging words on social media or any other platform, I want to acknowledge you, for, without you, this book would not exist. Thank you from the bottom of my heart. As long as you'll keep reading, I'll keep writing.

MEET THE AUTHOR

CHRISTINA KAYE

From The Horse Capitol of the World, Kentucky, Christina Kaye was born to a family of creative right-brainers. She enjoyed creative writing, even in school, and always received A's on her essays in high school.

During a twenty-two-year career as a paralegal, Christina Kaye sharpened her writing skills, and when she was asked to write an article for an online magazine for lawyers, she jumped at the chance. After rave reviews and many comments stating she should write a book, she decided to do just that, and she hasn't stopped since.

Her debut novel, LIKE FATHER, LIKE DAUGHTER (Book 1 of the Flesh & Blood Trilogy) was named Suspense Finalist by the 2017 Indie Excellence Awards, and she has penned six other novels, all of which fall in the suspense/thriller genre.

Christina also works as a book editor, author coach, and CEO/Founder of Write Your Best Book, which caters to authors of all skill-levels and helps them write, publish, and sell their best books.

She still lives in Kentucky with two rowdy pups and a very fat cat.

For more information about Christina Kaye, click Here
You can follow her on social media here:
https://www.facebook.com/xtinakayebroaddus
https://www.instagram.com/xtinakayebooks/
https://www.pinterest.com/xtinakayebooks0228/

Write your Best Book !

Thank You...

While Write Your Best Book has extensive experience with romance novels, we also specialize in other genres, including suspense, thrillers, fantasy, paranormal, horror, sci-fi, historical fiction, picture books, children's books, and much more!

In order to provide you with an accurate/fair quote, please email us at: info@writeyourbestbook.com

Ask us for a FREE (5-page) sample edit!
Average turnaround time for sample edits is less than 24 hours!

Average turnaround time for editing projects ranges from 4-6 weeks (though most finish much quicker).

Contact Information

Email:
info@writeyourbestbook.com
Website:
www.writeyourbestbook.com

Printed in Great Britain
by Amazon

21073697R00150